One Match

J.Y. Chung

Additive Credits
Cover Illustration: Jane Chung

ISBN: 0-692-86707-4
ISBN-13: 978-0-692-86707-5

TO MY FAMILY

Table of Contents

Chapter 1

Claire glanced at the white rose that she'd laid down on her table at Café Sauvignon. This would be the last time, she told herself. If the man she was about to meet was not the one, she was going to take a break from online dating for a while, possibly forever. There had been too many promising profiles that had turned out to be whack jobs, arrogant piss ants, and just flat-out boring men.

She grimaced thinking about her last date two months ago. Her date had suggested that they meet at the Lion and Eagle in Farringdon, a famous London pub. Just as she did for all her dates, she'd put in her best effort in looking nice for the evening. She'd worn her new navy blouse with a matching gray skirt and topped it off with her silver necklace and earrings. For the finishing touch, she'd gotten her hair and nails done at the posh Chloé Salon.

She'd spent a considerable sum for the date, but it'd been worth it, as she felt fabulous click-clacking her heels on the wood floors of the L&E. Her date's name was Harold, and he'd said he would be wearing a blue and white checkered shirt. She looked around the pub, searching for the handsome dark-haired man she'd recognize from Venus.co.uk.

A man in the corner waved to her, and relieved that he had shown up before her, Claire hurried over to him. But upon reaching his table, Claire noticed that the man's face and body didn't match his profile at all. He had dark hair, but instead of the strong chin and the piercing blue eyes that Claire had been dreaming about, he had slightly pointy ears and a noticeable overbite. Not terribly bad looking all in all, but he had some traits resembling a beaver. She also observed that he had a bit of a paunch, which was a contrast from the very fit and muscular Harold she'd lusted over online.

"You must be Claire," he said as he got up and greeted her. "You look lovely."

"Thank you, and you must be Harold."

"Yes, it's finally nice to meet you after all our conversations. It's always a bit nerve-racking meeting for the first time, isn't it?"

"Yes, it is," she said weakly. "You never know what to expect in person."

He pointed to the drinks menu on the table. "Why don't I order you a drink?"

She perused the menu briefly and said, "I think I'll have the cider on tap."

He smiled and his protruding teeth gleamed in the light. "We have similar tastes. I was going to go for the Strongbow myself." He got up and walked over to the bar. While he was getting the drinks, Claire quickly pulled out her phone and opened up her Venus app. She was not imagining things. The Harold on the phone was gorgeous and was decidedly not the Harold who was fetching her drinks.

When Harold came back with the pints, Claire decided that she'd best cut straight to the point. "Harold, I think there's been some sort of a mistake."

"I was afraid that you'd say something like that," he said as he put the drinks down. "It's about the profile picture, isn't it?"

She looked at him in surprise, and began to feel a bit nervous. "Yes, you don't look anything like your picture." Under the table she felt her hands begin to tremble. She thought, this may be one of those TV stories where I'm on a date with a psychotic murderer. They're going to find my bloody corpse in a dumpster somewhere tomorrow morning. She eyed the exit door that was about twenty feet away and wondered if she should make a run for it.

He said, "I can explain. Yes, that profile picture isn't me. I just uploaded a picture of an underwear model from a Marks and Spencer catalog."

"You what?" Claire was surprised by his blunt honesty, but the honesty eased her a bit. She asked, "Why would you do something like that?"

He laughed and said, "I'm not some lunatic, so don't be alarmed. Well, just look at me. Women like you wouldn't give me the time of day if I posted a true picture of myself. You have to admit that, don't you?"

Claire paused. She hated to think that appearance would play such a role, but Harold was a bit right. "But Harold, when you actually meet the person they realize that you're lying."

"Of course. But at least by that point we would have shared some conversations, and you might give me a chance if you can look past my little white lie."

Claire looked over him a little bit more and said, "The thing is, you're not that bad of a looking man. If you'd just posted a nice picture of yourself and had some clever line or two in your profile, it's likely that I would have agreed to meet up without this underwear model nonsense."

Harold snorted. "Now look at who's lying. I know women like you. A chap's got to have a handsome face, drive some fancy car, have lots of money. Fit birds like you don't go out with ordinary blokes like me."

"That's incredibly insulting," Claire responded. "You presume to know me, and you assume that I'm some superficial bitch."

Harold frowned. "I'm sorry, you're right. That's wrong of me. I'm just frustrated with the dating scene, that's all. Haven't had much luck over the years."

Claire softened at Harold's sad face. "I know what you mean. Things haven't been great for me either."

He said, "I hardly believe that. You're very pretty, and I'd think that you're getting asked out every day."

She replied, "Well, it's not so much being asked out that's the problem. I've just yet to find that true partner in life. Someone you can just be comfortable with and just be happy without all the emotional games. My last boyfriend was a bit of a narcissistic wanker at the end."

Harold perked up and said to her, "I know I didn't make the best first impression, but if you gave me a chance, I could try to make you happy. I haven't a narcissistic bone on my body. If anything, I'm a bit insecure as you might tell. I'd worship you, and you have to remember that when you thought I was Mr. Underwear that we shared some fun email conversations. Remember when we both agreed that we may be a match because we're the only Brits who can't stand the show *Sherlock*?"

Claire laughed. "Yes, I remember that. Honestly, Sherlock Holmes is a real arse on that show." She thought for a moment, and said to Harold, "Thanks for this drink, but I'm going to have to pass."

"Really? I thought this is the part where you'd say yes." Harold looked hurt.

Claire gathered her purse. "Harold, you told me in our email conversations that you liked poetry like I did. Which poets do you like?"

Harold was silent.

Claire wanted to laugh out loud. Men and their lies. This was a scene that had played out countless times before. She was almost tempted to give him a go out of sheer pity. Instead, she got up and laid a five quid note on the table. "The truth is Harold, even three years ago I would have said yes and given you a chance. But what I didn't tell you was that I had another boyfriend before the narcissist boyfriend who was insecure and lied often in our relationship to make up for his insecurities. I won't date you, but I want to tell you that you should be yourself and gain some confidence, and I think you'll be okay. Good-bye, Harold."

"Wait, what was he so insecure about it?"

"Stereotypical—he had a small penis."

"And I'm guessing that it didn't matter to you at all, did it?"

"Are you kidding? I hated his small willy," said Claire. She cupped her mouth in horror. The words had tumbled out unexpectedly, and embarrassed by what she'd said, Claire quickly turned around and walked away.

Chapter 2

Harold had been the disaster two months ago, and Claire was ready to quit online dating then. The day after the date, she'd met up with her best friend Maddie and described what had happened. Maddie tried not to laugh but failed miserably.

"I'm thrilled that my dating mishaps are at least a source of comedic amusement for you," Claire said as she watched Maddie crying from laughter.

"Honestly, Claire," Maddie said, as she wiped the tears from her eyes, "Why don't you quit being stubborn and sign up for One Match?"

Claire sighed. "I know it's worked for you, but it's just too much for me. I put a device on my head for a week so that it can scan my brain and then pair me up with someone? No thank you."

"It's completely harmless. Loads of people are signing up for it every day. It's not just Sarah and me who found men through it. Victoria was recently paired a couple of weeks ago, and I hear that Liana is quite happy with her boyfriend, too—she's been with him for over three months now."

"Liana? Really?" Liana was Claire's most fickle friend when it came to dating, dumping men for even the tiniest of reasons, and she was impressed that Liana had been with someone longer than a week.

Claire said, "I don't know. I know you and John have been happy together, and it's great that it worked out for you, but part of me would feel that I'd be giving up finding someone on my own. Am I ready to do that? Am I ready to admit that I am incapable of finding love on my own?"

Maddie nodded. "Yes, it's impossible these days. We are beautiful, smart women who are surrounded by the Harolds of this world. Plus, we've got careers—we haven't got the time to pick out the one decent guy in a sea of twats."

"'A sea of twats'. I rather like that phrase. Can I claim it as my own?"

"Stop it, Claire. Promise me that you'll at least check out the website."

Claire said, "Fine. I'll at least visit the website, but I'm not signing up. I'm not paying for yet another dating service."

Maddie gave her a piece of paper and said, "I've already signed up for you, and you should be receiving the device in a couple of days. Here's your username and password so that you can log into the website later and review the instructions once it's arrived. Think of this as an early birthday present."

"Maddie!"

"You have no excuses now. And if you'll excuse me, I have to run to meet up with John for dinner." And before Claire could protest further, Maddie walked away.

Claire received her device a few days after signing up on the site. It arrived in a plain white box without any instructions. She picked it up and examined it. The device was a small patch, no larger than a postage stamp, and the color of a Band-Aid. Not quite sure what to do next, she opened her laptop and went to the One Match website. It looked sleeks with its minimalist design. She entered the login credentials that Maddie had given her, and it took her to a page with menu options. She selected the option that read "Instructions for One Match" and read the following:

Once you sign up for One Match, you will receive the One Match device via the post in one to three business days. Simply attach it on one of your temples and keep it on for seven days. During this period, the device will act as both a camera that will survey your surroundings and as a neurological scanner that will determine the impact that various environments, activities, and interactions have on you. This information is then sent to our servers, and we will create a profile of you. After the initial seven days of information gathering, there will be an additional thirty day processing period to determine a pairing for you. At the end of the thirty days you will be able to log into the website to receive the date and location to meet your match.

The instructions were straightforward enough, but there was also a section titled "FAQs", so she clicked there:

FAQs

Q: I'm nervous about using One Match. What will you do with the information you gather about me?

A: We understand your concern. We are not interested in accumulating information about our customers. We just want to help people meet other compatible people and lead happy lives together. That's why we only temporarily store our customers' profile information to identify a match, and afterwards any data associations with a specific customer are erased. We have opened up access to our source code to all the government regulatory agencies in the countries we operate in so that they may review our technology at any given time.

Q: What should I do during the seven days of scanning?

A: You should engage in your regular activities. Don't suddenly go skydiving or bungee jumping unless that's part of your everyday activity. The core of who we are is shaped around the mundane minutiae of everyday life. Your behavior and response in simple activities such as cleaning your house, talking to friends and family, or watching television provide the central foundation for your profile.

Q: Why do you only reveal one match at the end? And why do I have to meet my match in person to find out anything about him or her?

A: We pair you up with just one other person because too many choices can be a bad thing. And we're pretty confident that we'll get it right the first time. But if we're wrong, you can come back to us and we'll pair you up again, free of charge. As for meeting your match in person, we believe that meeting your match without biases is the best way to meet.

After reading the instructions and the FAQs, Claire still felt nervous about the idea of a patch latched onto her head, recording and analyzing the activities going through her brain. What if it was all a fraudulent scam? What if it read your thoughts and then somehow found out personal details such as your National Insurance number?

She continued scrolling through the website and saw a section titled, "The Founder's Letter." Curious, she clicked on it and read the following:

Dear customer,

Thank you for signing up for One Match. My name is Jorgen Magnussen, and I wrote this letter because I know that One Match is radically different from the other dating services out there. I want to tell you a little bit about myself. I'm a neuroscientist who has studied the human brain for over fifteen years. I'm also someone who signed up for online and offline dating services over the years, and I was quite frustrated by them. I filled out questionnaires and listed hobbies and preferences on these services, only to be paired up with women with whom I had little in common. Sometimes we shared interests at a surface level, but the deeper connections were missing. I initially blamed these dating services for my failures, but I came to believe that perhaps I didn't know enough about myself when I answered the questionnaires. What if I wasn't an introvert as

I believed myself to be? What if I didn't really want someone who was an intellectual like I was?

I set out to create an objective method to determine who I was and the compatible traits of my ideal partner. One Match is the culmination of my life's work. While we are continually working on the algorithm to improve our matching capabilities, we have created the first instance in which the data of someone's behaviors, likes and dislikes, personality traits, and mental makeup can all be combined to find a compatible partner.

I launched One Match only after finding my wife Farrah, but I can testify that I was the first test subject. I used the original technology to come to a better understanding of who I was and who I was looking for. I don't fault people who are skeptical or even frightened of One Match. Surely I'm happy for the people who are able to find lasting love on their own. But for those of us who've been unlucky in love and just want to move on with building a life with a partner rather than participating over and over in the tired mating dance of habitual dating, I invite you to give One Match a chance. I invite you to find someone and move on with your lives together.

Cheers,

Jorgen

This Jorgen fellow seemed heartfelt in his letter, and some of what he said resonated with Claire, but she didn't quite feel ready to make the leap. She'd already received the patch, so she could put it on whenever she felt the urge to do so. She put the patch back on her kitchen table and went to bed that evening.

In the following days Claire would stare at the patch while eating her meals, or fiddle with it while talking on the phone with friends. It was only on a late Friday evening that she finally succumbed. She had made plans that evening to meet up with Maddie for dinner, and when she called Maddie to confirm their meeting time, Maddie yelped, "Oh shit! I'm so sorry Claire, but I totally forgot about our dinner tonight."

Claire tried to hide her disappointment as she said, "That's okay. Something going on? Not like you to forget."

"So sorry, Claire, but you won't believe where I'm at right now."

"Where?"

"I'm on the Eurostar on my way to Paris! It's our one-year anniversary and John surprised me with a weekend trip."

"Wow, Maddie. I'm so happy for you."

"Again, so sorry, but I promise I'll make it up to you when I'm back."

"Don't worry about it. Tell me about all the details when you get back."

After Claire hung up with Maddie, she scrambled to think of backup plans. She texted Sarah and Victoria, but they were both out on dates with their boyfriends. She thought of her single friends, and texted her co-worker and friend Lucy. Lucy texted back that she was out in Stoke Newington with some of their office mates if Claire wanted to join, but Claire decided that it'd be too much of a hassle to trek all the way there. She decided that she'd just change into her pajamas and stay in for the evening.

Claire heated up frozen pizza and resigned herself to a couple of hours of BBC One shows, none of which particularly held her interest. She brought out the butter pecan ice cream and felt sorry for herself. She was happy for Maddie that her sweet husband had surprised her with an anniversary trip, but it reminded her of her own status as a very single woman at home on a Friday evening. She got up from her sofa and looked out the window of her Swiss Cottage flat. Night had crept in and the line of cars snaked by below. So many Londoners, all dressed in their fancy attire, flush with anticipation of the parties and dinners that awaited them. We live for the weekends, she thought. And when those weekend plans were dashed, the existential questioning settled into the room in the form of a weary malaise. She was approaching thirty, having wasted time with men who'd all been wrong for her in some way or fashion. She'd always thought that she'd have found someone by her mid-twenties, but instead her life felt like a never ending reel of dates or meet-ups with friends after work to talk about the same old chatter. She'd traveled a bit during this time, and all those conversations and heartfelt moments with her friends at the pubs couldn't be considered a complete waste, but still, it felt like a lost decade that had sloshed away in wine glasses. She felt tears coming down her cheeks, and she wiped them away.

She sat back down on the couch with a second helping of ice cream, and she saw that a reality show of some spoiled brats living in Knightsbridge was now showing on the telly. She glanced at the patch on her table. She recalled the founder's letter, and she remembered the last sentence: I invite you to find someone and move on with your lives together. The dream of finding the ideal man, so seemingly attainable in the emergence of her adulthood, had proven to be a rope beyond reach. Defeated, she sighed and said out loud, "Oh fine, let's get on with it."

She peeled off the patch, and after a final pause, placed it on her left temple. The patch emitted a green light as if to indicate that it was now activated, and it then returned to its original color. There was nothing that followed, no sounds nor sensations, but Claire had expected this based on her friends' descriptions of wearing the patch. Despite the lack of sensory signals, Claire felt as if some part of her had just changed by affixing the patch to her body. As she dozed off to sleep later that night, she couldn't help but feel a tingle of excitement picturing who her match might be.

In the seven days of wearing the patch, Claire followed the instructions on the FAQs and carried on with her regular weekly routines. On Saturday she took a stroll through Hampstead Heath, met up with Lucy for lunch, and gathered with a group of friends at SoHo for dinner at the trendy sushi restaurant Marasaki. She spent a good portion of Sunday at the Columbia Road Flower Market buying daffodils, and she brought them over to her Aunt Lizzie and her family for Sunday Roast. The weekdays were filled with mostly work, but in the mornings she made time for quick runs, and on some of the evenings she went out with co-workers to pubs in the area or read her books. During this weekly stretch, Claire was acutely aware of her surroundings and her interactions with the people around her. She tried to be especially considerate and generous this week so that she might increase her chances of being paired with an equally kind and generous person. But no one remarked that she was doing anything outside the ordinary, and it pleased Claire to think that she might be kind to others all the time.

The week passed by quickly, and thereafter the agonizing period of waiting for a month to find her match began. Claire thought about what she wanted in her ideal man. He would be funny. He would make her laugh all the time and appreciate her sense of humor. He would be clever and well-educated, and they would be able to have witty conversations on books and politics. He would be adventurous—perhaps not so adventurous that he'd want them to live outside England, but they would go on lots of trips around the world and sample exotic foods in fancy restaurants. He would be kind, thoughtful, and caring. He would do the dishes in the evenings, be attentive when she was sick, and sweep her off her feet repeatedly with romantic gestures. But he would still be a masculine man who wouldn't be afraid to take charge when necessary and protect her in times of trouble. As for looks, Claire thought of her date with Harold and told herself that looks wouldn't matter so much, but she admitted secretly that she wouldn't mind if he was tall and handsome.

Finally, the long awaited day of her match announcement arrived. Claire woke up that morning and immediately checked the email on her phone. Sure enough, there was a message from One Match declaring that her match was set. Almost dizzy with anticipation, she logged into the One Match app and entered her username and password. The app opened and presented the following instructions:

Congratulations, Claire! We have found a match for you. You are to meet your match at Café Sauvignon in London, England. Please show up with a white rose at three o'clock in the afternoon on May 4.

Chapter 3

Claire sat at Café Sauvignon and looked at her watch. It was a quarter past three and still no sign of her mysterious match. She was about to get up to freshen up in the loo when a woman sat in front of her and laid down a white rose on her table.

"Hello," the woman said as she extended her hand. "I'm Rebecca Kennedy. Sorry I'm late. Had some trouble finding this place."

"Hello," Claire said. She was befuddled as to why the woman had sat down, but reflexively she shook her hand. "I'm Claire Moore."

"Claire, that's a pretty name. My favorite aunt's name is Claire as well."

Claire looked at the woman in front of her. She had short, cropped dark hair with a tinge of auburn highlights. Claire then looked again at the white rose that the woman had set down on the table and realized what was happening.

"Oh my god; you're my match," she said. Claire suddenly felt dizzy as she tried to make sense of the situation.

It was now the woman who looked at her in a puzzled state. "Yes, I think so. Is there something wrong?"

Claire put her hand to her mouth and said, "I'm so sorry, Rebecca, but I think there's been some mistake. I wasn't looking to be paired with another woman. I'm not a lesbian."

"You're not?"

"No."

Claire and Rebecca stared at each for a brief moment, and then they both burst out laughing.

"Oh good lord! This is madness!" Rebecca said.

"Yes, wait until I tell my friends," Claire said. "I knew that the site sounded too good to be true. It couldn't even guess my sex preference!"

Rebecca continued to laugh, and she said, "And to think, I came all the way from the Cotswolds for this date."

"I'm so sorry," Claire said. "The site's a real piece of rubbish, isn't it?"

"Yes, and I had such high hopes for it too, what with all my mates having success with it. What a story I'll have to tell." Rebecca got up to leave and said, "I suppose I best get going. I'm so sorry for this confusion."

Claire felt bad that the woman had come so far for the date. Despite herself, she said, "Wait, please don't go. You came all the way here, so why don't we just have a drink together?"

Rebecca looked uncertain, so Claire said once more, "Please, Rebecca, stay. I'd feel awful if you just went straight back after having come all the way to London."

Rebecca sat down. "Oh…okay. I'll stay, but just for one drink. And you can call me Becks by the way."

Claire observed her again a little more carefully. She wasn't what Claire would describe as fashion magazine-pretty, but she was pretty in her own way. She was slender and had a healthy look to her, as if she exercised regularly in some capacity outdoors. She didn't appear to have any makeup on, but she didn't look as if she needed any, as she lacked wrinkles and had flawless skin. She looked like she was a few years older than Claire—maybe in her early thirties. She was wearing a black shirt with no designs, and Claire noticed tattoo lettering on her right wrist that she couldn't quite make out.

"Brilliant," Claire said as the waiter came by. "What are you having? It's on me."

"You really don't have to, but I guess I'll have a glass of Chardonnay," Becks said.

"And let's make that two," Claire said to the waiter.

Once the waiter took the order and left, Claire asked her, "So what do you do in the Cotswolds?"

"I own a little gastropub up on Bourton-on-the-Hill. It's called The Happy Clam."

"I like that. The Happy Clam," Claire repeated. "I'll have to visit your pub someday if I'm ever there. Can you believe that I've lived in England all my life and have never visited the Cotswolds?"

"You have to come by then. It's absolutely lovely up there, and it's just a train ride from Paddington," Becks said. "And what do you do?"

"I'm a financial analyst at Wyman."

"The high-end retailer?"

"Yes, it's quite boring, really. I help with forecasting projections and making sure that our stores hit their quarterly targets. It's all just a bunch of numbers and Excel sheets. Nothing as exciting as running your own gastropub."

"Then why do you do it?"

Claire was taken aback by the blunt nature of the question. She felt a little defensive as she replied, "Well, because I have to make money to pay for my living expenses. Not everyone can own their business in the countryside."

Becks said, "I'm sorry, Claire, I didn't mean to offend you. You just seemed a bit forthright about how you feel about your job to a perfect stranger, so I thought you wouldn't mind if I asked such a question."

Claire accepted Becks's reply. "No, you raise a good point. The thing is, I've always liked numbers, but it's just that the ins and outs of working in a corporation with all the emails and meetings is driving me mad." Claire joked, "That's where One Match was supposed to save me by delivering a rich future husband."

Becks laughed, "Sorry to disappoint."

"A pity, but I suppose that's what I get for banking my future happiness in the hands of a computer program that I know nothing about. A bit ridiculous, really. How do you suppose its algorithms even work?"

Becks replied, "I bet it watches for your most nasty habits and tries to pair you up with another person who has the same nasty habits so that you can maintain some semblance of tolerance for each other. Isn't that what lasting relationships are about at the end? That we're able to tolerate waking up next to the person without wanting to kick her out of bed?"

"I'd hope for a little more than that," Claire said, "but what's your nasty habit?"

Becks said, "I don't have one."

"Of course you do, everyone does," said Claire. "I sometimes don't wash my hands in the loo."

"You can't be serious? That's terrible. You could spread all kinds of awful germs like that."

"I wash my hands most of the time. It's just that sometimes when I'm in a rush it's not the most urgent task in the world."

Becks said, "Well, I suppose I sometimes get food pieces stuck in my teeth. People never tell me. I'll find out about it later in the loo, and then I'm embarrassed to no end."

"Do you? I guess I should tell you now that you seem to have some food piece stuck near your front tooth."

Becks eyes widened in a look of abject horror, and Claire quickly raised her hands and said, "I'm only joking. I was just being cheeky. Sorry—didn't mean to embarrass you."

As Claire continued to laugh, Becks gave a wry smile and said, "You seem quite pleased with yourself. All right then, how do you suppose the technology pairs people up?"

Claire thought for a moment and said, "What about food? It watches the food that you eat, and matches you with someone who has the same tastes in cuisine. Can you imagine if you loved Indian food and your partner hated it? It would be the greatest tragedy. You'd be in the mood for some delicious tikka marsala, but he would put the kibosh on it. I'd break up with that chap in a jiff."

"That's ridiculous," Becks said. "I've seen loads of happy couples who have different tastes in food. If your partner didn't like Indian food, you'd just get it during your lunch hour or when you're out with your friends who did like Indian food."

"But it wouldn't be the same. I'd want to share everything with my boyfriend. What's the point of having someone you love when you can't go out together for a romantic meal of the food you love?"

Becks replied, "You're a bit melodramatic, aren't you?"

"One can't be dramatic enough when it comes to curry."

"Fair enough," Becks said.

There was a pause in their conversation, and at this point Claire realized just how much she was enjoying talking with this stranger. There was none of the awkwardness or tension of the typical first dates because it wasn't a date.

"In all seriousness," said Claire, "it's sort of a relief that the device did such a poor job of match making. Maybe it's just my fragile ego, but I like that I couldn't be analyzed and paired up after a week's analysis."

"I agree. It would have been demoralizing to think that some computer algorithm could unveil an ideal pairing after I'd failed so miserably at it myself. It's one of the reasons why it took me so long to actually wear the device."

"That's funny, it took me a while to put on the patch as well. Felt like I was throwing in the towel."

Becks looked as if she was holding back from asking her another question, so Claire implored her, "Go on, I feel like you want to ask me something."

"What were you hoping of your ideal man?"

Claire laughed. "I guess I'd hoped that he would be clever, funny, and kind—the usual boring traits that every woman wants in her man."

"Physical traits?"

"Well, let's just say that I was hoping that he'd look more like Prince William than Prince Charles. That is, Prince William before he lost all his hair."

"There was always so much commotion about how good-looking Prince William was, but I never saw it. Always thought he had kind of a horsey face."

"In his heyday Prince William was quite fit! Every teenage girl back in the day would have committed multiple murders to marry him."

"Hmm, if you say so."

Claire feigned indignation and said, "Okay, what about you then? What were you hoping you for in your perfect woman?"

She expected Becks to have some clever retort, but instead Becks was silent. Finally she said, "Not that exciting either. At this point in my life, I just want to find someone that I can be comfortable with."

Claire nodded. She also felt that this trait might be the most important thing at this point in her life.

Becks continued, "I'm embarrassed to admit it, but during my week of wearing One Match I did some things that I normally wouldn't do in the hopes that it'd raise the quality of the person I'd meet."

"Really?" Claire didn't mention her own little attempts at the tweak.

"Yes," Becks said, turning a shade pink in her cheeks, "I don't read many books, but I tried to read a novel and convince myself that I was enjoying it."

"What book did you read?"

"*Anna Karenina.* It was painful. How can one read so many pages about a woman contemplating her affair? Just die already and put us all out of misery."

Claire said, "'Just die already'? That's a rather cruel assessment of one of literature's first modern women. I do love *Anna Karenina*, but *War and Peace* is better. It's sweeping and epic, and, oh, the characters—Pierre and Prince Andrei are two of the best characters in any novel."

Becks laughed her full laugh again and said, "With such an enthusiastic endorsement, I guess I should give it a shot."

They soon launched into a conversation about books in which Claire gave her recommendations of her top favorites. She suggested Chekhov's plays, *East of Eden,* and *One Hundred Years of Solitude*, and Becks jotted down the suggestions. The talk of books then gave way to movies and TV shows in which they found some overlap in tastes. The conversation then somehow meandered to restaurants and food, and it was Claire's turn to write down Becks's recommendations on how to cook a proper fish stew with a Mediterranean twist. They had talked their way through two glasses of wine each before Becks looked down at her watch.

"Yikes. I can't believe how fast the time has gone by. It was a pleasure meeting you, but I must get going."

The time had flown by for Claire. She felt a shot of disappointment at the thought that Becks was leaving now, but she responded, "Of course."

Becks gathered up her purse. "Thanks for the wine and the conversation."

"Wait," Claire said. She saw with absolute clarity that if she didn't speak up now, she would never see Becks again for the rest of her life. She thought of all the casual acquaintances in her life, people with whom she'd had some hints of a small connection but had slipped by due to a lack of effort or courage from either side.

She said, "This might seem a bit odd to you, but I was just thinking that maybe we could be friends. I know we've just met, but I've enjoyed our conversation today, and I really think it'd be a shame if we gave it up with just a good-bye. And maybe nothing will come of it, but even if nothing does, I'd like to know that we at least tried. We're all so shy and lazy nowadays when it comes to meeting people outside of our own terms. We'll go on dates with people assigned to us through the internet but we can't be bothered to say hello to our neighbor. I thought we had a bond, and I hope you feel that way too."

Claire hadn't intended to go on this little tangent, so she caught herself and stopped. Becks said nothing, and immediately Claire felt like the biggest fool. But Becks then broke out into a wide grin and said to Claire, "Honestly, you really are quite melodramatic. If you wanted my email address, you could have just said so."

Relieved, Claire said, "Yes, there was a bit of a flourish in my request, wasn't there?"

"Just a tad, but I suppose my life can be filled with more flourishes." Becks pulled out a pen and paper from her purse and wrote down her email address. She handed the paper to Claire and said, "Claire, have you ever had a lesbian friend before?"

Claire was surprised by the question. "Yes, I have some colleagues and other friends from uni who are gay. Although, I guess none of my closest friends are gay. Does it matter?"

Becks paused as if she was debating her in mind, but then said, "No, I guess it doesn't matter."

They looked at each other, a bit clumsily, and Becks extended her hand out. "Again, nice meeting you, Claire."

Claire watched Becks walked out the café, and then looked down at the paper. Becks4@gmail.co.uk.

Later that day, Claire sent an email:

Hello Becks,

It was a pleasure meeting you today, and I hope you felt the same. I'll look you up if I'm ever in the Cotswolds, and please let me know if you're ever back in London.

Kind regards,

Claire

Becks replied back a few hours later:

Hello Claire,

Pleasure meeting you as well and thanks again for the wine. Please do give me a ring if you're in my neck of the woods, and the next round is on me.

Cheers,

Becks

Chapter 4

The following Monday Claire sat at her cubicle at work as she told Lucy about Becks.

Lucy said, "This is one more reason why I've never used One Match. It's creepy enough that they're scanning your brain with that scary patch thing, but I can't believe they set you up with another woman."

"I didn't meet the man of my dreams," Claire said, "but I had a pleasant time. It was really easy to talk to her. Maybe One Match should also try to help people find friends."

"I wouldn't touch it. Maybe they'll set you up with your siblings on accident."

As they laughed, Claire's boss Ronald walked by and said, "I see that you're hard at work here, but you little ladies better hurry on up to the bloody auditorium. The quarterly meeting is about to start, and I'll be damned if you're going to skip it."

Claire said, "We'll be right there, sir."

As Ronald walked away in a huff, Lucy said, "What's his problem this morning? He's nastier than usual. And to call us 'little ladies'. You'd think that we were secretaries in the fifties."

"Well, you are a secretary, and we should hurry over."

"That term is so outdated, Claire. I'm an executive assistant, thank you very much."

They followed some of the other office stragglers to the auditorium of Wyman's headquarters. It was packed with employees already in their seats, but Lucy and Claire managed to find two seats in the back.

Shortly after they sat down the presentation started. Like all the other quarterly all hands meetings, the CFO started off by talking about the company's quarterly numbers. Claire was already aware of them, but it was still disconcerting to see the downward trend in revenue and profits in the last few years. The numbers were followed by presentations from various teams on their accomplishments for the quarter.

Lucy pretended to yawn and said to Claire, "Wake me up when they turn on the lights."

Claire nodded and was thinking about taking a short nap herself when the CEO and chairman, John Wyman, then took the stage and said, "I know we're getting antsy here, but I've saved the best for last. As you all know, we've been looking for a new senior vice president of consumer operations for the past year. We searched far and wide and conducted numerous exhaustive interviews to find the right person to introduce bold new ideas and innovation to our company."

Claire rolled her eyes. It seemed as if they'd been searching for this unicorn SVP for forever now. But to her surprise, Mr. Wyman smiled and said, "Well, I'm pleased to announce that the search is over and we've finally found our man. I'd like all of you to give a warm welcome to Lewis Hardy."

The new senior vice president took the stage, and there was an immediate hush in the crowd. Claire was amazed. He was much younger than what she had anticipated. He looked like he was in his mid-thirties. He was very handsome, with blue eyes, a square jaw, and a classic side-parted haircut of full dark hair. He looked a little over six feet tall, and even in his expensive-looking tan suit, Claire could tell that he was trim and in shape. In short, he looked like the underwear model that Harold had pretended to be.

"Good lord, he's absolutely gorgeous," Lucy said. "I can't believe that people like him exist in real life."

Claire nodded in agreement and strained to get a better look.

John paused for the crowd to applaud and then continued. "Lewis was chief of operations at Biga's UK division for the last five years, where he led their turnaround efforts and produced a record £500 million in profits last year for that online retailer. As Wyman's new SVP of consumer operations, he'll be reporting directly to me. He has also come up with an exciting vision for our company moving forward, so I've asked him to share his plans with this group today."

Lucy poked Claire's arm and whispered, "I heard about Lewis Hardy from some of the other EAs. There's a rumor that we poached him by paying him £1 million a year and 5% of annual profits."

Claire murmured, "Christ, with a salary like that he better create the same kind of turnaround here."

Lewis gave a wave to the crowd and said, "Thank you all for welcoming me to Wyman. It is a true honor to join this venerable icon of retailing. I've been here for over three weeks now, and I've been overwhelmed already by the passion and talent that I've observed in its employees. It is truly humbling to be part of such a dedicated organization, and I can honestly say that I've never been more thrilled in my career than I am today."

Lucy whispered, "He lays it on thick, but I like it. Stroke my ego further, Lewis Hardy."

Claire elbowed her. "Shh, stop it, Luce."

Lewis went on, "I've also had a chance to speak with a number of employees at all rungs of all the departments. During this time, I've tried to speak as little as possible and only listen. I've listened to your feedback on the current state of the company—what we're doing well and what we're not doing so well, and where you think Wyman is headed. You've told me about the changes that you'd like to see and the policies you'd like for us to keep or return. You've told me everything I wanted to hear and more, and I think one of you even gave me a recipe for lamb chops that I tried and loved."

The crowd laughed. He's good, Claire thought. He had a commanding presence, but his little anecdote about the lamb chop recipe gave him a common touch that already had the crowd eating out of his hand.

"After receiving all this feedback, I feel obligated to share the results with you. I wish I was a good liar, but that has never been one of my strong suits. The news, unfortunately, is grim, but you already knew that. Many of you are frustrated by the amount of red tape to complete tasks. You've complained that there are too many meetings to prepare for meetings. You're tired of the committees and the sub-committees and the sub-sub committees that have formed a sort of bureaucratic nightmare for many of you. And let's not forget about the emails. Mountains and mountains of emails gushing into your inboxes every day, so much so that many of you can only tremble and stare at the screen in a state of glum paralysis. That paralysis has seeped all throughout the company like a hidden, gaseous poison that's ruining morale and preventing decision-making. You have all alluded to that paralysis in some form or another, and it's been the source of blame from everything from our phone shortages for this Christmas season to the lack of tissue in the toilets."

The crowd laughed again, and Claire could see nodding as they listened to him. Even though he hadn't interviewed her, she felt as if he'd received all the tidbits she would have given him.

"It was not always like this. I remember as a child when my parents would take me to a Wyman department store. It was always for special occasions when my father had saved enough money for my mum to buy a new dress or a nice piece of furniture for our small house. I would walk down the aisles of gleaming counters, marveling at the fancy displays of toys and board games, pretending that I was the prince of a palace. My imagination never had to work too hard; all Wyman stores were palaces in their own right."

Lewis paused, seemingly lost in the recollection of this memory, and then gathered himself. "People have asked me why I left Biga. They told me that I was mad. I had an enviable position at an enviable company growing by leaps and bounds. Why would I leave all of that for a sagging institution for which the papers were predicting an impending demise? I told them I left because I still remembered the palaces of my youth. They were not merely retail stores. They were dream makers. You only had to step into a Wyman to believe that a better life was out there, and that there were treasures to be obtained on this earth if you just wanted it enough."

The crowd was silent. Claire could feel the electricity as they all sat entranced by his speech. Lewis was just getting started. "In its two hundred year history, Wyman has been there to showcase the inventions of dreamers. The bicycle, the lawnmower, the chocolate bar, the washing machine, the radio, the telephone, the television, the bikini, the computer, and the cell phone among countless numerous other inventions have been sold in our magnificent storefronts, and we will continue to do so for another two hundred years over. Our customers will always view Wyman as that shining jewel in the mine, the palace where dreams come true, and we will say that it was during our watch that we restored the luster of its hallowed halls. We will do so by re-examining and re-imagining everything, item by item, shelf by shelf, floor by floor, store by store. We will not rest until our stores are shining with the pride of our blood and sweat!"

An employee near the front suddenly stood up to clap, and soon everyone was standing to give the new SVP a standing ovation. The thunderous applause was deafening. The crowd was taken over by a delirious frenzy of ecstasy. Claire herself felt the chills. She understood now what it felt like to listen to an inspiring leader firsthand. She wanted to go back to her desk now and work until she keeled over.

Lewis raised his hands up to quiet the crowd. He said, "Now, you may be asking, 'And exactly how will we turn things around here? It's one thing to sell the vision of a restoration, but it's another to actually execute on that vision.' Lean in closely then, because I'm about to share my mad plan. You're tired of the bureaucracy? Fine, we're taking it all down. The entire company is getting rid of managers."

The crowd gasped. Claire herself sat stunned by his last sentence. Get rid of managers? How would the company possibly operate? Lewis nodded and said, "Yes, we're getting rid of managers, and we're forming family units instead. In the family units we'll have two employees working together, and they'll be overseeing two junior employees in tandem. These 'families' will decide what projects they'll be involved in and tackle these projects together. While the two senior employees in the family are responsible for the growth and development of the two junior employees, they won't have the power to promote or terminate their employment. Instead, we will have assigned HR employees who'll remain independent of families and will have the task of evaluating each unit. They will measure the performance of the family groups and decide the compensation for the groups as well as individuals in the families."

The auditorium was filled with muttering and whispering between people. Lucy turned to Claire and said, "Has he gone mad? Families in the workplace? I can't stand my own family, and now I'll have to deal with one at work as well?"

Lewis raised his hands to ask for silence once more, and said through the noise, "I imagine that you all must have many questions, and in the next couple of days there will be emails and HR representatives providing all the details. Answers to questions such as, 'Do employees get to pick their family members?' and 'Do employees get to move on from their families?' will all get answered. I can also assure you that all current managers will be able to stay on and join the family units. But for now, I want to explain why we're taking such a radical approach. If history has shown us anything, it's that as companies get larger, they get mired in bureaucracy and tend to die. Consider this fact: 87% of the companies that were in America's Fortune 500 list in 1955 no longer exist today. It's a testament to the Wyman family that Wyman has existed for so long, but even now Wyman looks as if it has run its course if it continues down its current path. If we operate as other companies, our inevitable end has already been written for us."

He paused to let the thought sink in, and the auditorium was silent. "But we have other models of sustained continuity, and none other is a better example than cities. Yes, as they get bigger, corporations calcify but cities thrive. We only need to look in our backyard to see that London is flourishing after nearly two thousand years. And the backbone of these cities are families, families that willingly participate in the daily scrum of keeping the city humming because they're given transparency of decisions, forums to voice their concerns, and choices to volunteer in areas of interest to make their living area a better place for their loved ones. We will strive to do the same here at Wyman. We will create a company that's not just about receiving payment for a job well done, but rather, a gathered union of people who want to work alongside others they genuinely care for as we re-invent our stores. My hope is that the families will unite with other families to create and build in ways that cities have built for centuries without the stranglehold of top-down management. I know that this bold experimentation won't be for everyone, and in the months ahead, I'm prepared for the attrition that we'll face. But for those who are tired of the same corporate culture, for those who are wondering if there's got to be a better way, I ask you to stay here and participate in this grand experiment. If we fail, we'll fail knowing that we failed spectacularly. And if we succeed, this new Wyman Way will uphold this company through the years ahead so that we might be purveyor of dreams as it once was for this humble lad who stands before you now."

A beat after he finished his speech, the crowd broke out into applause once more, but Claire could sense the air of uncertainty that hung over all of them. The lights of the auditorium were turned back on, and she could hear the breathless conversations about the speech breaking out all around her. When she got back to her cubicle, her office mates were all chattering about the new family model with Ronald.

"His speech was a bit grandiose for my taste, but I think his idea is worth a shot," her co-worker Daniel said.

Ronald replied, "A bit grandiose? He's so far removed from reality that they should lock him up in a mental asylum."

"That's harsh, don't you think? We don't even know the details of the plan. I thought he made a good point about companies not lasting over the years."

Ronald gave Daniel a smirk and said, "It's all rubbish. Family units. Ha, he sounded like a bloody communist to me. And cities. Cities don't have to deal with fickle customers and competitors who're out there licking their chops like wolves. These young hotshots think they have all the answers, but I bet they'll kick him to the curb in six months when his 'grand experiment' proves to be a 'grand failure'."

Claire joined in, "Maybe it will fail, but you can't call him a communist. If anything, the current corporate models of top down management mirrors the Stalinist planned economies."

Ronald snorted and said, "I'm not going into some stupid debate about communism. That's it. Everyone back to work. Until this stupid idea starts I'm still the one in charge here, and I'm ordering that everyone provide me their weekly finance reports by end of today. And if you think I'm resembling Joseph Stalin with this top down order, you can thank Ms. Moore for it."

Everyone moaned as they returned to their desks. Some of them gave

Claire dirty looks, but she didn't mind, as she recalled Lewis Hardy's speech in her head. His plan was certainly bold, and she was unsure as to whether it would work out, but she knew that she'd be one of the ones to stay to find out.

Chapter 5

A few weeks after the company meeting, on an unusually warm May afternoon, Claire decided to go to Hampstead Heath and enjoy the sun. She sat on the lawn of Kenwood House Manor and watched families having picnics and children chasing each other between shrieks of glee. Delighted by the scene, she pulled out the book she'd brought, *Lord Byron: The Major Works*, and began to read. A few minutes later, a voice behind her said, "She walks in beauty, like the night, of cloudless climes and starry skies."

Startled, Claire turned around and saw a man crouched near her. He had a mop of brown curls on his head and large brown eyes. Despite his goatee, she thought he had a rather youthful face, probably aided by the impish smile he wore at the moment. She said to him, "I beg your pardon?"

"Lord Byron. 'She Walks In Beauty'. The first few lines, isn't it?" He carried an American accent.

"Oh, I don't know. I've just started reading it."

"Check it out," the man opened his hand out to her to ask for the book, to which she hesitatingly obliged. He flipped to the first page to scan the table of contents, and then flipped some more. He gave the book back to Claire with his saved location: "She Walks in Beauty". Claire scanned the first couple of lines and saw that he'd recited the first lines of the poem word for word.

"That's pretty impressive."

"Thanks," he replied, and he sat down beside her. He was lanky, as if working out wasn't one of his hobbies, and he wore a t-shirt that read: Chicago Jazz Festival. The casual manner in which this man carried himself, the way he'd plopped himself uninvited onto Claire's grassy space, amused and irritated Claire simultaneously.

She asked, "Is this how you pick up women in America? You just go up to them, cite some poetry, and they swoon for you?"

He seemed unfazed by her question, and if anything, his smile seemed to grow wider. "Women in America don't read poetry. And no, I don't approach women. They approach me."

Claire bristled. "You're disgusting. Can you please go away and let me read in peace?"

He ignored her request and said, "I'm not trying to be disgusting. I'm telling you the truth. Are you disgusted by the truth?"

"If so many women approach you, why aren't you with them right now? Why are you here?"

"Just because women approach me doesn't mean I comply, and I'm here because I saw a very beautiful woman reading Lord Byron, on whom I wrote my doctorate dissertation. Can you blame me then for coming up to you?"

Claire told herself she should get up and leave, but instead she found herself asking, "So you're a professor then?"

He shook his head. "Not yet. I'm doing some postdoc work at King's College." He stuck out his hand and said, "Will Adams."

Claire ignored the gesture and said, "You're quite smooth, Will Adams. You're one of those types in the movies, those American men who lay on the charm thick and get the girls to fall in love with them. Never seems to end well for those girls."

Will's smiled faded. "I don't know what movies you're watching, but in the few rom-coms I've seen, the boy eventually convinces the girl that he's not a jerk, and they live happily ever after. *Pride and Prejudice,* for example."

His comment set her off. She felt her cheeks flush as she said, "*Pride and Prejudice* is not some 'rom-com'. It's about class hierarchies and gender struggles. It's about women trying to pave their lives in a period when they were treated like nothing more than property and keys to familial alliances and money."

Will held up his hands, "Whoa. Look, no need to get worked up. I'm a pretty straightforward guy. I saw you reading Lord Byron, so I had to come over. I didn't mean to get you riled up."

His explanation was straightforward, although perhaps still a bit too forward. "It's a bit clichéd of me, really," she said, her anger cooling a little. "Reading poetry in the park."

"I think it's nice."

Despite herself, Claire offered her hand. "Claire Moore."

Will's boyish smile returned and he shook her hand. "Nice to meet you, Claire Moore."

"You can just call me Claire."

"Sounds good, Claire. By the way, I might have called *Pride and Prejudice* a romantic comedy, but I also agreed with everything you said about it. Jane Austen was a genius."

"Right. I somehow doubt that you're an admirer of Jane Austen."

Will furrowed his brows. "Let's see: Born in 1775 and grew up in a gentry household with seven siblings. Had a little bit of formal education but was primarily educated through her father's vast library of books. Wrote three novels by the time she was twenty-three, and died at the age of forty-one in 1817. Quite a shame that it was such a short life, as she was a genius."

Claire replied, "I suppose that I should be mesmerized, but I can look up facts on Wikipedia as well."

Will grinned. "I know I'm coming across as a show-off, but I don't mean to. I'm obviously trying too hard to impress you."

Despite herself Claire couldn't help but laugh. "Just a tad bit."

He said, "I took a class on Austen once, so I remember some facts, but how about if I just say that I enjoy her books, and that *Persuasion* is my favorite?"

She replied, "And I will have to politely disagree with you and say that *Emma* is her best work."

"I didn't say that *Persuasion* was her best work but that it was my favorite."

"But by saying so I think you'd be implying that it's her best."

"Not really. You could think that one novel is technically sounder but enjoy another one better."

Claire rolled her eyes. "Fine then, so what do you think is her best work?"

"*Mansfield Park*."

Claire said, "*Mansfield Park*? I don't know anyone who would say that's even in the top three."

"Well, you know someone now."

Will and Claire then proceeded to get into a long debate about Austen's novels, going back and forth on the merits of the writer's top stories, and before Claire knew it, her serene afternoon at Hampstead Heath passed by in a flash.

Chapter 6

After the initial encounter, Claire and Will began seeing each other. They started off with the hip coffee shops around Shoreditch and Brick Lane. Will always had plenty of things to say on his dates. He was well-read, had traveled a lot. He'd taught middle school through Teach for America and had spent time in Haiti building homes. He spoke of his adventures through South Asia and Africa and had a defined opinion on every current event. He introduced her to his friends, a literary group of professors, authors, playwrights, and actors who thrilled and intimidated Claire. She attended some of their salon parties in which they debated the latest books and plays while smoking cigarettes.

A couple of weeks into their relationship, Will took her to a party in Bethnal Green that was hosted by one of his ex-pat friends. There were several Americans, and one of them, a philosophy grad student named Lennie, asked the group, "Have you guys read the editorial in *The Times* this week, the one about expanding the concept of reparations not just to blacks but to other previously discriminated groups such as LGBTQs?"

One of them responded, "Yes, I know it'll never happen, but I thought it was an interesting thought exercise. The idea of America wiping the slate clean for everyone so that we could start anew as a purer representation of equality certainly has a noble appeal to it—the New World restored to its proper vision, so to speak."

Will snorted and said, "It was a stupid article. Every liberal will post it on Facebook and pat himself on the back for doing so, and it'll be a topic of conversation in parties like these for a few days, but it'll go away because it's ridiculous."

"That's a bit defeatist, isn't it?" asked Lennie. "I thought when Ta-Nehisi Coates made the case for reparations for blacks in *The Atlantic* there was some thoughtful dialogue that came out of it."

Will replied, "'Thoughtful dialogue'? You're so delusional. Any discussion of black reparations was strictly between intellectual liberals like ourselves, and now we want to throw gays and other minority groups into a reparations proposal that was already a pipe dream? It's ridiculous."

Lennie countered, "That's so cynical. Ideas kindled among intellectuals have sparked revolutions. Democracy. Emancipation. Universal suffrage."

Will waved him off and said, "Let's not pretend we're revolutionists; I'm talking about the specific issue of reparations itself. There might be some argument for reparations for blacks for repayment of services rendered through slavery, but even then there was no way that we were going to figure out how much money to give to individuals. Now we're adding everyone else? For what? For general discrimination over the centuries? Hell, I'm a quarter Jewish—would I be eligible for some payment?"

As Will and Lennie continued on in their debate, Lennie's girlfriend Ada announced, "While you two go at it, Claire and I are going to get some more drinks from the kitchen."

Relieved to get away from such a contentious argument that she knew little about, Claire got up and followed Ada, but Ada walked past the kitchen and out to a small balcony. The air was cool outside, and it felt good to be out of the stuffy living room.

"God, I can't stand those two sometimes," Ada said. "Seriously, the way they wave their dicks at each other makes me want to puke."

Claire laughed in agreement. She said, "Do they do this all the time?"

"Not all the time, but it happens enough. I haven't seen Will be this aggressive in a while, though. He must really like you, because he's doing his best to show off."

As Claire blushed, Ada handed her a rolled-up piece of white paper and said, "Do you want to go to Mexico with me?"

"I beg your pardon?"

"Sorry, I meant if you want to smoke a joint with me."

Claire stared at the joint and said, "No thank you."

Ada shrugged and said, "Okay, but I'll just say that it makes sitting through their pissing contests a little more bearable."

Claire watched as Ada smoked her joint, and after a few minutes she said, "Oh, all right. Pass me one."

Ada smiled, and handed her one and lit it for her. Claire held it in her hands and said, "So how do you do this?"

"It's not that different from a cigarette. You just inhale a little bit, and then you exhale. And try not to cough."

"This is going to be embarrassing, but I've never smoked a cigarette."

"Jesus. Here let me show you." Ada demonstrated with her joint, and Claire followed suit. She coughed a tearful bit at the first few attempts but eventually got the hang of it. The effects started settling in, and she started to feel sleepy. At the same time, however, she was fearful that she'd be arrested any moment. She asked Ada, "You're not an undercover policewoman are you?"

Ada laughed hard, and after calming down, she said, "Oh my god. That's one of the funniest things I've ever heard. You're funny."

"I am funny, aren't I?"

Feeling a bit loosened up, she asked Ada, "So what do you think about the whole reparations issue?"

Ada took a hit and said, "It seems to me that if you've fucked over groups of people for a long time, you ought to do something to make it right." She paused and asked Claire, "What about you? What do you think about this unfortunate issue?"

"I don't know. I think you're right, but Will seems adamant against it."

"Ha, Will's just trying to piss off Lennie because he's an asshole like that sometimes. If Lennie had said that he was against reparations Will would have just chosen the other side to hear himself talk."

Ada then seemed to see the concerned look on Claire's face because she added, "But I'm not saying that Will's an asshole, just that he likes to act like an asshole sometimes, you know what I mean? He's actually lovable in that asshole way."

Claire wasn't sure that she wanted to be with someone who was loveable in an "asshole way", but she kept silent. She finished up her joint with Ada, and they joined the living room once more, where Will and Lennie were continuing to debate while the others listened. Claire sat in the corner of the room next to Ada, trying to remain quiet as to not attract attention, but she and Ada would burst out into a fit of giggling every now and then.

Will and Claire left the party an hour or so later, and when they stepped outside, he said to her, "What the hell was all that laughing about?"

Still feeling the effects, Claire smiled wide and said, "I think I might be high."

"What?"

"Ada and I smoked some marijuana on the balcony while you guys were talking."

Will looked at her and said, "Really? Damn, Claire, I wouldn't have pictured that in a million years."

"It's your fault," she said, "you were boring me to tears."

They both laughed, and when they got on the Tube, Claire felt loose and unlike herself. She pawed Will's thigh, and soon they both started to grope and kiss each other. She sensed the other passengers gawking at them, but she paid them no mind as they made out during the entire Tube ride.

They got off at the Swiss Cottage stop and walked to her flat. When they got to the steps of her Victorian building, the cool air sobered her up a little. She said to him, "Will, that was so much fun. I had a lovely evening. I hope you have a good night."

"Perhaps I can come up? For a quick drink?"

"Not tonight, Will. I just need a little more time."

The disappointment in his face was noticeable. "Claire, we've been dating for nearly three weeks now."

She sighed. "I know. And I like you a lot, but it's just that my last break-up was a bit painful, and I just need some time."

She leaned in for a kiss, and he gave her a half-hearted attempt. "All right, I understand. Good night."

Claire watched Will's dejected silhouette recede into the night before she went into her flat. The happiness of the evening had disappeared. She changed into her pajamas and slumped in front of her laptop to check emails. Stupid, horny Will Adams. At the same time, it had been over three weeks—maybe it was time to put out? As these thoughts wandered through her mind, Claire saw in her Gmail that Becks was online for chatting. She was surprised that Becks would show up in her account, but she remembered that she'd sent Becks a quick email through Gmail, and that correspondence had likely added her to her Google Chat. On a whim, she clicked on Becks's name, and typed, "Hi Becks, you there?"

A moment later, there was a response. "hi claire how are u?"

Somewhat surprised by the response, Claire stopped to think what she'd say next. "Doing well. I hope I'm not bothering you?"

"its eleven in the evening in the english country. what could be more important than speaking with my algorithmically paired london lover?"

"When you put it that way, I suppose I deserve your undivided attention."

Becks wrote back, "to what do i owe the occasion?"

"Nothing. I just saw you online and thought I'd see what you were up to. Just writing after a bad ending to an odd night."

"oh?"

"Yes, I've been seeing someone. An American. Charming guy and all, but he wanted to have sex tonight and I wasn't quite ready. Plus one of his friends got me high, and I wasn't in the right frame of mind."

"christ, serves you right for dating an american. what were you thinking doing drugs?"

"It was just weed, but I don't know what I was thinking. It was really stupid of me, trying marijuana for the first time at my age. Just trying to fit in with his crowd, I guess."

"how long have you been dating him?"

"Over three weeks. Maybe two to three times each of those weeks. You think it was about time for us to start having sex?

There was a pause. Claire then saw Becks type, "no, no i dont. if you werent ready it wasnt time."

Claire felt a sense of relief at the response. "Thank you." She then added, "It's not that I don't want to have sex, but I'm just afraid of what's down the road."

"what do u mean?"

"He's fun, but I'm not sure if he's a match for me. We're very different." She could foresee all the energy and time that would go into the relationship, and it felt tiring.

"so why not break it up now?"

Claire thought for a moment. "Because I've been feeling lonely."

The response read, "thats tough. i feel the same things sometimes."

"So, do you think I should break it off or go in for the full plunge?"

There was a pause, but the typing picked up again. "the full plunge? you've now forever ruined the word plunge for me. but I think you should do neither. why do u have to make a decision now when you r unsure? if you r having fun stick with him, and u will know if hes mr right or wrong"

Claire smiled and wrote back, "Sounds sensible enough. I'll follow it. Perhaps you can become my love advice dispensing lesbian friend."

"tempting—always wanted to be known as the love advice dispensing lesbian"

"Enough about me, how are you?"

"i'm doing fine. happy to tell you about all of my life, but im afraid i have to get back to mindlessly surfing the internet"

Claire laughed. "Fine, I was just being polite, anyway. By the way, do you always avoid capitalization when you type?"

"just be glad that i dont use smiley faces and the other rubbish. and do u always type in perfect grammar on chats? its irritating as hell."

Claire sent her reply: "= P"

She then wrote, "When will we see each other again?" She'd wanted to propose a time and place to meet up again but couldn't quite get herself to do so.

There was a lengthy pause again, and then the response came. "i dont know. someday"

Claire was a bit disappointed, but she wrote, "Yes, someday. In the meantime, thanks for listening today. Good night."

"good night claire"

Chapter 7

Claire woke up the next morning and remembered Will's disappointment. From her bed she called Will and asked if they could meet up at Primrose Hill for brunch. At the Greenwich Café, between forkfuls of eggs Florentine, Claire explained that while she wasn't quite ready to sleep with him, she liked him. They were a little different, especially when it came to friends, but she thought that a few differences were fine and she hoped that Will wanted to stay in the relationship. Will listened to what she had to say, and once she was done, he cupped his hands around hers and said, "I get it. I completely get it."

"You do?" Claire was relieved. She'd thought that he'd be standoffish or even angry from the previous night, but Will looked as if he was in an excellent mood.

"Here, let me show you something," Will said. He reached into his wallet and pulled out two tickets.

"What's this?"

"They're two train tickets to Moreton-in-Marsh in the Cotswolds for this upcoming weekend. I've also booked us a bed and breakfast there for a couple of nights, and there's a couple of hikes that we can do."

Claire was puzzled. Had Will not heard her just tell him that she wanted to take it a little slow? He seemed to understand the perplexed look she must be giving him, because he added, "I was thinking about you last night, and I think part of the reason you don't feel as comfortable in our relationship yet is because we've been hanging around my friends a lot. So I thought it'd be nice to spend some time away from London on our own. And since you've mentioned the last couple of weeks that you wanted to see the Cotswolds at some point, I bought the train tickets."

He waited for her response and she hesitated. "I don't know, Will."

Undeterred, Will said, "I want you to feel totally comfortable. If I'm being honest, yeah, I hope something happens between us this weekend, but if you're not ready, I promise you that I won't pressure you. I like you a lot, Claire, and I really would love to spend some quality time together."

She was torn. It didn't feel as if Will was taking it slow and giving her space, but she could see that he thought he was being thoughtful. He'd gone out of his way to surprise her, and she did want to visit the Cotswolds.

She also remembered Becks's advice from the previous night to give him a chance.

"All right then. Cotswolds it is."

"Really? That's great," he said. His face was glowing, like a pubescent boy who'd just finished opening his loot of Christmas presents. "I promise you that it'll be a memorable time for us."

As Claire rode the bus back home, she wondered if she'd made a mistake by giving in. She had an uneasy feeling that Will had too high of expectations as to what might come out of the weekend. She sensed that he viewed the weekend as a sort of challenge, a chance to prove his considerate attentiveness, for which he'd be rewarded with some glorious shag at the end. She felt exhausted just thinking about it.

But her focus shifted when a Facebook friend request from Becks appeared on her phone. Claire was thrilled to see the request and accepted it right away. She looked at Becks's profile and saw that she didn't post much, but she'd put up some photos. There were pictures of her with friends in outdoor hills and meadows that Claire presumed to be of the Cotswolds, and it whet her appetite to see the land directly. There were also some indoor pictures in pub and restaurant settings, and Claire wondered which of them were photos of the The Happy Clam, but she saw no outright giveaway.

It was always a strange feeling to see the profile info and the pictures of a new Facebook friend. Yes, she'd been invited by her new friend into her private garden, but she still felt like a spy digging through memories that she was never part of and would never completely understand. Claire supposed that it was not too different from the friend showing her a physical photo album, but in those situations the friend acted as a narrator and provider of context as she carefully leafed through the pages. Instead, Claire had received a full download of Becks's personal history in one dump, and she felt as if she was equipped with half-knowledge that only piqued her curiosity further.

She continued to swipe through the pictures and saw some photos of Becks in other parts of the world. She'd been to Europe, parts of Asia. There were a few that seemed to have been taken in India in which Becks looked much younger, perhaps in her early twenties or even late teens. In many of those photos she was accompanied by another young woman with red hair. They looked so carefree together mugging for the camera, trotting out silly faces and poses while landmarks like the Taj Mahal stood in the background. She couldn't find the mysterious redhead in later pictures of

Becks, and so she guessed that she may have been one of Becks's earlier girlfriends. Claire wondered what had happened to the relationship.

After perusing through Becks's photos, Claire sent her a quick Facebook message saying, "Facebook friends? Guess that officially makes us friends then."

A couple hours later she received a reply from Becks that read, "only official now? not when i became your love advice dispensing lesbian friend?"

Claire laughed out loud at the retort and wrote back, "No, we all know that you have to come out on Facebook to make the friendship official."

"Come out? is that some lesbian joke?"

Claire was terrified at the thought of having offended Becks and immediately wrote back, "I'm so sorry. I didn't mean it that way."

After a few excruciating minutes had passed, she received the response, "i was just being cheeky"

Claire breathed a sigh of relief and wrote back, "Piss off. ;)"

Throughout the week they continued to trade short messages to each other. They were simple and mindless chit chats, along the lines of, "Tube caused a 2 hour delay to work today—you're so lucky to live in the country" or "just dealt with an arse of a visitor at the pub. aargh!" Their banter was nothing memorable, but it made Claire's week. She couldn't quite put her finger on it, but she thought it was the unusual start of their friendship and the relative ease with which they had become familiar with each other that had made their conversations so fun. It almost felt like a game of virtual masquerade to message with someone she felt she knew so well and yet really didn't know at all.

In those messages, however, Claire didn't mention that she was heading to the Cotswolds that weekend. She'd told Will that that she wanted to stop by The Happy Clam during their getaway, and it was what she was anticipating the most for the trip. She imagined what a surprise it'd be to Becks to spot her order something at her pub. Claire could picture the scene: Becks would be busy at the bar attending to the many customers ordering drinks. Claire would walk up to the bar and order a glass of red wine very casually. Becks would fill the order not recognizing her at first, but upon recognition, she would be delighted by Claire's surprise visit. She would introduce Claire to all the waitstaff and tell them about how they became friends. It tickled Claire to think that such a happy unfolding was a definite possibility for the upcoming weekend.

That Friday evening Claire and Will met in Paddington and took First Great Western's evening line to Moreton-in-Marsh. During the train ride Claire could feel the excitement build. She'd been having second thoughts about spending time alone with Will for a whole weekend, but now that they were on their way, she admitted to herself that the idea of going away to the country was quite romantic.

They arrived at Moreton at half past nine in the evening, and the sky was ablaze in pinkish purple tones as the night slowly nudged the day away. The first stars that began to dot the expansive canvas illuminated Moreton's high street of corner shops and pubs. As Claire strolled hand-in-hand with Will, they peered at windows of tea rooms and antique stores with exquisite china sets, and they walked by cozy-looking pubs with ancient signs that read Black Bear and Redesdale Arms.

The smells coming from the pubs made them realize how hungry they were, so they entered the Redesdale Arms. They sat at a table by the window, where they could see the final descent of the day into the horizon. A low fire was burning in a hearth on the opposite corner of the small room, and rowdy football fans with ales in hands were cheering at the flat screens in the bar area as Chelsea and Arsenal faced off.

Claire and Will ordered mussels and a burger to share, and when their food arrived, Claire said to him, "This is wonderful. I'm so glad that you brought me out here this weekend."

"I'm happy to hear it. This is a pretty cool place."

Will drank his beer and looked quite pleased with himself. Claire thought it was an opportune time to bring up a subject had been on her mind the past week. She picked at her chips and said, "Will, remember Ada and Lennie's party? Remember what you said about reparations?"

Will gave her a searching look as if trying to recall the party and then said, "Yeah, I remember. Why?"

"Did you mean it?"

Will said, "Of course I did. Why would I say it if I didn't?"

Claire shrugged. "I don't know. It's just that Ada said that sometimes you'll say things that you don't mean just to have a debate with Lennie and rile him up."

"Ha! Ada said that? She knows me too well. I don't know. Maybe I was too much of a prick with Lennie. I think reparations is a noble idea, but it'd be an uphill battle."

"But don't you think there are some uphill battles that are still worth fighting?"

Will replied, "Yes, I do. Just not that one."

Satisfied with the answer, Claire smiled at him, and they went on to talk about other topics during the meal. Once they finished, they checked into their bed and breakfast just off of the high street, a cottage called The Silver Bells. The owners of the bnb were an older couple who greeted them warmly and showed them around. The inside looked like something out of the fairy tales Claire had read as a little girl. The dining room contained oak tables and hand-carved wood chairs accompanied by plates with intricate designs and silverware that looked like museum pieces. They were then led into a sunroom with high ceilings and large bay windows that looked out into a garden. Claire loved how cozy the room felt, and she thought that perhaps if there was time later she and Will could spend an afternoon reading in there.

At the end of the tour, the owners handed them a silver key for their room. Claire and Will went inside and saw a queen-sized bed covered with a comforter with blue and white floral prints. There was a copper tea set by the nightstand, and two mint chocolates next to it. There were also two paintings in the room, both depicting scenes of life in the countryside, one of young girls playing in the meadows and the other a farmer and his cow. Between the paintings there was a window that looked out into the garden they'd seen from the sun room. As Claire looked out into the bright yellow moon from the window, Will came up to her and asked, "Well, what do you think? Have I done good?"

Claire turned around and kissed him. "You've done very well. This, all of this, is perfect."

They unpacked their bags, and Will pulled out a bottle of wine and two glasses and began to pour. Claire said, "You've thought of everything, haven't you?"

"I've learned over the years that you can only do your best with what you can control, and then let the chips fall as they may."

As Claire pulled out some lace lingerie she'd brought for the trip, she said, "I think that's wise learning on your part. You may find yourself getting lucky this weekend, Will Adams."

She saw Will's eyes widen as he saw her red lingerie, and she laughed and said, "But not tonight. I'm tired from the train ride. Let's see how we get on tomorrow." She reached for her glass of wine and took a sip.

He said, "You're killing me, but I suppose the wait will be worth it." He clinked glasses with her, and took a swallow himself. They took their time finishing the wine that evening as they planned out the next day, and they cuddled in bed for a little bit while gazing out into the moon and stars. As Claire drifted off to sleep, she felt relaxed and happy.

Chapter 8

The next day Claire and Will woke up at six in the morning to the sound of a rooster's crow. They dressed and went downstairs to the dining room, where they were greeted by the smells and display of a full English breakfast, including the black pudding and fried bread that the London cafés often left out. They took their time enjoying their breakfast and tea, and by the time they stepped out of the bnb, Claire felt ready to hike all day.

They bought a walking map to Bourton-on-the-Hill at the tourist center and found the back road hiking trail behind the parking lot of the Redesdale Arms pub. The hike took them through fields that seemed forgotten from the rest of the world. The only hint of man's touch upon these secluded meadows were the occasional wooden fences and gate posts. An hour into the hike Claire stopped to bask in the scene. There were green hills upon green hills in the distance, and the low-hanging cumulus clouds converged down upon them. Claire said to Will, "Isn't this gorgeous? I don't think I've been surrounded in so much beauty in my life."

He gazed towards the same direction and said, "Yes. It reminds me of a scene from the book *Travels with Charley*, in which the author John Steinbeck takes his dog up to the mountains near his hometown and says to the dog, 'There's the smell of heaven up here.'"

She joked, "What are you saying? That I'm your dog companion?"

"No, seeing how you're the one who proclaimed the beauty of the land, I think that would make you Steinbeck and I your dog."

They hiked on for another half hour, and soon they hit the main road to Bourton. It was a quaint village riding up a hill, and as they walked up the hilly road, Claire saw charming Tudor cottages hugging the side of the road. They passed by an old church building, and just as she wondered when they would reach Becks's pub, she saw it at the top of the hill. It was a rather large building in the same architectural style as that of the cottages they'd walked past, and attached to the building was the sign in bold lettering, The Happy Clam.

When they entered the pub, Claire observed the interior. The floors were new hardwood floors of a lighter wood shade, and combined with the stone walls they gave the pub a rustic, clean vibe. There was a wood-burning stove in the corner of the building, and above it, there was a large clock with the letters "The Happy Clam" decorating its edges. In the back area of the pub large windows looked out to Bourton's descending village and the valleys and hills beyond it.

Claire went up to the bar area where there was a woman serving drinks under a sign that read "Good people drink good beer."—Hunter S. Thompson

"Excused me, is Rebecca Kennedy around?"

The barmaid was pretty and looked like she was a few years younger than Claire, maybe in her early to mid twenties. She had a slender nose and an oval face, and Claire wondered where Becks had found such a bartender to tend to her pub in the middle of the country. "Yes, she's in the back cooking. May I ask who's asking for her?"

"Could you tell her that her friend Claire Moore is here for a visit?"

The barmaid went through the kitchen door and a couple of minutes later both she and Becks came out. Becks exclaimed, "Claire! What are you doing here?"

Becks was wearing a plain black shirt like their first encounter, and her apron was covered in grease stains. Her sweat made her cropped hair stick to her forehead. Claire thought that Becks looked as if she were in her element, and she replied, "Well, I came by to finally see what the commotion about the Cotswolds was about."

"And?"

"It's astounding. Absolutely astounding. I can't believe you live in such beauty. And your pub is so exquisite. You didn't tell me that your pub is the finest pub in all of England."

Becks looked pleased by her compliments. She then nodded to Will and said, "You must be Will. I've heard a lot about you."

Will offered his hand and said, "Pleasure to meet you. Claire had told me several times that we had to visit her friend's pub in the Cotswolds, and now I understand why. This place is awesome."

The barmaid then cleared her throat, and Becks put a hand on her shoulder and said, "Oh, and this is Susan, my bartender."

Susan glanced over at Becks as if expecting her to say more, but Becks ignored her and went on to say to Claire, "Are you staying here in Bourton?"

"No, staying at Moreton. We arrived yesterday."

"That's lovely. You know, Moreton has a pub called the Bell Inn for which Tolkien modeled the Prancing Pony after in *Lord of the Rings*."

"Really?" Claire said. "I love those books. We'll definitely have to go. Does it look the way it's described in the books?"

Becks looked sheepish as she said, "I hate to admit it, but I've neither read the books nor seen the movies."

"Are you joking?"

"No, it wasn't quite presented as a joke, was it?"

"But that's preposterous. Every conscious person on earth has seen the movies."

"I bet there's at least an eighty-year old widow in a North Korean village somewhere who hasn't even heard of the *Lord of the Rings*."

Claire smiled at Becks as they both recognized that they were easing into the familiar banter of their online chatter, but Will picked up the menu and said, "The food here looks great. I think I'm ready for lunch."

Becks said, "Oh yes, please pick a table and sit down. Here we are pecking away at each like a pair of hens when you must be starved."

Claire wanted to talk longer with Becks, but she followed Will to a corner table and sat down. She looked over the menu and agreed with him that the food descriptions read deliciously. They settled on the goat cheese and green bean salad to share, and Will went with the longhorn ribeye steak for his entree while Claire selected the butternut squash risotto. As they waited for the food and sipped their Cotswolds Wheat Beers, she said to him, "I still can't believe that Becks hasn't watched *Lord of the Rings*."

Will shrugged. "Not everyone is into pop culture. I'm sure several of my friends haven't watched the movies either."

Precisely, Claire thought. She imagined some of Will's stuffy friends debating the fighting skills of an elf versus that of a dwarf, and she burst out laughing. Will asked her what the matter was, and she just shook her head as she continued to laugh.

The food then arrived, and Claire realized how hungry she'd been. She took one bite of the salad and felt a pleasurable release from the fresh taste of the green beans and the goat cheese, and her happy sensations took over as she dug into her risotto.

A few minutes later Becks swung by their table and asked, "How's everything?"

Claire replied, "Oh, Becks, it's brilliant. I'm not lying to you when I say that this might be the best meal that I've ever had."

Becks beamed, and then Will added, "It's good. The steak is quite good. It's almost as good as the steaks back in the US, and that's saying something."

Becks's smile looked as if it quivered just a brief bit, and Claire noticed it. But Becks laughed and said, "Cheers. I'm glad to hear it. I hope you both enjoy the rest of your meal."

When Becks was out of earshot, Claire said to Will, "Was it really necessary to say that? Couldn't you have said that it was delicious and left it at that?"

Will looked at Claire with a surprised expression and replied, "What's the big deal? I was giving her a compliment. It's the first steak that I've tried in the UK that I thought was decent, and I'd want to eat it again. I think she appreciated the comment."

Claire was exasperated at his utter lack of awareness, but she decided to drop it. "Yes, Becks did say she was glad to hear you enjoyed her steak."

Claire remained annoyed as they finished up their meal, but she didn't think Will seemed to notice. They went up to the bar to pay, and Susan brought Becks back out from the kitchen.

Claire said to the both of them, "I wanted to say again that our lunch was absolutely brilliant. I'm not sure if I can eat at another pub again."

Becks said, "Oh, stop it. Flattery won't get you anywhere with me. Well, maybe a bit. No need to bring out your purse, because your meal is on the house."

"No, we couldn't accept."

"I insist. I told you that I would buy the next round after our last meeting."

Before Claire could protest further, Will chimed in and said, "That's very generous of you. Thanks a lot. Also, do you know of any trails that we might take back to Moreton?" He took out their walking map.

Becks studied the map and asked Will, "How did you get here?"

Will showed her the route, and she nodded and said, "Try this route going back through this area of south of the A44 road. It's very scenic, and I doubt that you'll run into many people this time of day."

They thanked her, and before they left, Claire asked, "When will you come back to London for a visit? You should come up."

"Thanks, but I don't know. It's the busy season, but maybe in the fall."

Claire said, "I hope it's sooner, but until the next time, thank you so much for the meal."

They said a final round of good-byes, and after Claire took one last look back at her new favorite pub, they headed out the door.

Chapter 9

Claire and Will headed out the door and started the hike back to Moreton-in-Marsh. Claire remembered that she'd been irritated with Will for his comment on the meal, but she tried to let it go as they began walking downhill. Following the trail that Becks had outlined for them, they walked past the church they'd first seen coming up the hill, and took a right turn on what looked like a faint trail path. They traveled past a row of cottages and reached a large wooden gate. After struggling a bit to figure out how to open the gate, they were able to unlatch it, and they stepped onto the meadows beyond Bourton-on-the-Hill.

Claire found the downward hike through this field of grass with grazing cows to be equally divine as the trail up to The Happy Clam. The grass was tall with patches of daffodils and juniper scattered throughout, and Becks had been right in that there were no other hikers to be seen for miles on end.

They hiked further down the hills, and slightly off the path they stumbled upon a small farmhouse. It was a charming house with a bright coat of yellow paint on its door and fresh flowers on the porch. Peeking through the glass windows of the living room, Claire could see an older woman curled up on one of the sofas in the room as she read a book. Her only movements were to turn the pages or to flip the occasional wisp of silver hair back into place when it fell down. She was so absorbed in her book that she didn't notice the two hikers observing from outside. Claire admired how peaceful she looked.

Will asked her, "What's the matter?"

Claire shook her head and said, "Nothing. I just couldn't help but be envious of how content that woman looks."

"Aren't you content?"

"Right now I am. To be in this beautiful countryside is wonderful. But when this weekend is over it's back to the grind. Back to a world of cubicles and spreadsheets and me questioning what I'm doing with my life. Part of me wishes I could stay here forever."

"You'd get bored here. Sure, it's fun to prance about for a weekend, but you'd miss the energy of the city. Think of all the pubs and restaurants, the museums and theaters."

"Maybe you're right. But I wish I was like that woman. She looks so at peace, as if she figured out what she wanted in life and is living it through."

Will furrowed his brows and asked, "You're not even in your thirties yet. You still have time to do whatever you want."

Claire sighed. "I don't know...it sometimes feels as if life is just slipping away, and there's nothing that I can do about it." She paused and then said, "When we get back to Moreton, do you think we can sit in the inn's sunroom for a bit? Maybe we can read for a bit there?"

Will said, "Sure, but afterwards I can think of something else we can do in our room."

"Honestly," she said as she gave him a playful shove, "can't you think of something else other than sex?"

Will grinned and simply shrugged his shoulders. Claire took one last look through the window before Will gently nudged her to continue on their hike. They hiked on for another hour, and the white, fluffy clouds of the morning gave way to ominous, gray clouds. Claire thought it might begin to rain soon, but they made their way past the open fields and approached a grove of trees. Claire followed Will as he led her further south off of the trail, but she started to wonder where they were headed.

"Will," Claire said. "What's going on? Why are we walking away from the trail?"

Will didn't answer her immediately as he forged ahead, but after they'd walked a quarter mile into a shaded area under some foliage, he said to her, "Isn't this a romantic spot?"

Claire wasn't sure what Will had in mind, but she answered him, "Yes, it's romantic here."

Will put his arms around her waist and began to kiss her. He then slowly slid his fingers down from her waist, and Claire said to him, "Will, stop that. People might see us here."

He gave her a coy look as he said to her, "No one can see us here. We're way off the trail now, and we didn't see anyone when we were on the path." He resumed kissing her, and this time squeezed her behind more forcefully with his right hand as he thrust his weight against her chest.

Claire pulled away this time, and she said, "Will, I mean it. Stop that. What's wrong with you?"

Will took her arm, and he said, "Claire, let's make love right here. I've been so turned on ever since last night when you showed me your lingerie, and I don't think I can take it much longer. It doesn't get any more romantic than this, to be out in such beauty in nature, and we're going to regret it if we don't seize the opportunity."

With his right hand still gripping her arm, he pulled her back to him, and the force of his tug scared Claire. He grabbed her left wrist with his other hand, and his tight squeeze sent a shot of pain. He began kissing her hard, and she shoved him away.

"No, Will! Get away from me! I'm not going to have sex with you here. People might see us. You're scaring me." Claire began to feel the hot tears starting to stream down her face.

Will's face contorted into an expression of anger and frustration. "Claire, you're being such a dick tease. I've been patient this whole time, but it's starting to piss me off." He stepped towards her.

Claire yelled at him, "Don't you come near me! I'll scream if you come near me." She felt panic rising, and she picked up a tree branch that was nearby.

When he saw the branch Will stepped back with his hands up and said, "Whoa, what, are you crazy?"

Claire waved the stick at him, and she screamed, "Go away, Will! Go away!"

He retreated back and said, "C'mon, Claire, calm down a bit."

She shouted at him, "Get away from me!"

He stepped back as she continued to wave the tree branch with all her might. She felt hysterical as she blindly waved the tree, and finally Will stepped back several paces and said to her, "I'm through with this bullshit. You're fucking crazy!"

Shaking from her crying, she continued to hold the branch and said, "Go away! Get the fuck away from me!"

Will stared at her for a brief moment, and then shaking his head, he turned around and began to walk away. Claire held onto her branch as she watched Will's mirage disappear into the horizon.

Even after he was long gone, she saw that her hand was still shaking as she held her stick. When she was sure that he was nowhere near her, she released her stick slowly and slid down to the base of the tree. She had been spared, but she was now alone and lost.

Chapter 10

The trauma of the event settled in, and Claire sat on the ground. The initial shock of what had just occurred trickled into her system in fits and surges, and she started to cry. She examined her left wrist and saw that there was bruising from Will's hard grab. She wished that all of this was some sick nightmare and that she would wake up to find herself in her familiar flat in London. She blamed herself. She felt foolish for having allowed herself into such a situation. She'd known that the weekend trip was a mistake when he'd first shown her the tickets. She'd known all along that Will had never been right for her, but she hadn't had the heart to cut it off earlier, just like all her other boyfriends in her past.

She could have sat there and cried for hours, but soon it began to rain. Claire realized that she should seek out shelter to avoid catching a cold. Her body ached at the thought of the long hike that awaited her. She continued to lay by the tree as she summoned up the energy to get up. Part of her worried that if she left the grove, Will might be waiting for her. She eyed the tree branch that lay next to her and grabbed it. But she thought to herself that if Will had wanted to attack her, he would have come back and done so in this secluded clearing of trees rather than waiting in the open grass. Don't be afraid, she said to herself. She took a deep breath and finally got up from the ground.

When she came out of the grove, she saw grass fields in all directions. With the sun gone, she realized that she had no sense of direction on how to get back to Moreton. Trying to steady herself, she tried to recall the steps that she and Will had taken to the grove of trees. Generally they had hiked their way down eastward from Bourton, and near the farmhouse they had cut right to head south toward the grove. She decided to walk straight ahead then and look for the house, at which point she would hopefully find the trail once more or even ask for shelter.

The rain soon became a downpour, however, and it became very difficult to see even thirty yards ahead. There was no one in sight, and even the cows seemed to have scurried off somewhere to avoid the rain. Shivering and feeling as if she was the sole living creature in the world, she walked for an hour as water started to fill up her shoes and her socks became soggy and wet. She got to a patch of the fields in which she thought the farmhouse should be, but it was nowhere to be found. Claire circled around the perimeter of some fence posts to see if the farmhouse was in the horizon, but it was to no avail. She was lost.

Claire tried to maintain her calm in the midst of the rain. She tried to recall Will's map in her head, and she convinced herself that she was tracing her steps correctly; Bourton was west of Moreton, and she had to be in the meadows that lay south in between the two villages. If she could just figure out which way was north, she was bound to meet the A44 road. But thinking through the map a little more, she recalled that the fields were also fenced in a triangular manner by other roads in the other directions as well. She reassured herself that in the worst case scenario she would eventually meet one of the roads and hitch a ride back to Moreton.

With this little assurance to steady her mind, she decided to keep marching straight ahead with the hopes that she had picked the northern route. As she traveled on, she kept encouraging herself that it was just rain and that she'd walked through much worse rainstorms in London. Granted, in London she hadn't been so hopelessly lost with the nearest human being seemingly miles away. But Claire tried to focus on positive thoughts as she trudged along. She promised herself that once she got to Moreton she would head over to the Bell Inn for a hot cup of tea and a scone with plenty of jam. Two scones, she promised herself.

Claire couldn't remember the last time she'd felt so lost and afraid. Once when she was eight years old, she'd lost her parents while following them at Heathrow airport. One of the airline desk clerks found her crying and had used the intercom to find her parents. Even now she remembered what it was like to believe that she was orphaned forever. Her senses had become so heightened to the awareness of her own existence that she could count every beat of her thumping heart, but she had felt as if she was trapped in a bubble that made her invisible to the rest of the world. She felt the same feeling tugging at the edges of her mind now. She tried to fight the feeling for a bit, but then gave into the despair.

"For fuck's sake!" she said. She sat down on the grass and began to cry again. Tears flowed freely as she yelled out, "What the hell am I doing here?" She felt so tired, so she lay down and closed her eyes. Once her eyes were closed, she pictured the woman in the farmhouse. She remembered how beautiful and serene she looked in her old age.

I want to be like her, Claire thought as she lay on the grass.

I am desperate.

I'm so desperate that I could scream.

I want to change.

I don't want to have any regrets later in life.

I want to figure things out and become a woman that I'm proud to be.

I have to change.

Claire felt a calm feeling come over her after she made these declarations to herself. Soon she was able to muster up the energy to get up and walk again. She walked for another hour, and just when she was starting to lose faith that she'd ever get out of the fields, she saw that the fields started to slope upwards to hills. At last, something she recognized. Claire felt a wave of relief, as she remembered the hills and was able to orient herself. She was no longer lost, and her immediate thought was that she could walk straight ahead to meet the road and then walk alongside of it until she made it to Moreton or was picked up by a driver. But she then thought that Will had likely headed back to Moreton to gather his belongings. The mere thought of running into him made her weak.

Her other option then was to hike up the hills back to Bourton. Once in Bourton, she'd have to intrude upon Becks to go to Moreton with her to pick up her items. After some hesitation, Claire turned westward and decided to hike uphill back towards Bourton. She hated the thought of being a bother to Becks while she was overseeing the pub, but she couldn't risk seeing Will again.

She started the march back up the hilly fields and realized that it was so much more tiring when her clothes were soaked and she'd already been hiking for several hours. At one point she wanted to give up, but she willed herself to keep climbing up the hills. She pictured the warm stove of The Happy Clam and the comfortable chairs by the fire, and it gave her the strength to push ahead. She thought of Becks. She wasn't sure what she'd say to her once she got to her pub, but the thought of seeing her friendly face kept her focused on hiking up the trail.

Finally, when she thought she'd faint from exhaustion, she reached the familiar gate back into Bourton. She was now drenched, her hair and clothes covered in mud and her shoes squishing with water. Her teeth were clattering to no end, and she couldn't feel her feet. She pushed the gate open, and moving forward in small steps now, she repeated to herself, onward and onward.

Her mood lifted considerably now that she was walking along the main road to The Happy Clam. After a few minutes of walking up the village road she made it to the church landmark. Here she stopped for a bit under its roof to gather her bearings. She was going to make it to The Happy Clam, and she was ever so grateful. She replayed in her mind all the events that had transpired after she'd left that pub, and she was thankful that she hadn't been hurt or gotten lost. Who knew what Will would have done if she hadn't picked up the tree branch right in time? Or if she hadn't stumbled upon the hills just in the nick of time? She could have been lost for hours. You lucky bitch, she muttered to herself. She became aware that she was standing underneath a church building. She didn't think of herself as a religious person, as she'd stopped attending services as soon as she'd left for uni away from her parents, but she couldn't help but lift up a silent prayer of thanks.

After the brief respite, she hit the road once more. It was easier now, with the path clear and the known distance so short. High up the road she could see The Happy Clam rising tall up ahead like a distant lighthouse in the rain. It gave her renewed energy and vigor, and the steps up the road felt lighter. Eventually a car stopped by and the driver asked her if she wanted a ride, but she declined and kept hiking. The journey's end was near, and she wanted to savor in the fact that she'd made it back on her own.

After following the road through its upward curves, she at last reached the doorsteps of the now familiar pub. Any sense of feeling in her body had long left her, but she had made it back. After taking a quick breath, she pushed the door open to The Happy Clam.

Chapter 11

When Claire walked through the pub's doors, she saw Susan and Becks conversing at the bar area. They stopped and stared at her with shocked expressions, and Becks said, "Christ! What the hell happened to you?"

Claire felt relief from seeing her familiar face, and suddenly she felt exhausted. She slumped onto one of the chairs near her, and as Becks and Susan rushed to her, she began to cry uncontrollably. They quickly scooted her chair to near the warm fire, and in between her cries, she recounted what had just happened. When she was finished, Becks said to her, "We have to call the police."

Claire shook her head. "No, I don't want to talk to the police." At this point talking to the police to recount the situation in the grove was the last thing Claire wanted to do.

Becks replied, "Claire, he tried to rape you."

Claire shook her head once more. "No, he was horrible but he stopped trying to kiss me after the first couple of attempts."

"You're sure?"

"Yes, and nothing happened."

"Claire…"

Claire cut off Becks by saying, "But, if it's not too much of a bother, my bag is still at the bed and breakfast we were staying at."

Becks nodded and said, "What's the name of the place?"

"It's called The Silver Bells."

Becks turned to Susan and said, "The Silver Bells is off the corner of Bourton Road and the High Street. Go take Gary with you and bring back Claire's bag."

Susan motioned over to one of the waiters, and they hurried out of the pub. Becks went to the back of the pub and reappeared with a change of clothes and a towel. She said to Claire, "Go beyond those back stairs, and it'll take you up to my room. There's the shower next to it for you to use before you catch a cold."

Claire got up and did as Becks instructed. In the hot shower the soothing warmth of the water cleansed her body and mind. She got out of the shower and put on the clean T-shirt and jeans that Becks had provided her. They fit her well, and after drying her hair, she felt rejuvenated. When she came back down to the pub, she saw that Becks had brewed up a pot of tea for her.

"Drink," Becks instructed.

Feeling much better after her first sips of tea, Claire said, "Thank you. Thank you so much. I don't know how I can repay you."

"Shh. Don't worry about it. Just drink the tea and try to regain some of your strength."

Claire sat down on one of the nearby leather chairs. "I'm such a fool," she said. "I can't believe I got myself into such a situation."

Becks said to her, "You can't blame yourself. You did nothing wrong here. If there's anyone to blame, blame me. I'm the one who said that you should give this arsehole a chance."

Claire continued, "I'm such an idiot. I knew that he wasn't right for me. Even today, when he commented on the steak, I knew how hopelessly unaware he was, but I just kept fooling myself."

"Stop beating yourself up, Claire." Becks gave her a squeeze of her hand, and the warmth of her hands was comforting. Becks said to Claire, "There's no excuse for his behavior, and there's nothing you could have done to predict it. And I don't want to be overbearing, but now that you've got your wits about you, I want to ask you one more time if you're sure that you don't want to call the police."

Claire said, "I'm sure."

"But what if you hadn't waved the stick at him? He might have tried something."

"No, it all happened so fast, but I don't think he was thinking of harming me. Even before I grabbed the stick he could have done something if he'd wanted to."

When Becks continued to give her an incredulous stare, Claire said, "Honestly, I don't think he was going to try. I grabbed the stick just to make sure, but he'd stopped trying to kiss me. I think he was already about to walk away when I scared him with my branch."

Claire wasn't entirely sure of this last statement, but she wanted Becks to stop fretting. The incident already was a little hazy to her, so she chose to believe what she said.

Becks sighed. "All right then. You must be knackered. I have a guest room next to my room upstairs, so why don't you go back there and rest up while they come back with your suitcase?"

The offer appealed to her, so Claire went upstairs, and upon finding the guest room, she lay down on the bed. The wool blanket felt soft against her skin, and she fell asleep right away.

She woke up later in a disoriented state and looked at the time on her phone. It was nearly seven, which meant that she'd been asleep for nearly three hours. She got up from the bed, and as she opened the door of the guest room, she could hear voices coming from a nearby room and quickly identified that it was Becks and Susan.

"You care for her."

"Yes of course, she's a friend."

"No, I don't mean that. You have feelings for her. I saw the way you looked at her when she was here earlier for lunch."

"Don't be daft. I barely know her. I told you we met once and realized that we'd been set up incorrectly."

"Then why didn't you tell her that we were seeing each other?"

Claire was somewhat surprised to hear of Becks and Susan's relationship, but looking back now, she remembered some of the odd glances that Susan had given Becks.

Becks said, "There wasn't a proper time to mention it. They came in to have a meal. What would I have said? 'Claire, welcome to my pub. And by the way, allow me to introduce Susan, my bartender who also happens to be someone I'm dating.'"

Before they could argue further, Claire knocked because she was afraid that Susan and Becks might discover that she was listening outside their door. Becks opened the door, and Claire said, "Becks, I just woke up, and I was thinking that I better catch the train to London before it's too late."

Becks replied, "No, you should stay for the night. We can cook some dinner for you, and you can stay in the guest bed again." Susan nodded in agreement behind her.

"No, I best get going. You've already been so hospitable, and I don't want to be a bother. I also think I'll feel more comfortable when I'm back in my flat in London."

"Don't be silly. You wouldn't be a bother, and you need some rest."

"Please, Becks. I should get going."

Becks sighed and said, "You're a stubborn mule, aren't you? Well, all right then. Let me drive you to the station, and you should be able to catch the eight o'clock train back to London. But promise me that when you get back that you'll stay at a friend's place for the night to be safe."

Claire nodded and said, "Thank you. I'll call up my friend Maddie. Were you able to find my bag?"

Susan replied, "Yes, when we arrived the owners gave us the bag and said that Will had already left."

"Did they say anything about him?"

"They just said that he arrived soaking wet and said that he had to leave early but that you'd come for your bag later. He paid for the room and then left."

Becks said, "He's likely taken one of the afternoon trains back, but just in case, I'll stay with you at the station until the train comes."

The three of them walked downstairs to the pub area, and Becks gathered Claire's bag for her. Becks and Claire drove to the train station in relative silence, as Claire still felt a little unhinged from the afternoon incident, and Becks seemed to understand this and didn't attempt to engage in conversation.

They got to the train station and waited in silence on a bench. The night was clear and the bright moon was out. There were only a few others waiting around the benches near them. Claire said to Becks, "Thanks again. I don't know how, but I'll repay you again."

"Don't worry about it. Just have a safe trip back, and I'll talk to you when you're feeling better."

"I'm sure I'll be fine. I was just caught off guard by his actions. He didn't do anything wrong, really. Other than being a stupid, horny American."

Becks said, "I hope you don't let this ruin your opinion of the Cotswolds."

Claire replied, "No, it won't. Hopefully in due time I'll just remember the beauty of this place and forget that I was here with a complete twat."

"That's the spirit."

After some hesitation Claire said, "I didn't mean to eavesdrop, but after I woke up, I heard you and Susan talking in your room."

Becks's expression didn't change at all. She replied, "I assumed that you might have when you knocked on our door. She's right. I should have told you and Will at some point that we were seeing each other. Susan thinks I'm embarrassed of her."

Claire said nothing, and after a moment Becks said, "And she may be right."

Claire looked at her in surprise, and Becks sighed. "We met about two weeks ago online. She lives in Evesham, not too far from here. She was in between jobs but had bartended before, so I invited to help out here temporarily. Probably not my most clever move, serving as the boss of someone you've just started dating. She's fun, but she's so young and so silly at times."

Claire nodded and didn't mention the part where she'd heard Susan accusing Becks of having feelings for her. Her jealousy was likely part of the silliness that Becks just described. Claire wanted to tell Becks that she herself had dated many men who'd all turned out to be so silly in the end, and now Will was just another chapter of this silly parade. Or, maybe it was she who was the silly one. Whatever it was, she felt as if time was running out for her to find her match. People never told you that there was a very short window in your early adulthood to find your partner. They never told you that as you grow older you get quite settled in your ways, and any person that you're considering has to be worth the disruption or compromise of your set routines and habits. And to make it worse, the barrier to disruption only grows taller and taller as you settle in deeper over the years until the hope of finding a lifelong partner is quietly extinguished. She wanted to say this to Becks, but she felt shy; she didn't know this Becks sitting next to her as well as the online Becks. So instead, she sat in silence, turning over and over various thoughts on love and loneliness until her head hurt.

Soon the blare of the horn from the oncoming train sounded. Becks picked up Claire's bag and handed it to her. She and Claire made their way to one of the train cars with the other passengers. Becks waved and said, "Good-bye, Claire. Be safe."

"Good-bye, Becks."

They embraced, awkwardly, and for a brief moment Claire wanted to tell Becks that she'd changed her mind, and that she wanted to stay the night in Bourton after all. She thought of sitting by the warm fireplace in the cozy pub and drinking another pot of tea with a blanket draped over her. Back home, there was only her empty flat. But before she could contemplate it further, she was whisked into the stream of the crowd of passengers pushing their way into the car, and Claire eventually sat down. From the window she waved once more to Becks, and she closed her eyes as the evening line began its journey to her awaiting city.

Chapter 12

In the ensuing days after the Cotswolds debacle, Claire believed that life would return to what it had been before her relationship with Will, but she found that she suffered from sudden bouts of anxiety. She would be out with friends or by herself in different parts of London when she would suddenly think that she'd spotted Will in the crowd, and she would feel a sense of panic spring upon her. On one particular Saturday when she was out shopping at Portobello Market, she thought she saw Will buying some apples from across the street. She tried to run the other direction, but she felt a wave of dizziness as she ran, and she fell over onto the pavement. She was helped up by a couple of teenage boys who happened to be near her, and she had to sit at a nearby coffee shop for a while to gather herself.

Her panic attacks followed her to some degree to her workplace. She found it hard to concentrate, and her work suffered. She was often late in delivering her assignments and there were frequent errors when in the past her work had been immaculate.

One day Ronald stormed to her cubicle and smacked down a report that she'd turned in the previous day. In front of other employees around her, he berated her, shouting, "For fuck's sake, this is absolute shit. Your numbers on the last quarter were all wrong again. The gross revenue figures were mixed up with the net profit numbers and the margin figures were way off. And that's just from the few lines I quickly glanced over."

"I'm sorry, Ronald," Claire mumbled, "I'll get them fixed right away."

He replied, "Damn right you will. This is shit. You've been absolutely shitty, and if you hadn't been halfway decent for the last couple of years, I would have sacked you days ago. Now stop being a miserable wretch and get your act together."

Claire could feel the tears well up when a voice behind them said, "That's enough, Ronald. Why don't you leave her alone?"

They turned around and saw that it was Lewis Hardy. Ronald was flabbergasted and said, "Lewis. I didn't realize that you were standing there. I don't know how much you heard, but I was simply explaining to Claire here that there were some mistakes in her report that needed fixing."

Lewis stared at Ronald and said, "I came down here to find you, and I heard the whole exchange. That wasn't an explanation you were giving—it was outright verbal abuse. You're not going to be sacking anyone here at Wyman because I'm dismissing you right now for gross misconduct."

Ronald's eyes widened as he replied, "You can't be serious."

"I am, and I want you to gather up your belongings from your office and leave the premises now. Security can escort you out and will bring your cubicle materials to the lobby."

Ronald's face turned red, and Claire could see that he was about to have one of his explosions. On cue, he said, "I've been at this company for twenty-three years and have been minting money for Wyman while you were some little shit in secondary school. I'll be damned if some hotshot SVP boots me from this job. You'll be hearing from my attorney."

Lewis didn't flinch as he replied, "Good luck with that, as I think there were enough eyewitnesses to dispute whatever tale you might conjure up."

The security guard on the floor came over to Ronald to escort him away from the cubicle, but Ronald pulled away and yelled, "Don't touch me! How dare you touch me!"

At that moment Lewis grabbed Ronald by the collar with both hands and said to him, "I want you out. Now."

Claire and her officemates looked on, startled by Lewis's swift and firm response. Ronald was apparently shocked as well, as he looked back at Lewis in a timid silence. After a few seconds of pause, Ronald glared but kept quiet as he grabbed his briefcase and followed the security guard out of the floor.

Once Ronald had left the premises, Lewis turned to Claire and asked, "Are you okay? I'm sorry that you had to endure such nonsense."

Claire nodded, "Yes, I'm all right. Thank you for what you did."

He offered his hand and said, "I'm Lewis Hardy."

She replied, "Claire Moore. I saw you speak at our last all company meeting when they introduced you."

He waved his hand and said, "That was embarrassing. I hate it when they make a big fuss of those introductions."

She said, "I thought you were brilliant." She then added, "And I thought that your plan for the family units was bold."

"Really? What do you think then? Do you think it'll work?"

Claire nodded, "Yes, I do. We'll all work to make it work."

He looked as if he was blushing a little, but said, "Thank you. Anyway, I have to get going, but if there's anything that you need, don't hesitate to contact me."

After he left their area, Claire's office mates were abuzz with what just had transpired. They asked Claire if she was okay, and then celebrated the fact that Ronald had finally been sacked. They were all also in awe of how Lewis had handled the situation.

"Good god, did you see the way he remained so calm when Ronald was shouting at him?"

"Thank heavens that wanker's finally been sacked!"

"Ronald was bound to leave the company anyway. I doubt that he would have lasted long with the new 'family' plan Lewis is putting together."

"Lewis is awfully fit, isn't he? He must be one of those people who work twelve hours a day and goes home to run a marathon."

"I heard he's single. Wonder how a catch like that remains single all these years."

Claire tried to ignore the chatter around her, but she allowed herself the pleasure of recalling how Lewis fired Ronald on the spot. She also allowed herself that he was even better looking in person, but beyond that she tried to concentrate on fixing her report.

When Claire came home, she couldn't wait to share her story with someone. She initially thought of Maddie or Sarah, but she noticed her laptop sitting on her kitchen table. She'd had a quick chat with Becks the day after coming home from the Cotswolds, but hadn't talked to her since then. She opened her laptop and went to her Gmail account and was pleased to see that Becks was available to chat.

"Becks, it's me, Claire," she typed.

"hi claire, how are you?"

"I had an astounding day in the office today." Claire then went on to describe Lewis's rescue.

"so Mr. SVP was your knight in shining armor? is he as fit as prince will?"

"Very funny, Becks. If you must know, yes, he's quite handsome."

"you should ask him out then."

"What? Ask him out? You're joking. You just don't ask out the SVP of operations at your company. Besides, he'd be too good for me."

"with that kind of attitude youll get nowhere"

Claire wrote, "I wouldn't know how to behave around him. He's a brilliant man. He's currently leading us through an initiative in which we'll work in family units rather than reporting to managers."

"what? is he mad?"

"No, I think it's a good idea. You work with a partner and two junior associates whose skills you're supposed to develop."

"what if you hate your partner? can you get a work divorce?"

"Haha, very funny."

"and your kids? can you spank them if they misbehave? will the work police come lock you up if you mistreat them?"

Claire smiled at her laptop screen. She could almost picture Becks in front of her saying the words. She typed, "Go on, then. Laugh all you want, but we'll see who's laughing when it's all said and done. I think he's a visionary."

Becks wrote back, "when men come up with loony ideas they r visionaries and when women come up with the same ideas theyre mad cat ladies"

Claire agreed silently, but replied, "And what if you're a woman who's following a visionary?"

"A fool in love."

Claire wrote back, "Please. He might have been my knight today, but I'm hardly in love with him."

"we'll see."

Laughing, Claire typed, "Please, stop that nonsense."

After they ended their chat, Claire recalled the events of the day as she got ready for bed. She smiled as she thought of her so-called knight. It was unlikely that she'd ever see Lewis up close again, so it would be a fond but small memory she'd store away to trot out occasionally for herself. As for Ronald, it was such a relief that he was gone, and she thought that no longer having to deal with his verbal abuse might even make her anxiety attacks go away. Things are definitely looking up, she thought as she fell into a deep sleep.

Chapter 13

Claire and Becks chatted often through IM and texts in the ensuing weeks. Their online interactions were always the highlight of Claire's day. When she woke up in the mornings she brewed herself a cup of coffee and opened up the laptop at the kitchen table in the hopes that Becks would be available for a quick conversation before heading off to work. At work, she'd sneak off a quick text or two during her lunch break to say a quick hello or complain about her job. But the best part of the day was when she'd nestle into her bed in the evening after dinner to have a more drawn out conversation in her pajamas.

Claire found herself frequently declining invites from co-workers and friends to meet up at pubs after work so that she could spend more time on her laptop with Becks. She felt a little guilty for this neglect of her other social circles, but she was having too much fun in her conversations with her. Part of it was the anticipation of opening up her screen and hoping that Becks would be there to respond to her. Another aspect was the sense of security that Becks gave her after the Cotswolds incident. But most of all, Claire just felt at ease in talking about everything and nothing with Becks. Sometimes they talked about more serious and lengthy topics such as love or friendships, but sometimes it was just about the weather:

Claire Moore: It's cold yet again in London today. I've been wearing a coat to work. It could be the worst summer of all time.

Becks Kennedy: not much better at bourton. thought global warming was supposed to make it warmer?!?!

Claire Moore: I think I read that global warming sometimes makes it colder.

Becks Kennedy: then they shouldn't call it global warming, should they? maybe global volatility would be more appropriate?

Claire Moore: Well, I think on average it's gotten warmer.

Becks Kennedy: you r confusing me. do you even know what youre talking about?

Claire Moore: Of course I do. What's so confusing about knowing that it's warmer on average but there's a higher degree of deviation?

Becks Kennedy: didn't know that you were a weather expert now. perhaps you could send me a weather report each morning

Claire Moore: = p

Becks Kennedy: there goes that tongue again

or about movies:

Becks Kennedy: I finally got around to finishing the lord of the rings movies this weekend.

Claire Moore: And? Aren't they wonderful?

Becks Kennedy: did nothing for me. just a bunch of hobbits and dwarves and wizards running around for miles on end like a bunch of fools

Claire Moore: You're the fool. Millions of fans would beg to differ with you. I bet you're going to tell me next that you haven't read or watched *Harry Potter*.

Becks Kennedy: i havent. why would I want to watch kid wizards if I can't stand adult ones?

Claire Moore: Oh, good lord.

or about their work:

Claire Moore: I'm crushed in a mountain of work today. Bloody interns screwed up the numbers in our weekly reports, and I have to redo them all. :(

Becks Kennedy: when's that visionary family plan supposed to start?

Claire Moore: It's not for another month.

Becks Kennedy: u can come work for me then. its been very busy with all the tourists and its been utterly overwhelming. think its getting to susan.

Claire Moore: How is she anyway?

Becks Kennedy: fine. everythings fine

At times Claire thought of calling Becks or even paying another visit, but those actions seemed like an intrusion beyond the boundaries of their virtual world.

One evening in mid-September, Claire saw a GChat come in from

Becks that said, "claire u there?"

"Yes, I'm here," Claire typed.

"would you be willing to turn on the video camera function?"

Claire looked at the words in surprise. Something must be up, she thought. She clicked on the video option in the corner of chat window, and Becks popped up on the screen. She saw that Becks's eyes were red, as if she'd been crying. Alarmed, Claire asked, "What's wrong, Becks? What's happened?"

"We broke up. Susan and I. We had a fight this afternoon, and she packed up her bags and left. It was a bit of a silly fight over nothing, but it was a long time coming for us to part ways."

"I'm so sorry. You must be feeling awful."

"I knew it wouldn't last, but I was hoping it would be longer than a couple of months."

Claire felt helpless and wasn't sure quite how to console her. "I'm sorry. It must be very hard. Is there anything I can do to help?"

"I don't think so. I was feeling a bit down, and I thought talking with you might help."

"Well, I'm here for you now."

Becks said, "Thank you, Claire. Breaking up with Susan itself wasn't so bad. It's just that it's put me in one of those self-pity modes where I wonder if I'll ever find the right woman."

Claire nodded in understanding.

Becks continued, "Maybe it's me. I can be quite critical sometimes without even realizing it, and I think it can be too much for my partners. Susan was foolish at times, but maybe I could have just overlooked some of it rather than calling her out every time."

Claire shook her head. "I have a difficult time believing that you'd ever be that critical. It's easy to second guess yourself after a break-up. You'll find the right person yet."

The forlorn Becks on the screen looked inconsolable. Claire started to say something, but then stopped as an idea dawned. "Becks, I know you're busy with the pub and all, but why don't you come to London this upcoming weekend and spend a couple of nights at my place? We can tour the city a bit on Saturday, and then on Sunday I'm having a few of my friends over for a small dinner party. I'm sure they'd love to meet you."

Even on the laptop screen Claire could see that Becks was hesitant. She said, "I don't know. The pub has been very busy."

"Please, I think it'd do you good to get away for a bit. Isn't there someone who could watch the place for you?"

"Well, I suppose Gary could oversee it for a couple of days—"

"It's settled then," Claire interrupted. "You can have him watch the pub, and I'll come over to Paddington on Saturday morning to greet you at the station." Claire held her breath as she waited for her response.

Becks stared at the screen for what seemed like an eternity, but finally relented and said, "Oh fine, I'll be there Saturday. You can be so damn persistent."

"Brilliant." Claire felt excited despite reminding herself that Becks was in a state of mourning after her break-up. "You'll have forgotten about your break-up by the time we're through with this weekend."

After they hung up, the possibilities of the weekend bounced around in her mind. They could go watch a musical. Or a play. Or maybe even a concert. They'd have to go to one of the parks. If they went to Regents Park they might go to the top of Primrose Hill. Maybe Becks was into the museums, and it'd been several weeks since Claire had been to any of them. But then they'd have to go shopping too, either at Harrods or Wyman or Selfridges. And of course, there were the restaurants. Whether to take Becks to one of the trendy new ones or her favorites near her flat? There was the new Japanese restaurant that had set up shop in Islington that her friends were raving about, but Singapore Garden never failed to impress her guests.

Claire laughed as she caught a hold of herself thinking of all these plans in a thousand different directions all at once, and she told herself that she'd just present Becks with options and allow her to choose. Claire was so keen to show her a good time as a sort of payment for Becks's help and kindness during the Cotswolds visit, and she vowed to give her the greatest weekend ever to cheer her up.

Chapter 14

Becks arrived Saturday morning at nine wearing her standard black shirt and dark blue jeans along with a small backpack. Claire saw her step off the train, and as she waved, she felt a rush of joy in seeing her friend once more. She felt nervous, as it was their first reunion since the Cotswolds, and she wondered if Becks felt the same.

If Becks was nervous, she hid it well, as the first words out of her mouth upon reaching Claire were, "Christ, I can't believe you had me ride the seven o'clock train in. I never wake up this early, especially for holidays."

All feelings of shyness were erased as Claire replied on cue, "And a good morning to you too. Will you stop grumbling? It's a beautiful fall day in one of the great cities of the world, and I'm about to show you the time of your life."

"Your morning optimism is unbearable. You're like a cheerful, rabid squirrel."

Claire gave Becks a playful shove, and they headed down to the Tube. They got on the Bakerloo line, and on the Tube car Claire outlined the itinerary for the day that she'd meticulously planned out despite herself. "We're first going to go to Oxford Street, where I'll take you to Selfridges to browse around and try some macarons. Then I thought we could walk to Leicester Square and catch the Tube to Borough Market for lunch. Then we'll walk along the river and head over to the Tate Modern. We'll end the day by eating dinner near my flat at this wonderful restaurant called Singapore Garden."

Becks said, "That seems like an awful lot, Claire. I told you that I've been in London several times before. Mind you, it's been a while, not counting our little date, but we don't have to see a bunch of places. I came here just to see you and see what your life here is like."

"I know that. But we can have a more relaxed day tomorrow. Trust me, you'll love every minute of our tour today."

They got off the Oxford Circus station, and when they stepped on to the street, there were crowds of people on the sidewalks carrying their shopping bags. As they pushed their way through the masses, Claire turned to Becks and said, "It's usually pretty busy here because it's the main shopping street, but it's usually not this bad, especially in the morning. God, I can't stand the tourists."

"I'm sure you've never been a tourist in your life."

"When I am a tourist I have the courtesy to not take up entire swaths of the sidewalk or stop in the middle of the walk to check my city map."

"Boohoo, Claire. Stop your whining and lead on."

They walked into Selfridges via the food hall, and Claire delighted in seeing Becks's expressions of wonder as they pushed past the hanging rib joints and the tables of Pierre Marcolini chocolate boxes. It was very crowded, and Claire lost Becks a couple of times whenever Becks stopped to survey the fresh crab legs or the glass displays of the cakes and pies.

"It's quite something, isn't it?"

Becks nodded. "Everything is so polished and shiny. I mean, take that butcher's corner for instance. I think of blood and guts and knives when I think of my butcher back home, but here it looks like the cow might have been massaged and oiled before magically transforming into a pile of perfectly chopped meat. It's so crowded, though. How are there so many people here?"

Claire shrugged and said, "I don't know. Maybe they're here for the macarons like we are." She led Becks to the Pierre Hermé shop and said to Becks, "Have you had a macaron before? They're orgasmic. They're like mini cookie orgasms."

"Lovely image. And yes, I've tried macarons before, although I've just read about the ones here at Pierre Hermé. But christ, I've been meaning to watch my sugar intake."

"Oh, stop that rubbish and start picking some out." Claire selected some of the salted caramel and pistachio ones for herself, and helped Becks settle on some white truffle and mango flavored varieties.

She waited for Becks to try a bite, and asked, "Aren't they good?"

Becks had a dreamy look in her eyes. "Very good. You weren't lying about them. I'd gain five stones if I lived here in London."

They ate the macarons as they elbowed their way through the perfume and makeup section of the department store, and they ignored the disapproving looks they got from some of the store employees. Claire was about to lead them out the door, but Becks said to her, "Wait. I want to take a look at the makeup section for a bit."

"You what?"

Becks turned a shade of scarlet. "Close your mouth. I've been meaning to learn how to apply makeup without looking like a clown, and I figure that this might be a good time to do so."

Claire nodded, and trying not to embarrass Becks, she said, "Of course. Let's head on up to the counters."

They walked up to a makeup counter and the saleswoman behind the counter asked, "May I help you?" She was stick-skinny and had her hair up in an extreme bun.

Becks said, "I just wanted to look for some new makeup."

The saleswoman said, "What sort of makeup are you interested in?"

Becks gave a hopeless look and replied, "Well, I'm not quite sure..."

Claire stepped in and said, "My friend here is a bit tired of the same old look, and she wants to rethink how she applies her makeup from top to bottom. She wants to start completely fresh, and we're looking for some basic products to start her off."

The saleswoman nodded and said, "Very well. We'll start with the foundation and concealer, and then add some powder. We'll then add the eyeliner and eye shadow, mascara, add a little bit of blush and lipstick—"

Claire saw the petrified look on Becks's face and said to the saleswoman, "Let's maybe pare it down a bit. She's got beautiful skin already as you can see, so maybe we can just try some eyeliner, mascara, and a little lipstick?"

"Very well. We can start with those and add more later if she wishes." The makeup woman then explained each of the products as she applied them onto Becks, and after she was finished, Becks turned to Claire and asked, "What do you think?"

The saleswoman had done a good job of accentuating her eyes and lips without going overboard, and just those slight highlights made Becks look like a gorgeous actress rather than a sweaty proprietor of a country pub.

She said, "Becks, you look wonderful. You look like Kate Moss when she used to have her short hair."

"Kate who?"

"Kate Moss. The model. You have to be joking. Don't tell me that you don't know who Kate Moss."

Becks then grinned and said, "I'm kidding. Of course I know who Kate Moss is. It's not like we don't get the papers or the internet in the country."

She looked at herself in the counter mirror once more and said, "I do look nice, don't I?" She turned to the saleswoman and said, "I'll buy the lot of the products you just applied."

Looking pleased, the saleswoman said, "Very well. I'll package them up, madam."

After Becks paid for the makeup, they left Selfridges and started walking back on Oxford Street. Claire said, "I think the saleswoman might have been a cyborg, and a rather dull one at that. 'Very well' indeed. 'Very well, I'll piss off.'"

Becks laughed at Claire's imitation. "You're horrible. She was a little stiff but she was fine. I think she might have been annoyed with you for sparing me the full line of her products."

"You hardly needed it. Honestly, I can't believe how good you look. I'm absolutely jealous. People are staring at you as you parade down the street."

Becks looked as if she was blushing a little as she said, "Stop it. But thank you. I do feel nice. So where are we headed next?"

Claire replied, "Leicester Square. Now that you look like a model celebrity, you can strut along the red carpet there." When Becks gave her a confused look, Claire continued, "The Odeon Cinema there is where all the celebrities show up for their movie premieres."

They took the Tube once more and got off at Piccadilly Circus. There was the usual crowd of tourists sitting at the base of the Shaftesbury Memorial Fountain, and many of them stared at the enormous video display of a Samsung phone advert on the north side of the road junction.

Claire hurried Becks past the neon signs for the Angus Steakhouse and M&M World until they reached the garden of Leicester Square. Surrounding the garden were more of the restaurant chain ensembles they'd just pushed past, and discount theatre box offices were lined up side-by-side, selling tickets for the roll call of musicals playing on the West End: Wicked, Lion King, Les Misérables, Miss Saigon, Jersey Boys, Book of Mormon. Giant glittering signs for the Hippodrome Casino blazed on the north end and shone for Odeon Cinemas to the east. Street performers break danced around their booming speakers as mobs of tourists snapped pictures with their smart phones. Schoolboys scuttled around the square, passing out free drink cards for the nightclubs in the vicinity.

Claire said, "Oh, christ almighty. This place is a nightmare. Look at all these people."

Becks replied, "It's been a while, but I've been here before. It hasn't changed much."

"You know, it's like I have amnesia," Claire said, watching a teenage boy strumming a guitar for a crowd of girls. "I always tell myself that I'll never come here to avoid the tourists, but then somehow I end up here, and I'm always pissed off by the orgy of crowds milling all around me."

Becks laughed and said, "That's why I told you we didn't have to do all these things. I've told you I've been to London before. I just wanted to see you, and I want to go to the places that you hang out at. Where does Claire like to go on the weekend?"

Claire thought about it, and she said, "Well, if you're sure that you don't need to see those touristy bits, I guess we can go to Kilburn High Road."

"What's over there?"

"It's a busy street, and they've got all kinds of markets and shops. Lots of different kinds of people over there too, and none of the stuffiness of the high end areas of London."

"Do they have food there, because I'm starving. I believe we've had just macarons for breakfast, as delicious as they were."

Claire put her hand to her mouth. "Oh, so sorry, Becks. Now that you mention it, yes, I'm quite hungry myself."

She grabbed Becks's arm, and they pushed their way past the crowds back to Piccadilly Circus to get back on the Tube.

Chapter 15

Claire and Becks got on the Bakerloo line once more and stopped at Kilburn Park station. As they walked to the main road, they passed by a construction site of a new flat building. A wall was up to guard the site, and it had a quote from the author Zadie Smith describing Kilburn: "It's not perfect—where in London will you find perfection—but it's alive."

Once they got to Kilburn High Road, Claire directed them up north. They walked past some of the chains that were visible on any of London's other high streets, such as Poundland and Sainsburys, but many of the stores were unique to the street. They walked past Chinese herbal shops and a few Irish pubs like Sir Colin Campbell and the Black Lion, and there were several grocery stores with Arabic lettering offering halal meats. The street was busy with pedestrians, but unlike on Oxford Street, they walked with a sense of ease and direction of people who were familiar of their surroundings. Becks saw them and said, "It's a very interesting street. There's a little of bit of everything here. I feel like the entire world has been compressed and squeezed into this one street."

Claire nodded, "Yes, it's a very diverse place full of interesting people—none of that touristy nonsense. What do you think about it?

"I think it's nice. But I'm starving to death. Where's a good place to eat around here?"

Claire said, "None come off the top of my head, but we can look up some places on my phone."

Becks said, "Forget the phone. Look over there. What about that fish and chips shop? I think some fish and chips will do the trick."

Claire looked across the street to where Becks was pointing and saw a hole in the wall with a fading sign that read Cod Haven, Traditional Fish and Chips. She said, "I don't think we want to have lunch there. I doubt that it's offering London's finest culinary advancements."

"Will you stop being such an elitist," Becks said, and she began walking to the restaurant with Claire helplessly trailing after her. When they stepped inside, there were greeted by a couple of friendly Middle Eastern chaps behind the counter. They both selected the five quid cod meal with mushy peas, and they were able to sit down on one of the few tables with their fried fish in less than five minutes.

After the first couple of bites Becks said, "Artery clogging be damned, I could eat this every day."

Claire said, "You don't even serve it at your gastropub. It was noticeably missing on your menu."

"Of course not. I try to make food that you wouldn't get elsewhere."

"So who's the elitist now?"

"Shush. Just eat your fish and chips before I steal it away."

"Fine. I do wonder though, how you manage to look so fit if you enjoy all this fried rubbish?"

"Thank you, I think. I bike around the hills quite a bit, but that's about it."

"Do you? I've been meaning to buy a bike myself. Biking in the city has become a thing recently."

"I've noticed a lot of bikes on the streets. I can help you pick one out when you're ready."

"Thank you, I think I'd like that."

They ate in silence for a few minutes, and then Becks said, "Claire, I don't mean to offend you, but I get the sense that you don't spend a lot of time here at Kilburn."

Claire felt herself blushing and said, "Was it that obvious?"

Becks replied, "Kind of was. You didn't have that walk of purpose like you did at Oxford Street or Leicester Square. It's also a bit dodgy here, not terribly so, as it looks like it's being gentrified, but still not the kind of place where I picture you spending your leisure time. But the big tip-off was that you're into food, but you didn't have any restaurant suggestions."

Claire laughed. "You're right. I guess that was a dead giveaway. I don't come here often. But the thing is that I want to be someone who knows a place like Kilburn High Road well."

Becks said, "You want to feel like Zadie Smith when she says that this place is alive in its imperfections."

Claire said, "Yes, precisely—you understand me. I want to be someone who does her shopping at the halal corner market and gets her hair done at the salon owned by a Bangladeshi immigrant and has a best friend who's Afro-Caribbean. How cool would it be have a Jamaican best friend?"

"Good god, you're horrible."

"I know, but you get my point, though. Instead, I'm an incredibly white British female with my incredibly white friends, and I do all my shopping at Waitrose."

"You can work your way towards adding more 'color' in your life if that's what you want, but while you work on your intentional diversification, I just want to see your real places and habits."

"My real places?"

"Yes."

Claire sighed. "Well, I live in Swiss Cottage, which is about a fifteen, twenty minute bus ride from here. On nice days like this I like to go to Hampstead Heath, which isn't too far from my flat, and then afterwards I like to walk along Hampstead High Street. My friends tease me all the time because Hampstead is a really posh area, but I think it's quaint and lovely in its villagey set up."

Becks said, "Sounds wonderful. Let's head over there after lunch."

They finished up their lunch, and as they walked out the door, Claire said in half-jest to Becks, "Are you sure you don't want to look around some more in Kilburn before we leave? There's a tattoo parlor right there if you want a tattoo."

Becks said to her, "And why in the world would I want a tattoo?" She looked down at her wrist and smiled. "Is it because of this tattoo here?"

Claire nodded. "I noticed it in our first meeting. I'd wanted to ask you what it said, but I didn't."

Becks replied, "Ashleigh. It says 'Ashleigh.'"

Claire wanted to ask who Ashleigh was, but the short manner in Becks's answer made Claire think that now wasn't the appropriate time.

Becks pointed across the street and said, "I don't need another tattoo, but if you're up for it, we could go get a massage at that Thai massage parlor over there."

Claire looked at the small massage center. She didn't tell Becks that she actually dreaded receiving massages. Just the thought of a stranger rubbing her body in a vigorous manner sent chills up her spine. But in an effort to be the perfect host she said, "Let's go in then."

They walked inside to an elegant and clean lobby with Buddha statues standing next to mini waterfalls and potted plants. Soothing music played in the background. A petite Asian woman, presumably Thai, greeted them and gave them each a cup of tea along with a menu of options. Claire looked through the list and she saw that there were individual massages as well as couples' massages. She looked at Becks and said, "You know, I'm not sure if I'm in the mood for a massage myself, but how about if I wait for you here in the lobby while you get one?"

Becks said, "Come on, you have to get one with me. You could be waiting for an hour or so."

The Thai woman also tried to coax Claire by saying to them, "Are you a couple? I give you a couple's massage at discount."

In surprise, Claire repeated, "Are we a couple? No—"

Becks cut her off and said, "Yes, we are a couple and we'll take that couple's massage."

Claire shot her a look, but Becks was busy looking away from her. Claire then trained her ire at their hostess. You bloody damn well know that we're not a couple, she thought. But the hostess looked back at her with an innocuous smile, and Claire knew that she had lost this battle.

Claire and Becks were led down the hall and taken to a dimly-lit room with more statues and two raised beds in the center of the room. Another petite Thai woman greeted them and provided them with two pairs of robes to change into. There was a screen in a corner of the room, and the first hostess ushered them behind the screen to change out of their clothes.

When the two of them were behind the screen, Claire was about to ask Becks who should change out of her clothes first when Becks started stripping. Claire thought about looking away, but she thought doing so in such an obvious way would be awkward, so instead she started to change out of her own clothes as well. She turned towards Becks at one point and saw that she only had her knickers on. She was lean and muscular, and in particular, Claire noticed how her calf muscles arched out a little, likely from all her biking. Her eyes traced up her legs and saw the way that Becks's knickers hugged her small hips, and Claire was aroused. She was immediately embarrassed and turned away from Becks, hoping that Becks hadn't noticed that she'd been staring at her. As Claire concentrated on putting on her robe, she convinced herself it wasn't arousal at all but rather a feeling of admiration at Becks's beautiful shape. She then tried not to think about what she'd seen as they both finished up changing and stepped beyond the screen.

The initial part of the massage started off without a hitch. The Thai women started off by sitting them both on each table and rubbing their ankles and heels. Claire felt ticklish during this portion of the massage, but she was successful in suppressing her laughs. She looked over at Becks a couple of times, and she had her eyes closed with a peaceful smile on her face. Claire tried to mimic Becks's serenity as the women started the next phase of the massage. She tried to close her eyes, but in doing so, her mind wandered off to the image of Becks undressed. Stop it, she told herself. She tried to picture David Beckham's masculine body instead, but his torso kept morphing into Becks's figure, and so she finally gave up and stopped trying to picture bare bodies altogether.

While Claire struggled with her mind's imagination, her masseuse lay her on her stomach and then placed her two knees on Claire's back. She then grabbed Claire's arms and pulled her up. Claire felt an intense shooting pain as the masseuse's knees pressed against her back. She wanted to scream but bit her tongue just in time. She looked again at Becks, her eyes still closed and looking happy as a cat bathing in the sun, and Claire resolved to endure the pain for her sake.

An hour later they stepped out into the sun. Claire felt throbbing pain all over her body. Her masseuse, so unassuming and pleasant before the massage, had proven to be an expert in torture. A series of elbows and knees had pummeled Claire on her hips and back until the pain had elevated into a single numbing sensation that pulsated through every nerve of her beat-up body.

Becks said to her, "That was such a relaxing massage. Thanks for amusing me."

Claire weakly said, "My pleasure."

"Is everything all right, Claire? Did you enjoy the massage?"

Claire nodded, "Yes, everything was fine. Shall we head over to Hampstead Heath now?"

Becks looked at her a little reluctantly, but Claire pulled her along to the bus stop to wait for Bus 31.

Chapter 16

When they arrived at the Heath thirty minutes later, Claire had a bounce in her step in seeing her favorite park in all of London. They walked past the swan ponds at the southern entrance and made their way to Parliament Hill. There were several people up at the top of hill gazing at the London skyline, and Claire and Becks joined them. "Look," Claire said, "you can see St. Paul's Cathedral, and that's the Shard and the Gherkin."

Becks looked in the direction that Claire had pointed. After a few minutes of admiring the view, she motioned away from the skyline and to a collection of houses and buildings nestled on a hill beyond the ponds of the northeast end. "And what about that village area up there?"

"That part of London is Highgate, and I think that tall spire is St. Michael's. Do you like it?"

"It's beautiful up here. Seeing the orange and brown leaves and the smoke from chimneys of those houses—it feels as if some old and dear memory is being uncovered." Becks said. "And to think that you wouldn't have shown this park to me if I hadn't nagged you on end."

Claire said, "Yes, I'm glad that you did. This park might be my favorite spot in the world, and somehow it didn't occur to me to have it in our tour."

They lingered, staring at the view for a while, and then continued on the path down the hill. As they strolled through the fall foliage, Claire said, "Becks, do you remember our first meeting?"

Becks raised her eyebrows. "How could I forget?"

"Well, remember how at the end of the encounter you asked me if I'd had any lesbian friends?"

"Did I?"

"Yes, you did. I've been curious as to why you asked that question."

Becks said, "It's not that big a deal, really. I've sometimes had women wanting to befriend me because they think it'd be a novelty to have a gay friend, like I'm some rare figurine to be added to a doll collection. I then get asked the most stupid questions, like whether I'm 'the man' in my relationships or if I ever feel attracted to them because I'm a woman."

"But I've been good, haven't I?" In truth, Claire admitted to herself that those exact questions had popped into her head at one point or another, and she was glad that she'd never had the nerve to ask them.

"Yes, you've been good at not asking stupid questions."

Claire hesitated and said, "I gather it's still not easy sometimes?"

Becks looked at her in a bemused way and replied, "What, being gay? Sometimes it isn't, but who doesn't have their troubles? The hardest time is when a relationship doesn't work out and I'm left to ponder if I'll ever find another partner. My neighborhood isn't exactly brimming with gay single women."

"I meant to ask you how you're getting on after your break-up. I was going to ask you when you got off the train, but I didn't want to pry."

"I'm fine, and thanks for asking. There was a lot of screaming and crying before Susan left in a huff, but I saw it coming for a long time. She was so young and we were so different. I'm not sure what I was thinking when I invited her to come work and live with me at the pub."

Claire ventured, "To be honest, I didn't know what you were thinking in having her work with you. And to have her live with you after a couple of weeks of dating."

Becks replied back in good-nature, "Well, you're not the only one who'd been feeling lonely. She was fun and attractive, and she needed a place to live. And at least I didn't date some twat American."

"Ugh, let's not bring up my twat American."

"Sorry, a little too soon?"

Claire nodded. "A little too soon."

They continued on the path, and it took them to Kenwood House Manor. Claire turned to Becks and said, "That white mansion there is Kenwood House. You can go inside for free, and there's a café attached to the main house if you want any food or drinks."

Becks viewed the meadow landscape around the house, and they sat down near a shaded area near the southern end of the manor. "It's like paradise here. This park is filled with wonder."

Claire said, "I used to think that. But I stopped coming here." She continued, "You see, it's where I first met Will, and I was afraid that I might bump into him again. This is the first time I've been here since that incident."

Becks reached out to touch her arm and said, "Oh, Claire."

"Sometimes I'll be walking down a street, and I'll think that I see his face in the crowd, and I'll start to panic and go hide somewhere for a few minutes until I've regained my composure." Claire said, "I hate that I get that way. I sometimes wonder if I should go to therapy, but I just haven't been able to get myself to do so."

Claire felt tears coming down. Becks handed her a handkerchief, and she wiped her eyes. Becks said, "I'm sorry, Claire. When I made my earlier comment about you dating a twat American, I thought that—"

Claire interrupted. "You don't have to apologize, Becks. I told you from the beginning it was just a scare and nothing more, and I've been putting on airs to you and others since then that I've been fine. In fact, most days I'm fine, but it's just sometimes when I see reminders of him that I get anxious."

Becks asked softly, "Did he try to rape you that day?"

"No, I don't think so. I've replayed the scene countless times in my head. I don't think he was trying to, but maybe it would have been different if I hadn't grabbed the branch. I'm not sure if I'll ever know."

Becks said, "It's not too late to go to the police."

Claire shook her head, "I've thought about it, but he was just a little aggressive in the beginning, and he didn't really touch me once I told him to stop. The funny thing is that his aggressiveness was one of the traits that I found attractive initially. He was just a little friskier than the other men I've dated, and he just surprised me because I wasn't ready for it."

"I'm not sure 'frisky' quite describes his behavior."

Claire felt tired and said, "Let's talk about something else."

Becks continued to give her a concerned look but said, "Yes, but at least please consider getting some counseling or therapy about your panic attacks."

Claire didn't respond, and they sat in silence on the lawn for a while. Finally she said, "I'm glad you're here. I feel safe with you here."

Becks replied, "I hope you'll be able to find a way to come back here on your own again."

Claire said, "It's a start to even come here with someone else. But let's move on, shall we?"

Becks nodded as they dusted off the grass and got up. "Yes, let's move on."

They left the Kenwood House area and strolled to the western exit of the park. The grass was taller in this area, and they saw a few children flying kites as they ran around the meadow. Observing them, Becks said, "I understand now why people live in London. To have this scene and something like Kilburn or even Leicester Square just a Tube ride away is a real luxury, isn't it?"

"Yes, I never tire of London. Do you ever think you could live here?"

Becks laughed. "And what would I do here? Run a pub? There must be a pub on every block."

"Not like yours, Becks. It would stand out as the greatest among the city's pubs."

"Thank you, you're generous, but I'd settle for just visiting you every now and then for the weekend like this."

As they were talking, a man jogged past them. Becks grabbed Claire's arm and started saying, "Oh my gosh! That was Ronnie James! The actor!"

Claire gave a shrug. "Yes, I see him running in the Heath all the time. He must live in Hampstead."

"How can you be so nonchalant about it? He's one of Britain's most famous actors! And he's so funny. Let's go chase after him."

Before Becks could run ahead, Claire pulled her arm. "No, we can't do that. When you see a celebrity here in Hampstead you have to act all natural about it. They're like timid squirrels; you glance at them from the side of your eyes as to not scare them off. You can't act like some silly girl at a concert."

"Sigh. Well, now you've done it. You've ruined me by letting me spot a peek of Ronnie James, and I'm now under London's spell. It's going to be hard for me to go back to my tiny little hamlet."

Claire replied, "I'm glad that you're having a good time. And it's just getting started. Wait until you see where we're going for dinner tonight. It's the best pizza place in the world, and it's not too far outside of this park."

Becks said, "Oh, I'm definitely going to gain a few kilos on this trip, but I suppose I can't say no. How do we get out of this damn park and make our way over?"

Claire laughed and said, "Onward march."

As they exited the park, they saw Ronnie James by the sidewalk stretching his legs. Claire could see Becks's eyes getting bigger, but she motioned her to continue on. Becks gave Claire a pouting look but followed her lead. As they walked past Ronnie, however, he glanced up at them and gave them a wink. They continued to walk, but after they were out of his earshot, Becks made squealing noises that resembled a teenage girl sounding a mating call to a whale. Claire rolled her eyes and ushered Becks along.

Chapter 17

Claire and Becks soon made their way to Hampstead's High Street. They walked past the landmarks of Le Creperie and the Coffee Cup, and Becks stopped often to observe the shops and the twinklings lights of the alley of Flask Walk. They walked into an antique bookshop on the street because Becks mentioned she'd never been in one. Claire felt an unabashed happiness as Becks ran her hands down the spine of some of the books and smelled the pages. Seeing Becks's sense of wonderment and discovery, Claire thought to herself that one of life's greatest joys was sharing something very precious with a friend and seeing that friend regard it with the same level of reverence and care.

Eventually Becks picked out a book and paid for it at the counter. Claire asked her what book she'd selected, and Becks responded, "*One Hundred Years of Solitude.* A friend once recommended it to me."

Claire smiled as she recalled their first encounter in which she had suggested the book. She said, "Your friend has fabulous tastes."

They stepped outside the bookstore, and after a few minutes of further walking they reached the small restaurant of L'Antica Pizzeria. The restaurant was a favorite of Claire's, and she sometimes stopped by herself to eat pizza and watch people out the restaurant's front windows. There was a large wood-burning oven at the back of the restaurant, and the young Italian waitresses wore red and white checkered aprons.

Becks said, "What a cute little restaurant. Now this is the kind of place that I imagine you come to often."

Claire said, "Am I really that predictable? I come here all the time."

"Let's see: A hidden gem kind of a restaurant that probably has something like a 4.5 rating on Zomato. Tourists aren't aware of it and even only some of the locals come here. A pretty decor without being pretentious. A little pricier than the equivalent chain, but a great bargain based on the quality of the ingredients. Does that sum it up?"

Claire laughed. "You hit it on the nose. My goodness, I really am that predictable."

"Don't despair. Restaurant choices reflect the personality of a lot of people."

Claire said, "Really? I think I liked the description of my personality then. Especially the bit about 'a pretty decor without being pretentious.'"

Becks teased, "I should have added, 'the kind of place where the owner is overly proud of the compliments she receives.'"

They ordered two individual pies, and when the Neapolitan pizzas arrived, they dug into thin slices layered with fresh tomato sauce, mozzarella, basil, and black olives. Every now and then one of them would let out a contented sigh, and the other gave a knowing nod in return.

In the middle of the meal Claire said, "I'm envious of the people who work here. There must be tremendous satisfaction in knowing that you're creating something top notch for customers who'll come and enjoy what you've created. You must feel the same way at the pub."

Becks said, "Yes, it's a lot of hard work, and it's not always fun and games, but all in all, I do love what I do."

"How did you even become a pub owner in the first place? Was it a family operation?"

"Yes and no. My uncle owned it, and when he died, he passed it on to me because he had no direct heirs. I was his only niece, and we were very close. It was really run down when I inherited it, though."

"You're kidding. It's such a beautiful pub now. I can't imagine it being in such a state."

"You should have seen it. It was filthy. The toilets had an awful smell, and the floors were a grimy carpet that had been there since the Dark Ages. It was dark inside, and the chef cooked up some awful dishes that may have contained the rodents he captured in the mouse traps. I think even the local drunks refused to touch the place."

Claire laughed and asked, "So how did you turn it around? It must have been an awful lot of work."

"Once I realized that I was in this for the long haul, I traveled all over Britain and Europe to see other restaurants and pubs, and then I formed a vision for my place. It would be clean and inviting, with hardwood floors and stone walls and a stove. It would have many large windows so that customers could see the beauty of the surrounding lands. We would only have beers from the local breweries on tap. We would source locally to have the freshest ingredients, and we would serve inventive dishes that you'd expect from the more daring restaurants. Most of all, both locals and tourists would feel as if they were coming home when they visited, like the kind of place in olden days where pilgrims could rest after a long day's journey.

"Amazing," said Claire, "and you made it happen. I was just astonished when I saw your pub. There's no pub in all of England like it."

"Thank you, but it took years. I started off by making sure I kept the toilets clean every day, and bit by bit I slowly added the other pieces. And there were many times when I thought I was going to quit. I came close to running out of money several times, and I had to take loans out from the banks and friends. People told me I was mad and that no one wanted fancy food in some pub in the country. There were tough moments, especially those first years, when I would scrub the toilets and wonder what I was doing with my life. But I told myself that I had to keep at it until I saw my vision through—if I could just realize the vision I had in my head, I felt that I could move on if the pub failed."

Claire pictured Becks scrubbing the toilet bowls and wrinkled her nose. "So once you completed your vision did people start pouring in?"

Becks shook her head. "No, it wasn't that easy—it's never that easy."

Becks ate another bite of pizza and looked deep in thought as she added, "I'm trying to remember how I felt at that time. When you're in that process of trying to make something happen, you think it can be a success if you just do everything that you believe should be done, but you never know for sure—know what I mean? It's scary as hell because there's no one to tell you if what you're doing will bring people in, and you feel utterly helpless at times. But you just keep going and try to have faith that you're doing the right thing. I know what I'm saying must not make much sense, but does any of this make sense?"

Claire nodded, even though she only understood it to just some degree and didn't feel that she'd ever understand it fully. When she'd seen the pub it looked like the handiwork of an artist who held mastery over every impeccable detail, so it was surprising to hear her express her initial doubts.

Becks continued, "And somehow, I learned over time. There were plenty of lumps and wasted money along the way, but I learned, and the customers eventually started to come bit by bit."

Claire sat back and said, "That's just such a brilliant story."

"The thing is," Becks said, "the pub has been doing really well for a few years now, and although it's busy, it's kind of on auto-pilot thanks to the competent staff that I've got with me. I've been thinking for some time that I might sell it and try something else."

Claire was stunned to hear this. She couldn't imagine that Becks was possibly serious after all the work she'd put into the place. "Really? What would you do?"

"You're going to think I'm mad, but I've been thinking about possibly opening a restaurant on a small island in Thailand called Koh Tao. I visited there once, and it was very beautiful. White beaches, blue waters where you can go scuba diving and see colorful coral. I always thought I'd like to go back, so why not have a restaurant there?"

Claire was taken aback. Becks's plan was getting wilder by the second. "Thailand? That would be halfway across the globe."

Becks said, "I know, and I haven't given it a lot of thought, but it's in the back of my mind. What I noticed on my visit was that a lot of English people visit there, and if I could create some dishes that were a fusion of Thai and English flavors, maybe like a fish and chips dish seasoned with Thai flavors and sauces, there could be a niche for it."

Claire said, "I'm sure your restaurant would do well, but it would be so far away. I would miss you." She could feel herself blush after that last sentence, and she hoped that Becks wouldn't notice.

Becks replied, "It's just a thought for now. It probably won't even happen."

"I don't know how you're able to come up with these grand ideas," Claire said. "Look at me. I'm stuck in my job, and I don't know where I want to go with my career."

"Suppose you could do anything. What would you do?"

Claire was surprised by the question as she'd not given it much thought before. She racked her brain a little as Becks looked at her curiously.

"I guess I like analyzing data, so my current job is along those lines, but I hate how I spend all my time dealing with big corporate admin tasks like attending meetings and writing email replies," Claire said. "The American retailer Target analyzed their data and came up with a way to guess when their customers were pregnant even before the customers knew. I'd love to do something like that, but for small businesses."

She became more excited as she thought about the idea on the fly. She continued, "Take your pub, for example. What if there was a way to know all the demographic information for your customers, and you were able to figure out what kinds of customers visited at different parts of the year and what kind of food and drink they liked to consume? For example, you might find out that in February you received a lot of visitors from London that were couples looking for a weekend getaway, and they preferred to drink more wine. You could analyze what kinds of wines were popular and decide what food dishes would work with those wines."

Becks said, "I've sort of figured out that kind of information out in my head from serving the guests directly all these years, but I can see how having that kind of exact data might be useful. Maybe there would be surprises I didn't know."

"Yes, precisely. You might know most of the facts already, but just finding out a few tidbits of information here and there might add a few percentage points of business each month, and that might make a large difference over time."

"So why don't you start out your own company providing this kind of analysis for small businesses?"

Claire said, "Well, I don't know the first thing about starting my own business. I'd be overwhelmed just figuring out where to start. And then if larger companies started to offer these kinds of analyses as part of standard analytics software, I'd have to stay one step ahead, and I'm not sure if I can do that."

Becks shook her head and said, "You just have to take it one step at a time, and I could even help you. If you really wanted to do it, I think you could make it happen."

Claire felt her cheeks turning red once more. "You flatter me. You have a lot more faith in me than I do in myself."

"We all need someone who believes in us more than we believe in ourselves."

Claire thought that Becks might have more to say on that statement, but she didn't prod. Instead, she responded, "I might not leave if this family model at the office works out. Maybe it'll address all my complaints about working in a big corporation."

Becks nodded. "Perhaps, but I'm not holding my breath. Nothing beats the freedom to set your own path in life."

They finished up their pizza and stepped out into the street after splitting the bill. It was dark and cold now, and the street lamps of Hampstead were brightly lit. Claire said, "There's one more place I want to show you if you're up for it."

Becks said, "Lead the way, Claire. I could use the walk to work off all this pizza." They walked over to the bus stop and sat on a bench. Her body shivering from the wind, Claire hugged Becks for the heat, and Becks laughed. She put her arm around Claire in response, and her skin felt warm against her. They said nothing as they waited on the bus stop bench.

Chapter 18

Claire and Becks rode the bus and got off at Chalk Farm, and they walked down Regents Park Road until they were at the foot of Primrose Hill.

"Up there," Claire said, pointing to the top of the hill, "you get the best view of London."

They hiked up the main foot path to the top of the hill where there were several people. There were tourists and families, but many were couples who were huddled together on blankets as they looked out to the London skyline. The evening lights illuminated the scene, and the Shard, BT Tower, and the Eye were particularly discernible. Closer to the hill the yellow street lamps of Regents Park and Primrose Hill were lit up like a maze of candle lights holding vigil for all those lost in the night.

Claire said, "I come here all the time. It's not too far from my flat, so I like to come here whenever I can. Looking out to all of the city, I'm always reminded of how much I love it in all its busy and messy happenings. One could never leave London and see the full world."

Becks pointed to a spot on the hill and said, "I came here with Ashleigh once. We came here on a cold evening like this and had no coats. We were both so foolish then. We sat huddled together until some kind couple loaned us their blankets."

It was the first time that Becks had mentioned the name of the woman inscribed on her wrist. Seizing the opportunity, Claire gathered up the nerve to ask her, "Was Ashleigh one of your girlfriends?"

Becks nodded her head. "Yes. Ashleigh was my first girlfriend."

Claire waited to see if Becks would explain a bit more, and she was rewarded as Becks went on to tell their story. Ashleigh and Becks met during her gap year before she was to start university at Glasgow. Becks had decided to spend some time in India, and so she'd joined a touring company that was to travel around the subcontinent for several months. Many in the company were gap year travelers such as herself, and they'd been forewarned that they weren't going to stay in the best accommodations, but they stayed in hostels of the worst conditions in slums of cities such as Mumbai and Bangalore. In these unbearable spaces the group quickly bonded with one another, and Becks became friends with a student named Ashleigh on a gap year herself. But one week into

Mumbai, Becks came down with malaria, and she was hospitalized for several days while suffering from high fever and vomiting.

While Becks remained bed-ridden, the itinerary reached a point when the tour group was supposed to move on to Hyderabad. As a group they decided to wait for a few days to see if Becks would heal enough to carry on, but when she remained sick, Ashleigh volunteered to stay behind to be with her and then join the rest of the group later. She never left Becks's bedside for several days as she fed her soup and shared stories until Becks was well enough to travel again.

During those hospital chats, they came to know each other intimately. They talked about their families and friends, their childhood experiences, dreams they had for the rest of their bright lives. Ashleigh eventually revealed that she was gay, that she'd come out to her parents right before her graduation, and she was intent on being open about it once uni started. Becks opened up that even around the age of twelve she'd been attracted to other girls, but she'd never shared this with anyone. An attraction between the two quickly developed, and by the time that Becks was well enough to travel again, they decided to abandon the tour group and travel around India on their own.

They traveled around India for six months. They traveled freely, on whims rather than any pre-determined schedule, staying or moving on from location to location as the mood hit them. They traveled through the major cities, saw the landmark sights, and toured the rural areas both deep in the heart of the country as well as near the surrounding seas. They spent their money frugally to make it last, but when they needed more, they found it easy for two nubile English girls to find jobs as hostesses in restaurants and hotels. During their whirlwind travels, their romance bloomed into a passionate love affair. They uncovered each other as they discovered themselves, and many nights were tangled with sheets and sweat as they groped and bit in the darkness, hungry for the other's twisting, quivering body. They emerged from their journey as changed women whose lenses of the world had expanded and altered beyond their wildest imaginations, and the thought of returning home to further schooling and then respectable careers seemed ordinary and mundane.

Claire was riveted. The story seemed like something out of a book. Becks had a faraway look on her face as she said, "It was the most amazing time. I was in love for the first time, and for a girl like me who'd grown up in Chipping Norton all her life, to travel around India and see places and things I'd never even dreamed of before was an education in itself. It was such a beautiful country, so full of life and excitement everywhere we went. We saw the Taj Mahal and the Caves of Ajanta. We saw oxen on beaches in

Goa. We rode the crowded trains, the kind where you push your way through and hang on for dear life on the rail car and pray that you don't fall off onto the tracks. We rode them into remote villages along the Ganges River, where I saw hundreds of women bathing in sarees. I will never forget the river of colors, the way they held their noses as they bobbed up and down. I experienced a lifetime in that short period."

Claire had always been curious about Becks's background, and now that it was all tumbling out, it was more than what she'd expected. She recalled the redhead from Becks's Facebook photos. She felt a twinge of envy that someone had been so close to Becks. Her mind was racing as she asked, "And what was Ashleigh like?"

Becks shook her head and smiled. "Ashleigh was fearless. She was clever and funny, but most of all, she was fearless. She wasn't bothered by what anyone thought of her. When we were traveling she'd march right on up to shopkeepers and bargain the hell out of them. I couldn't believe that someone like her could love me, but she did, and I decided that I would follow her anywhere. Those months were the happiest days of my life."

"It sounds magical. To be traveling with someone you love in some foreign place—I think I would have wanted it to last forever."

"Yes, I felt the same way, but I was in contact with my parents periodically during that time, and one day I received the call from them stating that my uncle had passed away and had left me his pub."

Claire was surprised, as she'd pictured Becks to be on her own during those early years. She said, "Ashleigh was there with you as you worked on the pub?"

"Yes, when I came back home I told my parents that I was gay. They disowned me and kicked me out of the house, so as the new owner of my uncle's shitty pub, I asked Ashleigh to forego uni and run the pub with me. She obliged and stayed by my side as we scrubbed those toilets and waited on tables and experimented with different dishes."

Claire's image of Becks slaving away on her own to renovate the pub was now replaced by a joyful partnership of two lovers happily working together side-by-side. She wondered what had happened to Ashleigh, but she didn't dare ask.

As if reading her mind, Becks said, "You're probably wondering what happened between us."

Claire said nothing but nodded.

Becks didn't say anything for a bit as she looked out into the city, and Claire followed her line of sight to see the red orbs of the BT Tower blinking in the distance.

She said quietly, "She decided one day that she didn't want to be gay anymore. She told me it was too hard to maintain a lesbian lifestyle, and that she thought that she might be able to like a man and have a family. She left me, and two years later she was married to a farmer named James, and I believe that she has a child now."

Claire put her hand to her mouth in shock. "Oh, I'm so sorry, Becks."

Becks continued, "I was devastated initially. I asked her what 'lesbian lifestyle' she was talking about, as we just lived in Bourton together like an old married couple. I wondered whether she'd tired of me specifically. But she insisted that it wasn't me, that she just wanted a normal life with a husband and a family without being defined by her sexual identity. It was a dark time for me after the breakup. I questioned everything about myself after she left me. I wondered if I really liked women, or if it was a phase, or something I could switch off like Ashleigh had done."

"And?"

"And the verdict was that I'd only loved a woman and had only ever been attracted to women, and that wasn't something I could change. More importantly, it was not something I wanted to change."

Claire sat down on a nearby bench and shook her head. "What kind of a person does what she did? To say one day that you want something completely different?"

Becks sat next to her and said, "It happens. You hear regular stories about husbands or wives telling their spouses that they're gay, so why couldn't it happen the other way around?"

Claire said to her, "You're awfully forgiving of Ashleigh given what she's done to you."

"It's been five years now so I've had time to move on, but at the time, it nearly killed me. I haven't talked to her since she left me."

Claire began to feel tears rolling down her cheek. She wiped them with her hand and said, "I'm sorry. I brought you here thinking that it would be a happy viewing, but instead it's brought back painful memories."

Becks squeezed Claire's hand. "Claire, this entire day has been perfect. Thank you. I will treasure this day for the rest of my life."

They sat on the bench together for several more minutes, and stared out into the expanse of the city below them. She'd taken Becks to many places today, but there was so much more she wished that she could have shown her. If we were only birds, thought Claire, we could quickly fly through some of the areas that she should have seen as well. They'd fly east from the hill towards Islington, and trail the revelers down Upper Street to the late night chicken shops and banker pubs of Farringdon and further south to the Dome of St Paul's. And then they'd flit back east to the narrow ends of Covent Garden, past all the retail stores and her favorite gelato shop and through the alleyway of St Martin's Court where the post-musical crowds would be filing out and spilling into the tourist restaurants in the surrounding streets of Soho. They'd head down south past Admiral Nelson and the blue cockerel in Trafalgar Square and fly up to Big Ben and Parliament, and upon reaching the banks of the Thames River, they'd start to rise higher, flying high above the London Eye, soaring higher and higher, until when they looked down from the night sky, the dotted lights of the city would be but a galactic grid of electricity shining up at them from below. Then and only then, would she have been satisfied that she'd fully shared her immense love of the city in one beautiful and perfect day.

Soon the cold sank in to wipe away this dream from Claire's mind. Looking at each other, Becks and Claire wordlessly got up and made their way to Swiss Cottage. They walked home in relative silence.

When they reached Claire's flat, she gave Becks a quick tour around her place. It was a simple flat with a kitchen and a bedroom. Claire felt self-conscious of how small and insignificant her home felt compared to the stories that Becks had shared in the evening. She had spent a lot of time and energy decorating her place with an array of neatly arranged books and framed posters scattered between pieces of IKEA furniture, but her efforts seemed trivial now.

As Becks sat on her white couch and surveyed the room, she remarked, "I like it. Charming, and everything is so neat and organized. It fits you."

Claire asked, "Would you like a night cap to end the day?"

"No, I better go to bed. It's been a very fun, but very exhausting day."

Claire didn't object as she felt the weight of the long day herself. She showed Becks the guest room and gave her a towel. Claire said to her, "If there's anything more that you need, don't hesitate to knock."

Becks said, "Cheers, Claire. Have a good night."

"Good night, Becks."

Claire went to her own room and washed up for the night. She then lay in her bed, the melancholy air from Primrose Hill still hovering over. She thought of Becks and Ashleigh. Their story saddened her, so instead she tried to imagine mighty oxen on beaches as she drifted to sleep.

Chapter 19

Claire woke up the next morning and looked at her alarm clock. Nine o'clock. She didn't hear any stirrings outside her bedroom, so she tiptoed out to the living room. She saw Becks curled up on a chair by the living room window. Becks was showered and dressed in a yellow sundress with pretty blue flowers. She had a notebook with her and was scribbling something inside. The morning sun shining through the window pane cast a gentle light over Becks, and Claire felt as if she was witnessing a painting. Seeing Becks's long legs revealed, she felt the same feeling of arousal that she'd felt at the massage parlor in Kilburn, but this time she didn't try to fight it away. She was not sure what the feeling meant, but she tried not to worry too much about it as she lingered in the pleasure of observing this beautiful woman. Becks looked up and saw her and smiled.

"Good morning," Becks said.

"Good morning to you. You look lovely in your dress. I hope I didn't bother you."

"Thank you, and no, you didn't bother me. Journaling some thoughts about yesterday, that's all. I like to jot down the good memories."

"Would you like me to make you some breakfast? I have some toast and bacon I can fry up."

Becks looked at her watch and said, "Yes, but I was also hoping to try and make it to church this morning."

Claire blinked as Becks waited for her. "Church? I haven't been to church in ages. I don't even know where the nearest one is."

Becks replied, "I guess we'd better find one then."

To Claire's dismay, Becks pulled out her phone and began browsing for churches. She found one called Swiss Cottage Christ Church that was a ten minute walk on Finchley Road and started at ten.

"That'll do," Becks said. "And it's close enough where I'm sure I can make it over and back without getting lost."

Claire was a bit bewildered by the unexpected plans for church but decided that she had nothing better to do. "Wait. I guess it won't kill me to go to church once. Let me just get ready, and I'll go with you."

Once Claire was ready, they had a quick breakfast and walked out the door. When they reached the main entrance of the church, they were greeted by two elderly ladies who handed them programs with cheerful smiles. Upon entering the sanctuary, Claire surveyed the scene. Unlike its older exterior, the interior looked modern with brick walls and a simple cross on the main stage behind the glass podium of the vicar. The five musicians on the stage looked fairly young, probably in their late twenties and early thirties, but the parishioners were an older lot. It seemed as if everyone was looking at her and Becks, and she felt an unease as they searched for a place to sit. They can probably smell the stench of my lapsed religion, she thought.

Claire and Becks sat towards the back of the church, and when the band began their singing, Becks stood up to sing with the others, and Claire followed suit. The band led them through some vigorous rock music that Claire wouldn't have recognized as church music if it weren't for the lyrics. The modernity in the music and the overall service thus far were a jarring contrast from the traditional Anglican services of her childhood, and she felt further unsettled.

The vicar then took the stage. He was a tall bearded man, and he had a jovial countenance as he first discussed the church's news and then proceeded to give a sermon on the apostle Paul. Claire listened with one ear to the message, as she was more intently peeking at Becks next to her. Becks looked as if she was listening with her full attention, so Claire tried to focus. The vicar droned on and on, talking about the Apostle Paul's various plights in his missionary trips. They were vaguely familiar stories that Claire had heard in church as a child, and she began to doze.

She woke up from her little reverie about forty-five minutes later when she heard the vicar say, "So in closing, let us recap the extraordinary life of Paul. Formerly Saul of Tarsus and a student of the great Jewish teacher Gamaliel, he persecuted Christians until he was blinded by Jesus on the road to Damascus. After his vision was restored by Ananias, he embarked on one of the greatest journeys ever known to mankind. He traveled over thirteen thousand miles over multiple missionary trips on foot and ship to spread the gospel. He preached in front of market crowds and Roman governors, and he endured stonings, floggings, imprisonments, and shipwrecks before his ultimate death. But because he stayed the course, the germs of Christianity were flung across churches in two continents, and the epistles of Paul the Apostle remain the bedrock of our Christian faith today.

"It is unlikely that any of us will be blinded by a sudden light that will transform our lives. But I am convinced that all of us at some point or another encounter the life-altering moments that invite us to change. And when those opportunities come along, I hope you seize upon them, and tell yourself, 'something has to change'. Because if we do not change, we will wander aimlessly through our lives, never knowing what impact we could have had on those around us and ourselves. But if we choose to embark on that journey, we travel with the hope that we might end it with the very words that Paul uttered at the end of his life: I have fought the good fight, I have finished the race, and I have kept the faith."

The words moved Claire, pinned her to her seat. The phrase, *something has to change*, triggered some feeling within her, but she couldn't quite pinpoint what it was. She racked her brain, and then she remembered: lost in the meadows of the Cotswolds she had vowed to change. She sat up in rapt attention, but it was too late now, as the vicar stepped down and the music team took the stage once more.

When the service ended, Claire hurried for the exit, but she had to wait a few minutes as Becks conversed with the women who'd greeted them at the door. After what seemed like an eternity of cheerful pleasantries, Becks joined her in leaving.

As they walked back to Claire's flat, Becks said, "That was a very nice service wasn't it? The music is a little different from the traditional hymns back home, but it was still nice."

Claire said to her, "This is all so bizarre. How can you go to church when Christians have been so oppressive to gays? It's one of the reasons I stopped going awhile ago."

"The greeters at the door seemed quite friendly to me."

Claire replied, "Stop it. It's not funny."

Becks said, "My fundamental belief in the existence of God didn't change just because I realized that I was attracted to the same sex."

Claire was silent, so Becks continued, "I know where you're coming from, and I don't take it lightly. There have been moments in my life where I stopped going myself, but I will tell you this: when my parents disowned me and I was struggling to get my pub running, it was some of the local churchgoers who supported Ashleigh and me and helped us along with their patronage. And they knew we were gay. We were never explicit about our relationship, but everyone in a small town knows, and they came anyway and treated us well."

"People might act politely, but I think privately a lot of them are still bigoted wankers."

Becks shrugged. "It's changing so quickly now. When I was in my early twenties I never thought I'd see same-sex marriage allowed in this country, and then it just happened one day."

Claire said, “Yes, but is that enough?”

Becks responded, “Maybe not, but we’ve made major strides. Here’s a quote that I often say to myself: ‘The arc of the moral universe is long, but it bends towards justice.’”

“Winston Churchill?”

“Worse. An American. Martin Luther King Jr.”

Claire laughed. Then thinking about the sermon, she then asked, “So how did Paul end up dying?”

Becks replied, “No one knows for sure, but the common belief is that he was beheaded by the Roman emperor Nero.”

“Christ,” said Claire, “not a life I would have traded for. Even the death was painful.”

“Maybe not. But then again, when you’ve found your purpose in life, maybe nothing else really matters,” said Becks. As Claire pondered what she meant by this, they continued on the walk back to her flat.

Chapter 20

They arrived back at Claire's flat, and Claire changed out of her Sunday clothes and Becks changed back into her standard black shirt and jeans. They then ate a simple lunch of chicken salad and tomato soup at home. As they sipped their soups, Becks said, "So, your dinner party is this evening?"

"Yes, I can't wait for it," said Claire. "It's a small party with five people I've invited. My best friend Maddie will be coming with her husband John. They met through One Match. Then there's Sarah and her boyfriend Cormack—they met a year ago on One Match as well. Cormack can be a bit of an arse sometimes, but hopefully he'll behave. And finally there's my friend Lucy who works as the receptionist and executive assistant on my office floor. She's yet to be partnered up."

"She hasn't tried One Match?"

"Maddie and the others have urged her, but she's resisted. She cites my funny encounter with you as one of the reasons why."

Claire added, "No offense."

"None taken," Becks said. "I'm looking forward to meeting them. And what are you serving for dinner?"

Claire clasped her hands and said, "I'm going all out. We'll start off with some smoked salmon and cream cheese for hor d'oeuvres. I'll then serve pumpkin soup and spinach salad with bleu cheese and pine nuts for starters. Main entree will be a rack of lamb with a plum sauce, and dessert will be my mum's famous chocolate cake." Claire enjoyed hosting dinner parties in her flat, and rattling off the dinner menu gave her a shiver of excitement.

Becks said, "When are your guests coming? Shouldn't we get started now?"

"They're coming at six. I was planning to start at about two o'clock."

"Claire, it's two thirty now."

She looked down at her watch and saw that Becks was right. "Yikes—that damn church service. We have to get started now."

Becks began to clean up their lunch dishes and said, "Don't damn the church service. You've got no one to blame but yourself for losing track of the time."

"Yes ma'am."

For the next few hours, Claire and Becks remained anchored in Claire's tiny kitchen as they sliced and peeled and chopped amid a flurry of pots and pans. Becks's sure-handed assistance in cooking the food made the time pass quickly, and they finished early even after taking ample time to test sauces and feed each other bites of the dishes they were making. After tasting some of the preview morsels of the delicious food, Claire knew that her friends would be floored by their dinner tonight.

When they'd finished cooking, Becks announced, "I'm going to go change for your party."

Claire was taken aback. "It's not necessary," Claire said. "In fact, I'm not sure I'd recognize you outside of your black shirt and blue jeans."

"Always the comedian, aren't you? Never mind that I was just wearing a dress for church."

Becks went into her room for what seemed like half an hour, and just as Claire started to worry, she came out in her new outfit. Gone was the plain black shirt, and in its stead was a sleeveless, v-neck dress of a scarlet color that stopped several inches before her knees and revealed her long legs. She had a silver necklace around her neck and a matching bracelet on her left wrist, and she wore open-toed black stiletto pumps. She had her makeup on, applied even better than the saleswoman's handiwork from yesterday.

Becks looked nervous as she said, "What do you think?"

Claire was speechless. Becks was very beautiful. She recalled their first meeting at Café Sauvignon. She had thought then that Becks had been on the pretty side, but she had not seen her the way she did now. Was it really just some make-up and a nice dress that made all the difference? She knew that was only partially true even as she asked herself the question

Claire said, "You literally took my breath away. You are absolutely gorgeous. Who are you? What have you done with my Becks and her black shirts?"

Becks laughed, "Oh stop it."

"Seriously, do you realize how beautiful you look? If I had legs like yours, I'd wear nothing but dresses."

Becks said, "I wonder if I dressed up too much? You said it was a dinner party, so I didn't want to come under-dressed."

Claire replied, "It's perfect. Here, I'm going to go change into something nicer myself."

She hurried into her room and slipped into her blue dress that she wore on special occasions. She observed herself in the mirror and pictured them sitting next to each other at the dinner table. Her guests would marvel at the two of them together.

Claire's thought was interrupted by the sound of the first doorbell ring. She opened the door, and she was greeted by Maddie and John. Maddie saw Claire and Becks's attire and said, "Oh no! Were we supposed to dress up? I must have missed it when you invited us over."

Claire laughed and said, "No, you didn't have to. Becks and I thought it'd be sheer fun to be glittering hostesses together."

Seemingly relieved, Maddie embraced Becks and said, "Pleasure to meet you, Becks. Claire has told me so much about you. But she never told me how stunning you look."

Becks replied, "So nice to meet you too, Maddie. You can blame me for our uppity clothes. When Claire said it'd be a dinner party I thought formal wear was required."

Maddie squeezed her hand and said, "I'm glad that you look so nice. It adds a special air to our regular suppers."

As Claire went to the kitchen to bring out the wine, she heard the doorbell ring again, and this time the remaining three guests of Sarah, Cormack, and Lucy were at the door together. Claire ushered them in, and as they were introduced to Becks, they made the same remarks on how beautiful she and Claire looked in their evening dresses.

The dinner party moved into the living room, and Claire passed around the hor d'oeuvres. They nibbled on the smoked salmon and crackers and made small talk with Becks. Lucy said to her, "Claire told us that you live in the Cotswolds. I'm so jealous. It's so beautiful out there."

Becks nodded, "Yes, it's quite nice."

Sarah pointed to Cormack and said, "We've been to The Happy Clam. We can't believe that you're the owner. We had a lovely meal when we there a couple of years ago."

Becks quipped, "It must have been a day when I was on holiday and left the others in charge."

The guests laughed merrily at the joke. Claire thought her friends were a little stiff in their conversation but understood that they were getting acquainted. She summoned them to the small dining table at the corner of the living room and said, "Let's have dinner, shall we?"

Once the guests were seated at the table, Claire raised her glass of wine and said, "I'd like to say a toast. To friends, old and new, and the merging of the two."

"Hear, hear," they said, and they clinked their glasses with each other and commenced dinner. They complimented Claire and Becks on the delicious food and continued with small talk about the weather and the traffic. But during the entree portion of the meal, Cormack cleared his throat and said to Becks, "So you're a lesbian?"

Sarah said to him quickly, "Cormack!" But Becks replied, "Yes, I am a lesbian."

He said, "And how was it when you found out that you were paired with Claire on One Match?"

Becks said, "Claire was a good sport. She could have walked out on me, but she invited me to have a drink nonetheless, and here we are now."

He pressed, "But how did you feel when you saw a beautiful woman like Claire only to realize that she wasn't a lesbian like yourself? I imagine it would have been a sore disappointment?"

Sarah had a mortified expression on her face, and Claire felt the same way. Just as she was about to jump in, John intervened by saying, "You know, the programmer who created One Match gave an interview for the first time the other day."

Lucy chimed in, "Yes, I read that interview in *The Guardian.* What an odd fellow that Jorgen Magnussen is."

Grateful for the change in topic, Claire asked, "What did he say?"

John said, "He talked about the algorithm and how it's been more successful than he'd imagined, but as of now there's about an 80% success rate, and he's hoping to get that to 95% in the next three years. Some of it will happen naturally as more people join the service and widen the pool of potential matches, but a good portion of it will be with him tinkering with the algorithm as he gathers more data. The interesting part was that of the 20% non-matches, he said that there had been some very comedic mix-ups, such as heterosexual men getting paired with other heterosexual men, gays being paired with non-gays, or even cousins getting matched."

The entire table had a good laugh, and Maddie said, "And to think when Claire first told us her story with One Match we thought it was a very unique case, but it turns out that it happens often enough."

Lucy said, "And that's why I'm holding off from joining. 95% seems much better odds than 80%."

Claire replied, "I don't know. I didn't meet the man of my dreams, but I still got a good friend out of it." She gave a wink to Becks across the table and Becks smiled back at her.

John continued, "This Magnussen fellow is just such a clever chap. I feel that it's the future. Our children won't even bother dating. At the age of ten they'll sign-up for One Match, find out who their future spouse is, and then wait until they're grown up and just get married."

Sarah added, "Why wait until they're ten? I bet they'll do it in the hospitals as they're delivering the babies."

Becks had been sitting quietly through the conversation, but she then spoke up, "I suppose it won't have to be limited to just partner matching? Couldn't we come to a future where they scan your brain to find out your best match for your career, the place you should live, the people you should befriend and avoid?"

Cormack perked up and said, "Oh ho, our new friend has both beauty and brains. Yes, and from what I've read, there are companies working on those kinds of technology right now as we speak to make sure they get employees that are the best fit for the corporations."

Sarah said, "That seems miserable to me. We would lose our free will in making all the big decisions of our lives."

John replied, "Or, it could be an aid to uncovering the truths of our lives. One Match helped me to find Maddie, and it helped you in finding Cormack."

Maddie said, "That is the fundamental question, isn't it? Did it help us in realizing the truth that we were meant to be together, or did we succumb to the algorithm's decision to make that choice for us?"

"Whatever it was," John said, "you're stuck with me now, darling."

The table again cracked up at that final declaration. They moved on from the topic, and they finished eating their meal. After the dessert they retired to the living room to have tea and play a quick game or two of cards. By ten o'clock Maddie nudged John that they should be going to get ready for the work week, and the rest of the party took that as a cue to leave as well.

As they put on their coats and opened the door to leave, Maddie hugged Becks and said, "It was wonderful to finally meet you. I hope to see more of you."

Becks said, "Same here. You're as lovely as Claire's descriptions."

Claire closed the door behind the guests, and the two of them were left alone in the flat.

Chapter 21

After the guests had cleared out, Becks helped Claire clean the table and wash the dishes. They then settled into the couch of the living room. Claire poured Becks a glass of wine and said, "This was fun, wasn't it?"

Becks took a sip and said, "Yes, thanks again for having me here this weekend. You have no idea how much this has lifted my spirits."

Claire waved her hand and said, "It was my pleasure."

They sat in comfortable silence as they drank their wine when Claire had an idea. She said, "Would you like to see the view from the top of this flat? I have a key that will take us to the rooftop, and you can get one final view of London."

"Now? It looks kind of cold outside."

"Stop acting so old. We'll put on some coats over our dresses, and then tomorrow you can go back to your uniform of black shirts and blue jeans."

"Oh fine," Becks said, "perhaps for just a little bit."

They grabbed the wine bottle and glasses and took the lift up to the tenth floor, and then walked up the stairs to the roof access. Claire opened the door, and they stepped outside. The air was cool, but not too chilly for a September evening in London. It was just the two of them on the roof deck, and Becks took in the panoramic scene.

"It's beautiful up here," Becks said. "We didn't even have to go up to Primrose Hill yesterday. You can see just as much from here."

"It is nice, isn't it?" Above the haze of the city's lights they could make out the faint light of stars and the moon high up above. Claire handed Becks another glass of wine.

Becks protested and said, "Goodness, Claire, I'm sloshed enough already. I must have had five or six drinks by now."

Claire also felt drunk from the wine, but she felt good. Their isolation on the rooftop encouraged a feeling of boldness. "We'll both feel it tomorrow, but let's cap off a fitting weekend."

Becks looked hesitant, but she took the glass and began to drink.

Claire said to her, "By the way, I wanted to apologize for Cormack tonight. I warned you that he was a bit of an ass, but he really outdid himself."

"He was fine. I rather liked his straightforward approach. Cleared the way for a more interesting talk beyond the small chit-chat."

"Yes, it was an interesting discussion, wasn't it? What did you make of all of this future technology in our lives?"

Becks said, "'Future'? It's happened—it's happening. Your friends used One Match and so did we. I'd never given much thought about the question of free will when I signed up for it, but now I'm glad that I didn't find someone through the service. I think I would have felt the relationship was always a little tainted because I didn't find the person on my own."

"Perhaps," Claire replied, "but there are other online dating services. They might not be as sophisticated, but they're offering the same thing, and I don't think the millions of people who meet their partners through them feel as if their relationships are tainted. Or what about if you're introduced to someone through mutual friends? Is that relationship tainted because your friends helped you?"

"Those are good points, but you have to draw the line somewhere. Something about this technology feels different."

Claire could feel her words slur, and she felt too tired to argue further. She knew she should go to bed, but she wanted the moment to last, to see Becks like this, with her coat over her red dress and her bare legs peeking out from underneath the coat. She said, "Tell me what India was like."

Becks said to her without sounding displeased, "I already told you last night. It was a beautiful place, full of chaos and energy."

"What about those caves you talked about? I'd never heard of them before."

Becks's eyes lit up. "Ah, the Caves of Ajanta. They were enormous Buddhist temples carved into the side of a cliff. It was impossible to know how they could have carved on rock in such a treacherous location. And inside, such intricate depictions and patterns riding up high to the ceiling—it was so astounding that that were moments in which I thought I'd fall down in sheer stupor. To be inside such a sacred and holy place that's lasted over thousands of years...I felt as if I had stumbled onto a gateway to another world. I'd like to go visit again someday."

Claire felt shivers listening to her and said, "I wish I can see them, too. Will you take me the next time you go?"

"Yes, of course."

Feeling a bit daring, Claire changed the subject and said, "You never really answered Cormack's question. What were your feelings in our first meeting?"

Becks had a glazed look on her face, and she answered as she sipped her wine, "Cormack was right. It was a sore disappointment. When I first saw you, I thought you were so lovely. I couldn't imagine my luck being paired with such a beautiful woman."

"Really? You thought I was pretty?" Claire felt a tingling excitement upon hearing this admission.

"Oh stop it. Of course I thought so. I noticed your beautiful brown hair and your green eyes, and I was so excited. It was such a disappointment when I found out that it was a mistake. And then we had our short conversation, and you were lively and funny, and it made it harder. It's partly why I wondered if I wanted to give you my email address, as I thought it might be too hard to be friends."

"Then why did you give it to me?"

"I didn't think you'd contact me." They both laughed, and they clinked their glasses and drank some more.

Claire said, "I know we've assumed that our match was a mistake, but have you ever wondered if it wasn't?"

Becks gave her a surprised glance. She seemed to hesitate before saying, "Yes, the thought had crossed my mind."

Some part of Claire knew that she was very inebriated and should go to sleep, but she ignored it. She was fully turned on now, and her inhibitions suspended by the wine, she pressed on. She said, "Lucy used to tell me that most women, whether gay or not, can feel some kind of attraction to another woman."

Becks was silent.

Claire continued, "I would always tell her that I'd never experienced such an attraction. Until I met you. When I saw you in your dress. Actually, it was even before that when we were at the massage parlor..."

"Claire..."

"I've never kissed another woman before, but I've always wondered about it."

"Claire, I think we should go back down before we regret this later." Becks had a fretful look on her face, but Claire could tell that she also did not want to move.

"Please, Becks. Stay."

Becks looked hesitant, so Claire drew closer and whispered, "Kiss me."

Becks stood there, but then a moment later Claire felt her lips upon hers.

She felt chills run down her back and to her feet.

The kiss was tentative and quick. Becks stepped back and glanced at her with a quizzing look. To assure her that she wanted to continue, Claire kissed her back and lingered a bit on her lips.

They stared at each other briefly, and then wordlessly tried another kiss that lasted longer. Becks said nothing afterwards. Claire kept her silence, too, fearful that a spoken word would snap either of them out of their trance.

Claire then reached over and kissed her lips again. They slowly began to embrace each other in their kissing. She felt Becks's hands against her back as she did the same. Their hands crawled to the smalls of their backs, and she felt the warmth of her body as they pressed their fingers against each other.

Becks's lips were soft, much softer than a man's. Claire kissed her with a little more force, refusing to let go. Becks responded in kind, and she could feel her heavy breathing in between their kisses.

They paused once more to look at each other again. They smiled at each other and Becks stroked her hair ever so lightly. Claire then began kissing Becks on her neck, and as she kissed her there, she inched her fingers down and traced them along Becks's naked thigh. Her skin felt smooth and soft, and Claire pressed her hand against her thigh as they kissed.

The rhythm of Becks's breaths became heavier and shortened, and with this cue, Claire dared to travel her right hand behind the thigh. She then pulled up her dress and hooked her thumb to her knickers to bring it down slightly as she touched her skin. Becks did not pull back, and Claire felt a delirious shiver as she lay her hand there. She then felt Becks's hands descend upon her own rear, and the feel of her hand against her there aroused her madly. Becks stroked her gently with her hand, and Claire heard herself give a slight moan as all her repressed urges unraveled. Claire knew that she was stupidly drunk, but her entire body was tingling with a ravenous desire for the woman in front of her, and she continued kissing her hard and long under the cover of the night sky.

Chapter 22

The next morning Claire woke up to a hand shaking her. "Wake up, Claire. It's seven o'clock. I need to head to the train station soon, and you need to get ready for work."

Claire peeked her eyes open and saw Becks standing over her, dressed in her black shirt and jeans, packed up and ready to leave. She felt a throbbing pain beating rhythmically against the side of her head, and the events of last night returned to her. She looked at Becks, and then remembered that her last recollection was the kiss on the rooftop. The shock of that realization began to sink in, and she said, "We kissed last night."

Becks nodded and said, "Yes, we kissed."

"Did we..." Claire looked down and saw that she was still in her blue dress from last night.

"No," Becks said, "we didn't do anything beyond that. You were drowsy, but we managed to make it back down, and I helped you into your bed."

Claire felt disoriented and her throat felt dry. On cue, Becks handed her a cup of coffee and some Tylenol. Claire thanked her and sat up on her bed.

Becks put a hand on her shoulder and said, "I know we were both quite sloshed yesterday. Perhaps it'd be best if we both pretend that last night didn't happen."

Claire looked at Becks and saw that she was giving her a gentle path out of whatever complications lay ahead. But she saw in her hopeful face that Becks didn't regret the kiss from last night.

"No," said Claire. "I knew what I was doing." Even as she said these words, Claire wasn't quite sure if this was a lie or not. The night out on the balcony felt as if it had occurred days ago.

"I don't know, Claire. We were both so pissed."

"Becks, I'm sure." Claire was not sure at all, but she felt the need to be adamant to avoid embarrassing her friend.

Becks said nothing. Claire said to her, "So what do we do now?"

Becks responded, "I have to go now and catch the train, and you have to finish your coffee and get ready for work. But I'll give you a call later and we can figure it out from there."

Claire nodded, and Becks gave her a squeeze of her hand before heading out the door. Once Becks left, Claire started the arduous task of getting ready for work with a massive hangover pounding away at her. She sat motionless throughout the entire Tube ride to work, and it was only when she got to her desk at the office that the enormity of the events that had transpired the previous night began to settle in.

Portions of the conversations on the balcony that had been cordoned off in a dizzy haze were starting to unlock into focus. Claire remembered that she'd been flirty and then had even asked Becks to kiss her. Becks had complied, but she kissed her back. What a drunk fool she'd been.

Her immediate thought was to call Becks after work and tell her that she was right, everything had been a mistake, and that she had been too drunk to know what she was doing. But as the day wore on, Claire started to have second thoughts. She thought about the larger events of the weekend and everything that had led to the balcony kiss. She thought about how much she'd enjoyed spending time with Becks, how Saturday and Sunday had flown by talking about both intimate and silly topics. She felt that she could tell Becks anything at this point. And if it was purely the conversations, it would be easy to categorize their relationship as friendship and nothing more, but Claire admitted that she felt an attraction. She recalled her arousal when she saw her in her knickers before their massages, or when she'd spied Becks journaling in her sundress. She couldn't remember the last time she'd been so desirous of someone.

But even if I am attracted to her, I can't really be with her, thought Claire. To get into a relationship with Becks wouldn't just be dating another person, but it would change a part of her identity. What would it mean to be gay? Would everything change? She remembered Becks's own tempestuous journey when she came out.

All of these thoughts ran through Claire's mind as she went about her work. Just as she thought that her head would explode, Lucy stopped by with an excited look on her face.

"What is it, Luce?"

"Claire, you won't believe just what happened. I got a ring from Lewis Hardy's executive assistant. He wants you to come up to his office tomorrow at eleven for a quick chat."

Claire frowned. "What? Why would Lewis Hardy want to see me?"

"I have no idea, but I told her that you'd be free."

"This is all so bizarre. Do you think I'm in trouble after what happened with Ronald? Maybe he found out that I had been making mistakes and Ronald was justified to yell at me?"

Lucy replied, "Don't be a twat. Of course not. Maybe he wants to ask you out."

Claire rolled her eyes. "Now who's being the twat? You should stop reading all those silly romance novels."

"Well, whatever it's about, I told the EA that you'd be up there at eleven tomorrow, so mark it on your calendar."

"Okay, fine. But if I'm in trouble, I'm blaming you."

"And if he asks you out, you're taking me out to dinner."

"Deal. I hope you're ready to splurge because I haven't had lobster in a while."

After Lucy left, Claire remained worried for the rest of the day that she was in some kind of trouble. Perhaps he would even sack her as he'd done so quickly with Ronald. It was only when she got on the Tube that she remembered that she also had the issue with Becks to deal with. When she got to her flat, Claire felt exhausted. She lay on her bed for a little, and even though she hadn't quite figured out what she'd say to Becks, she thought she'd better call her.

Claire called her, and Becks picked up right away. "Hello," she said.

"Hello."

"How are you feeling?"

"I'm feeling much better now. It was a terrible hangover, though. I couldn't get anything done pretty much the whole day." Claire thought that Becks sounded shy, and she felt shy herself.

Becks said, "Good to hear you're better. And listen, about last night. I know you said you were aware of what happened, but I want to say again that I understand if you want to remain just friends. You must understand what it might mean otherwise."

Claire felt some relief when Becks said this. A voice inside her told her that she should accept this proposal and make things easier. But Claire was touched by the way Becks thought about her; she didn't think any of her previous boyfriends would have been as considerate in thinking of the situation from her perspective.

"Thanks, Becks. But it's okay. I'm a big girl, and I know what this all means. I don't know how to even begin, but I'd like to see you again." She knew that she had no idea what this all meant, but it was true that she'd wanted to see her again. It would be good to see her again just to be able to chart the next direction in their relationship.

Becks was silent on the other line, and just when Claire thought she'd lost connection, Becks said, "I want to see you again, too."

Claire said, "How about this weekend? I can come down to Bourton since you were up in London."

"It happens that I'm going to be back in London this weekend to run a few errands. How about if I meet you afterwards? I'll actually be near your neighborhood Saturday, so how about if I meet you at your flat at three?"

"Sure, that's easy enough for me."

"Good then. Good night."

"Good night." When she hung up the phone, Claire felt tired again. Everything seemed to be happening so quickly. What had she gotten herself into? Plus, she had the meeting with Lewis Hardy to deal with tomorrow, and what could he possibly want? The questions jabbed at her from all angles, so she took some Tylenol, and after cooking herself a quick meal of chicken and rice, decided to call it an early night.

Chapter 23

The next day at eleven o'clock, Claire took the lift to the twentieth floor. She was a nervous wreck the whole ride up, thinking, Lewis has found out what a mess I've been making the last several weeks and decided it was a mistake to fire Ronald. He's calling me up to sack me instead. Claire felt herself shaking, but when she arrived on the floor she told his executive assistant her name. The assistant pointed to his glass office and said, "Lewis is waiting for you."

Claire walked into his office, and saw Lewis sitting in his leather chair behind his desk. There were rows of shelves behind him filled with books. Along the edges of the office there were memorabilia such as signed jerseys and footballs. She recognized the Manchester United logo on one of the jerseys. Lewis himself was wearing a baby blue dress shirt with the top button undone and dark blue jeans, looking as handsome as ever. He went up to her and said, "Claire, thanks for coming over. Please take a seat."

She sat on the chair in front of the desk. He sat down in his leather chair and said, "Are you doing well these days?"

"Yes," she said. And then thinking that it may be better to be upfront, she added, "I want to thank you again for stepping in a few weeks ago. But you should know that I've been having some issues with my work lately. Ronald was right when he said I should be sacked."

Lewis said, "Ronald had no business treating you like that. I'd also been looking into the many complaints about him from others. If he tries to sue me or this company, I won't lose any sleep over it. But why has your performance been suffering recently?"

Claire demurred. "I've just been dealing with a personal matter outside of work, but I'm confident that I can return to my previous productivity."

Lewis pointed to a manila folder on his desk and said, "I looked over your previous annual performance reports. Four straight years of an 'excellent' grading. Your colleagues rave about you. And yet you've been promoted just once to a senior analyst level."

Claire said, "I don't know. I guess I figured that I'll be promoted once again when I'm ready for it."

"I think you've been held back, and it certainly didn't help to have had a neanderthal like Ronald as your manager. You know that my family unit model is starting in three days, and employees will be meeting their partners."

Claire nodded. Employees had been allowed to make partner requests, but they also had to take personality and interest surveys that the company would examine to determine the best matches.

Lewis said, "Well, I'm personally choosing your partner. I've asked Harriet Fisher to be your partner, and she's agreed. I think she'll be good for your career development and help you to really thrive here. How do you feel about this?"

Claire was stunned. Harriet Fisher was one of the superstars in the M&A department. Her colleagues in finance often talked in awe about some of the multi-million dollar deals she'd brokered. She'd come into his office expecting to get fired, and now she was being partnered up with a legend. "Yes," she said, "yes, I'd be honored to be her partner, but I'm not sure if I'd be qualified. If anything, I'd think I'd be lucky to be her junior partner."

Lewis chuckled. "You see, that's one of the advantages of the family model I'm creating. You don't have to think of her as some corporate deity. Harriet may have accomplished quite a bit in her time here, but I'm convinced that she can learn quite a good deal from you as well."

Still a bit in shock, Claire said, "If you think so, I'll take your word for it."

"Good," he said, "because the pairing has been made, and if you'd said no, it would have had a domino effect on all the other matches."

"Thank you, thank you so much."

She was exultant, and she couldn't wait to go tell Lucy the reason for the visit. She got up to leave, but Lewis held his hand up and said, "There's also one more thing." He cleared his throat, and Claire noticed that he seemed to be the one looking a little nervous. He said, "I was wondering if you might join me for dinner this Friday evening. I've already brought it up with HR to gauge the conflict of interest, and given that I'll be far removed from any of your tasks or performance, they've given the green light."

Claire was now really confused. "I'm sorry, I'm not comprehending. Are you talking about a date?"

Lewis said, "Yes, unless you're already seeing someone, I was thinking it'd be a date."

Claire flinched but replied, "No, I'm not seeing anyone at the moment." She felt a little guilty thinking about Becks, but it was true that she was not yet seeing her.

"Does that mean that it's a yes?"

She nodded weakly. "Yes, I'll be free."

"Good then," Lewis said, his confident air returning, "I'll pick you up at seven, and I'll take you to one of my favorite restaurants."

Claire left his office and got back on the lift down. She wondered what had just happened. The entire conversation seemed so surreal that she was still playing it to herself when the lift landed her back on the fourth floor. She walked over to Lucy's desk and said, "You won't believe what's just happened."

They hurried over to a meeting room, and when Claire finished telling her story to Lucy, she said, "Good lord, Claire, you've hit the jackpot! He's completely into you."

Claire said, "As strange as it seems, I think he might be."

"It looks like you're the one who owes me dinner. Now that you've said it, I think lobster sounds good to me."

"This is all so overwhelming."

Lucy had a dreamy look in her eyes. "Lewis Hardy. Oh god—that man is sex incarnate. I would murder someone to see his naked body."

"Stop it. You're awful."

"But in all seriousness, I'm so glad that this has happened to you. You deserve better after what happened with Will."

"I don't know how I feel about dating Lewis."

"What are you talking about?"

"The thing with Will was only a couple of months ago, and Lewis is a SVP here. It feels very weird. It's a little intimidating. What would we talk about?"

Lucy rolled her eyes and said, "Claire, you're overthinking it. Every woman would die to be in your shoes right now."

"And what about the fact that he personally assigned me to Harriet Fisher without asking me first? Of course I wanted it, but is this the fifties where the man can dictate big decisions to a woman?"

"Stop it, Claire. Stop it right now!"

Claire said, "Okay, okay, I've already said yes to the date, but don't be surprised if it doesn't lead to anything."

She thought about telling Lucy about her date with Becks on Saturday, but she decided that she'd better not for fear that Lucy would have a seizure. Everything in Lewis's office had happened in a flash, and she didn't know what that meant for her situation with Becks, but she decided that she'd better just take it one date at a time.

Chapter 24

Friday was the big family match day at Wyman. There was a festive atmosphere across all the halls of the company as the HR team had decorated meeting rooms and open areas with balloons and food and drinks to mark the beginning of a new era. Some of Claire's colleagues grumbled about the idea of being placed into a family unit, but many of them waited eagerly to find out their fate.

They'd all received emails that morning with the room numbers they were to go to meet their partners. Claire showed up to room 6.104 on the sixth floor as instructed, and as Lewis had said, Harriet Fisher was there waiting for her. She had her graying hair in a tight bun, and she wore a black, two-button suit that looked classic and sharp. The epitome of what a successful businesswoman looks like, Claire thought. Harriet extended her hand and said, "Claire, it's nice to meet you."

Claire shook her hand and said, "Ms. Fisher, it's an honor to be partnered with you."

Harriet waved her hand and said, "Claire, if we're going to be partners, you're going to have to get used to calling me Harriet."

"Yes, Harriet, but I think it might take time to get used to it."

Harriet gave her a wink and said, "You better get used to it quickly, because I won't tolerate stuffy nonsense. Now, where do you suppose our little junior partners are hiding?"

Claire laughed and said, "I don't know. While we wait, I have to ask you how you feel about all of this. I'd imagine that someone like you would feel that we're all just a burden for you to carry along."

"I'm not the pope, Claire. If anything, the older I get, the more I realize that there's so much I don't know and things to learn from people around me. I'm looking forward to working with this younger 'family' of mine. And you, Claire. Lewis must have seen something in you to personally intervene."

Before Claire could protest that there was nothing special about her, two young men showed up at the door. They both looked as if they were straight out of university; one had tousled brown hair with trousers that looked a size too big, and the other had one of those fashionable undercut haircuts. He wore a T-shirt with a large taco on it and that read, "Do you wanna Taco 'bout it?"

The one with the brown hair waved and said, "Sorry we're a tad late. My name's Jeffrey Hurst and he's Sam Parker. We ran into each other in the hallways on this floor and saw that we're in the same room, but we had a hard time finding it."

Harriet squinted at both of them and said, "Can Sam Parker speak?"

Sam spoke up. "Yes ma'am."

"Then why the bloody hell are you speaking for him?" said Harriet to Jeffrey.

Claire suppressed the urge to giggle and remained quiet. Assured that she'd given the lads a good scare, Harriet extended her hand and said, "My name is Harriet Fisher, and I'm one of your senior partners."

Following her lead, Claire said, "And I'm Claire Moore, your other senior partner."

Harriet continued. "Gentlemen, I don't know what kind of training you've received in the past, but your official first day as contributing human beings in this world starts today. Claire and I are going to see to it that you make something of yourselves, and we will expect you to adhere to our guidance and discipline. We will teach you how to properly work, and once you've proven that you have some semblance of being able to follow our instruction, we will give you the opportunities to thrive in this company. Do we have ourselves a deal?"

They both nodded. "Yes, ma'am."

"Now then, it seems that our first lesson next week will be on how to dress properly and show up on time. As much as I enjoy a taco or two for lunch, it's hardly the proper attire for the shining gatekeepers of Wyman's future."

This time Claire couldn't suppress her laughter. Harriet paused for a moment at Claire's laughter, and then joined in. Sam and Jeffrey looked at them in bewilderment but managed to smile.

After the initial introductions the four of them moved into their seating arrangements. Claire and Harriet had cubicles next to each other, and their junior partners were seated not too far from them. Claire assumed that Harriet had a corner office before this new family arrangement, but Harriet didn't complain about her new cubicle setup. After settling in, they went out for lunch as a new family, and they then spent the rest of the afternoon talking about their interests and strengths and some of the projects they could join as a family unit.

Given Harriet's background in M&A and Claire's skills in finance, the family decided that they'd be best suited for opportunities in business development. If they partnered up with a family focused on marketing and another one on supply chain and logistics, they could potentially cut deals and execute them end-to-end. The thought of doing so with just a total group of twelve excited Harriet and Claire, and the boys only nodded and listened as the elder partners explained how such a three family partnership might work.

Before Claire knew it, it was already six o'clock. She'd had so much fun with the family match day that she'd almost forgotten that she had her dinner date with Lewis in the evening. She hurried home and changed into her cap-sleeved Versace dress, a dress that was form-fitting but tasteful. She also decided that this occasion warranted her Jimmy Choos that she kept hidden in the back of her wardrobe. She got ready just in time, as at seven on the dot she heard the doorbell ring.

She opened the door, and Lewis greeted her with a bouquet of tulips. He was freshly shaved, and looked dapper in his gray chinos and navy blue sports jacket. He said to her, "You look very lovely, Claire."

"Thank you. You look nice yourself." She accepted the flowers, and she could smell his aftershave. She felt her heart beating quickly and for a moment was afraid that Lewis would notice this somehow.

After she put the flowers in a vase, he led her outside, where his black BMW was parked. Claire didn't know much about cars, but even she could tell that it was the kind of car that tourists stopped to gawk at in Chelsea and Knightsbridge. They got in the car, and the combination of the black leather and the gadgetry inside made Claire feel as if she was in the Batmobile.

Lewis said to her, "I'm excited to take you to one of my favorite places tonight."

As he drove, she wondered about the places he might take her. She listed all the Michelin starred restaurants in her head and entertained the idea of spotting a celebrity at one of them. She'd never been to the really fancy places, and she was nervous and excited at the thought of eating at one of these fine establishments.

Claire expected them to head south to Central London, but to her surprise, they headed west, and before she knew it, they were driving up on Kilburn High Road. She looked over to Lewis, but he said nothing, and then he parked the car on a side street off of Kilburn.

"Kilburn?" she asked.

"Yes," he said. "A couple of blocks up the street."

A true gentleman, he opened her door and held her hand as she got out. The evening air was chilly, and when Lewis noticed that Claire was shivering, he took off his jacket and put it over her. Kilburn High Road was in a fine state. The street was humming with Friday carousers heading to restaurants and clubs on the street. They passed by the busy outdoor kebab stands where the hot smoke rose in plumes, and they parted through the line for the night clubs as Lebanese and Egyptian hipsters with faux hawk cuts held their shivering dates in skimpy skirts. Just as Claire wondered how far they would walk in the cold, he led her inside a pub titled O'Neill's.

Inside, the atmosphere was cramped and lively. Lewis led her past the throngs of people drinking at the bar and sat her down at a table marked as reserved. The bartender saw them and waved to Lewis, and he waved back.

Lewis said, "So what do you think?"

Claire looked around and said, "I like it. I have to admit that it was a bit of a surprise. I was picturing you eating at fancier restaurants. But I love Kilburn, and I haven't been here before." Claire briefly thought of Becks and the Thai massage torture.

He said, "I'm glad. I do take out dates to the so-called 'fancy' restaurants, but there was something about you that made me think that you'd appreciate O'Neill's. I grew up not too far from here, and this place is dear to me."

"In Kilburn? That's wonderful."

"Yes, people are always surprised when I tell them, but I'm proud of my roots here. I have a working class background in that my dad was a barber on the street and my mum was a cleaning lady in one of the hotels. I had to work to pay my way through uni, and my first job was in the mailroom at Marks and Spencer."

Claire said, "A real rags-to-riches story. I'd love to hear more about how you made it to SVP of Wyman in such a short amount of time."

"I'm happy to, but I want to hear your story while we eat. Shall we?" Lewis handed her a menu, and Claire saw that they were mainly Irish pub food items. She ordered the corned beef and cabbage to go with her ale, and he ordered a steak and Guinness pie. He then said to her, "So where does one start with Claire Moore? How did you end up at Wyman?"

"My story isn't that exciting. Grew up in a two-parent home in Watford as an only child, and my parents still live there. I went to uni at Newcastle and received a degree in finance. I then spent a couple of years at an accounting firm before being recruited over to Wyman."

"You have a modesty about you that I've noticed," he said. "You undersell yourself. I had a chat with some of your colleagues in the finance department, and they think that you're a star. Even Harriet had heard of you."

"Really?" said Claire, "I never knew they felt that way about me."

"It's why I didn't hesitate at all in partnering you with Harriet." He then said, "By the way, I apologize that I partnered you before even asking. I should have asked you first, but I just knew it would be a good fit, and there were so many other things to take care of leading up to today."

Claire felt a bit of comfort upon hearing Lewis explain himself. "That's fine—Harriet's been wonderful."

Lewis said, "That's good to hear. What's the first day of the new re-org been like? What's everyone saying?"

"I think it's all been pretty positive. People are excited about the chance to work collaboratively and decide what to work on within their group. In our own little group we decided that we were interested in some business development areas, and we're going to look for other groups who might be interested in partnering up with us."

Lewis nodded his head. "Yes, I'm glad to hear that. So much planning has gone into all of this..." He seemed to gaze off into the distance, as if he was being pulled back into the work. Claire imagined that he must be under a lot of stress. He was the golden boy with the golden plan, brought in to turn everything around, and who knew what would happen if it all failed.

She tried to distract him and said, "I'm curious as to how everyone else got matched up. Did you have some complex algorithms to complement the surveys that we filled out?"

He shook his head and said, "We brought in some behavioral experts, but it was nothing too sophisticated. You saw the surveys. We tried to honor people's requests for partners as much as possible, and then tried to match people by the preferences they filled out. The HR department conducted the initial matching so that we could get started as soon as possible, but in the future I'd like to find some way for employees to find their own groups by themselves."

She suggested, "Or, maybe you could license the technology that One Match uses for future matching."

"One Match? The dating service? Have you used it?"

She hesitated but said, "Yes, I have. I think it works pretty well, and it's been good at pairing my friends up as well."

Looking a bit confused, he asked, "If it's worked for you, are you seeing someone then?"

Trying not to blush she said, "It sort of worked for me, but no, I'm not seeing anyone right now." She thought that it was not a complete lie, as her date with Becks wasn't until tomorrow, and she didn't think their weekend together last week counted.

He said, "I'm glad to hear that. I have a good feeling about us."

"I'm very flattered, but you hardly know me. What if we're not a fit?"

"Well, that's what I intend to find out. But you can learn a lot about someone from even the slightest interactions. I believe there's a subconscious side to all of us that can pick up the level of attraction based on how a person speaks, moves, or even looks at you. I didn't ask you out just because of your looks, although they certainly played a part. I could see that you were grounded, demure. Not at all like the boorish, high-society women that my mates try to set me up with all the time."

It was Claire's time to blush. "And you think you're in tune with this subconscious self?"

Lewis shrugged and said, "Perhaps not better than anyone else, but I have a tendency to embrace it. Some might say it's going with an innate feel. Several years ago, I dated a woman for a couple of years, and it became serious enough that she expected to get married. Deep inside I didn't think she was the one from the beginning, but I obliged and proposed to her, and it was only a few days before our wedding that I finally called it off."

"That must have been terrible. That poor woman."

"It was, and I felt so sorry for her. Ever since then, I've decided to follow my intuitions. I hardly ask anyone out for a date unless I think it can really lead somewhere, and if it doesn't feel absolutely right from the beginning, I'll call it off after just a date or two so that there wouldn't be any attachments from either side."

Claire felt that this was a little extreme and said, "But don't you think there could be relationships that you've thrown away that might have blossomed later?"

Lewis nodded. "Yes, I don't deny that. But it's better than the alternative of what happened with Cecilia, and these gut intuitions have helped me in all aspects of my life, including business dealings."

"I don't doubt that, but I have to say that your approach makes me feel as if I'm on trial."

Lewis frowned and said, "I don't mean for you to feel that way. If we're being honest with ourselves, all dating is a form of trial, and you can think that you're deciding on me as well. We're equals in that regard."

Claire didn't feel like an equal at all given his stature, but she said, "I guess you're right."

"If anything, I'm hoping that it'll free both of us to be ourselves, and you would forget that I'm a senior leader at your company. If things don't work out after the first couple of dates, we can part ways without any regret or complications, and you will continue on with your new family group without having to run into me."

She was not completely convinced that Lewis's approach to dating was what she wanted, but she didn't argue with him. Their dishes soon arrived, and they dug into their food as they continued on their conversation about their backgrounds.

At about eight o'clock, a band gathered in a corner of the room. There was a keyboard player, a drummer, a couple of guitarists, and a woman singer. She started to sing a jazz standard from the 1950s, and Claire thought that her smoky alto voice sounded heavenly.

She recognized the song and said, "She's singing 'Misty'. I love that song."

"I'm impressed. You know jazz?"

She nodded. "My father is a big fan. I grew up listening to a lot of his albums."

Lewis grabbed her hand and said, "Would you like to dance?"

Claire looked around and said, "There's no one else who's dancing."

"Then why don't we be the first ones?" He led her to the dance floor, and they did a slow dance as the musicians smiled at them. Claire felt all the eyes of the pub's patrons looking at her and felt self-conscious at first, but she began to relax in Lewis's steady arms. She said to him as they danced, "You're someone who knows what he wants, aren't you?"

He replied, "I'm someone who chooses to have no regrets."

She said, "I hope you don't regret tonight."

"On the contrary, I'd like to ask you out again."

She looked at him and still couldn't believe that this was all happening. Claire thought briefly about her date with Becks the next day, but she nodded yes and said, "I think I may let you continue in my trial run."

Lewis laughed, and they continued to dance as the singer started her next song.

Chapter 25

It was dreary and wet the next day as Claire waited for Becks inside her flat. She thought about her date with Lewis the previous night and wasn't sure what she would say to Becks. Probably the truth would be best, but how would she explain that in less than a week's time she'd already gone on a date with someone else? And that she was leaning towards choosing him rather than her? She felt the anxiety that usually occurred with her pseudo Will sightings, and she tried to steady her trembling hands.

At three on the dot she heard the doorbell ring. Claire took a deep breath and opened the door. Becks stood in front of her, and she looked nice. She had her makeup and hair done, and she was wearing a green cardigan. Becks looked a little nervous, and Claire imagined that she portrayed some nervousness as well. They gave a slight hug, and Claire let her into the flat.

"Would you like some tea?"

Becks shook her head. "No, thank you. I shouldn't stay too long."

"I'm sorry to hear that. I thought we'd have some time together to talk."

Becks replied, "Yes, well I came into town to look at some furniture that I thought I might add to the pub, but it was all so bloody expensive. I really should get going back to my pub, but I thought it'd be best if we talked about what happened Sunday evening."

"Yes," Claire said, "you're right. It'd be good to talk." Their conversation was flat. She couldn't believe that just a week ago they'd gotten along so well, and now there was a stiff awkwardness that trailed every sentence they spoke. She felt the need to go outside with Becks to try and recapture some of their rhythm from the previous weekend. "How about if we take a walk to get some fresh air?"

Becks agreed, and they stepped out onto the street. They made their way out to Finchley Road and headed north. Neither was willing to take the first step to start the conversation, so they walked in silence. Claire could feel her frustration mount; she needed to make some move to understand her own feelings once and for all. She reached out and grabbed Becks's hand. Becks looked at her with a slightly surprised expression, but she held onto her hand as they walked.

Something felt different for Claire once they held hands. In the past

Claire had occasionally held hands with her female friends and had made nothing of it. She'd perhaps had even held Becks's hands during their previous weekend. But now she felt as if she was making a declaration to the world that she was a lesbian, but she wasn't sure if the declaration was truthful. She liked Becks, but she knew that she was going to choose Lewis; she thought that she'd perhaps already known this the moment he'd asked her out in his office.

Becks sensed her apprehension and asked, "What's wrong, Claire?"

"Nothing. I'm just feeling a little wobbly for some reason. Do you mind if we sit down at the café there?" She pointed to a nondescript coffee house across the street.

"Yes," said Becks as she gave a look of concern. "Maybe we should sit down for a little."

They walked over while still holding hands, and once inside, the metaphoric microscope loomed over her again as the other patrons stared at the two of them holding hands. The hostess sat them down in a nearby booth, and Claire felt a sense of reprieve when they dropped their hand holding to sit down and wait for the tea to arrive.

Becks's face was encouraging and patient. Claire tried to smile, but she could see that she saw through her facade. Becks said to her, "There must be so much going through your mind right now."

Feeling as if a stone was lodged inside her chest, Claire said, "Becks, I'm seeing someone else."

Becks's smile stayed on, but the expression in her eyes gave away a hint of surprise. Claire went on to explain how Lewis summoned to her office and how they then went to Kilburn for their date last night.

When Claire finished telling her story, she half expected Becks to yell at her or even storm out of the café. Instead, Becks held her steady gaze and said, "I understand, Claire. I'm happy for you."

Claire was surprised. "You are?"

Becks held her hand and said, "Yes, I am. Of course, I'm disappointed for myself, but it's the best for you. It's Mr. SVP himself, sweeping you off your feet. Something out of a fairy tale. It would be wrong of me to stand in the way."

Claire felt an enormous sense of relief, but at the same time, a sadness hit her, as she realized that she was letting go of something. "I'm so sorry. I really felt feelings for you. I thought I could change. I thought I could have your kind of courage when you realized that you were gay."

Becks said, "And look where that got me. No, you shouldn't change. Not for me, at least. If you're attracted to Mr. SVP, I think we both finally know that One Match was wrong in its assessment of us. You were swayed by its faulty algorithms and nothing more."

Claire shook her head and said, "I don't know. I know there were times when I felt something for you. Even now, I think you look beautiful."

"Don't say that. There's no need to make this hard."

Claire could feel the tears welling up. "We will still be friends, won't we?"

Becks nodded. "Of course. Who else will bother me when I'm trying to surf the internet?"

Claire laughed, thinking of all the IM sessions they'd had in the last couple of months. She then thought about their brief time together. Memories at The Happy Clam or Selfridges or even the smaller moments of sitting through church or cooking together flashed through her head. She saw through Becks, knew that even as Becks was promising a continued friendship, their time together was likely over.

"I remember," Claire said, "when you waited with me at the train station in Bourton. I think I fell for you then, but I didn't know it. If you'd been a man, perhaps I would have known, but that's the big joke of all of this, isn't it?"

"Please, Claire, stop. You're just being silly now. We hardly knew each other then. We were never meant to be together. Maybe there was a glimmer of promise, but the fact that Lewis swept you up just before our date today is proof that we were never destined for each other."

"I didn't know that you believed in destiny."

"I'm like everybody else. I believe in it when it helps me to cope."

Becks maintained a stoic disposition, but the glistening of her eyes betrayed her. Claire wanted to lean over and embrace Becks, but instead she asked her, "So what do we do now?"

Becks gave a small smile and said, "We step outside and wish each other luck. And then we say good-bye."

They paid for their coffee, and walked out the door. It was pouring now, and they stood under the red and white striped canopy of the café to avoid the rain but failed. Some part of Claire told her that it was a mistake, and that she should just tell Becks that she'd changed her mind, but she stood frozen. All she could do was stare at her, her mind trying so desperately to embed one final picture of Becks into her storage of memories.

Becks gave her a hug, and Claire felt chills run through her body from contact with the cold water on her skin. "Will I ever see you again?" Claire asked.

Becks shook her head. "I don't know," she said. "Perhaps someday."

Tears running freely now, Claire hugged her again for a long time and said, "Good-bye, Becks."

Becks whispered, "Good-bye, Claire." And with one last look, she turned around and walked away.

Chapter 26

After Claire's farewell with Becks, she continued to see Lewis. During this time Lewis showered her with many romantic gestures: flowers sent to her cubicle, chocolates and expensive wine brought spontaneously, and dinners at the fancy restaurants Claire had first envisioned. She was surprised that he hadn't tried to keep their relationship a secret, and her work family teased her every time some fancy gift was sent to her cubicle. Outside of work they developed a routine in which they saw each other two to three times a week, and on some nights she stayed at his flat in Kensington and he occasionally slept at her place.

Claire's enjoyment of work continued to gain traction as well, as her work family continued to coalesce and define their roles. She and Harriet solidified their initial plans to be the business development arm of a three family group that could function on its own. Using her vast network within the company, Harriet had secured an agreement with one family to handle the logistics and supply chain and another to carry out the marketing and store rollouts of their deals.

Meanwhile, the two of them started a rigorous training regimen for the two junior partners of their family. Claire focused on teaching the financials and the practical applications of their software tools. She spent long sessions teaching them how to conduct forecasts, put together P&L statements, use MS Office suite applications, and write SQL queries to pull numbers from databases. She found that she had a knack for teaching and enjoyed sharing her knowledge. Harriet taught them how to negotiate, present persuasive presentations, and write clear and succinct emails and documents. During Harriet's training seminars Claire paid careful attention herself, as she saw it as a fortuitous opportunity to learn from the most distinguished woman within the company.

The junior members were quick studies, and they absorbed everything that was thrown at them with vigor and gratitude. As Claire got to know them better, she was able to identify their two very distinct personalities. Jeffrey was rambunctious and outgoing. He asked lots of questions, sometimes challenged whether there were better ways to do the work, but he remained respectful of his senior partners' authority. In Wyman's old corporate structure Claire would have tagged Jeffrey as an employee who would have climbed the ladder rather quickly, and she wondered whether he'd chafe in the long run in this new family structure.

Sam was quieter than Jeffrey, and didn't have his bravado and energy. But upon close observation his talents couldn't be denied. He was very diligent and made sure that all his work was completed on time and without mistakes. He had a calm presence about him, and he never seemed to get flustered like Jeffrey did when encountering difficult problems. He was a careful listener who never got the first word in during meetings, but every now and then he would throw out a good question or an astute observation that showed that he'd been listening and thinking about the discussed issues very carefully. During lunch breaks Claire sometimes saw him strolling around nearby blocks, seemingly lost in a daydream. She liked both of them very much, but she felt a particular affinity for Sam.

One day, Harriet was reviewing a deal proposal that Jeffrey had written up in a group setting. She put down the paper and said, "Jeffrey, the overall content of the proposal is quite good, but it has too many simple mistakes. For example, on the first paragraph of page two, you wrote that Wyman had 20M customers visit our stores last year, but I explicitly told you that we use 'MM' rather than just a singular 'M' for millions."

Jeffrey groaned and said, "Yes, I'll fix it, but in the big scheme of things, does it matter? Do our vendors actually care or even notice that I'd used a singular 'M'?"

Harriet's eyes narrowed as they seemed to drill an invisible laser into Jeffrey's forehead. Claire tried to suppress a laugh as she imagined the tirade that Harriet was about to launch.

Harriet did not disappoint. "Jeffrey, it makes all the bloody difference in the world." She gathered up a lather as she continued, "Let me tell you something, boys, since you're still boys after all. The first lesson that we should have taught you is that life is difficult. You're either bored or overwhelmed, and on top of it all you spend the light of day toiling away in some bloody cubicle. Most people hate their jobs. Oh sure, when you ask them about it at parties they'll tell you that it's okay or that they even enjoy it, but next time you're on a Tube ride, take a long, hard at those faces—like cattle being taken to the slaughterhouse, dreading the tyranny that awaits them at their desks."

Claire glanced at Jeffrey and Sam. They appeared as transfixed as she was as their sage orator thundered on.

"The only way to make your job bearable, and perhaps even enjoyable, is to master it completely. You have to pour every ounce of your passion, your blood, and your sweat to all the details of all that you're tasked, and once you've done that, you'll become the best at what you do. And when you're the best at what you do, success comes, and with it, happiness. But it starts with that extra 10%. That extra 10% of making sure you're properly dressed and arriving on time for meetings, that extra 10% of checking all the dates and formats and spelling in a document or presentation, and the extra 10% of ensuring that you've written the correct abbreviation for fucking 'millions' when we instruct you to do so."

Jeffrey looked as if he wasn't sure whether to be terrified or to burst out laughing at the last line. Claire thought it was wise of him as he simply said, "Yes, Harriet. I'll remember next time."

Harriet waved her hand at them and said, "Now run along boys. It's nearly seven now and I can't be bothered anymore for today."

Claire was about to head out herself when Harriet said to her, "Wait, Claire. If you're not busy tonight, mind joining me for a drink?"

She was surprised by the request but delighted. They gathered up their belongings and headed over to the nearby Shakespeare pub. It was a popular place for Wyman employees, but when they stepped into the dimly lit pub they saw hardly anyone there. They sat down at the bar and ordered a couple of pints. Once they settled in with their beers, Claire said to her, "That speech was brilliant. I can't imagine either of them screwing up an abbreviation again."

Harriet took a long drink of her beer and replied, "That speech was shit. Don't believe a word of it."

"Oh, come off." Claire couldn't believe what Harriet was saying after the impassioned tirade she'd just given.

"Sure, for the lads it was the right thing to say. When you're young and impressionable, it's good to be taught to pay attention to the details. Whatever you do in life you have to give that extra 10%. But the rest of what I said, the idea that with mastery you'll find happiness, that's all rubbish. You can become an expert on your field and still not be happy. Or, you can never be good at what you do and still be the happiest person in the world—your work is just a component of happiness. And besides, happiness comes and goes for everyone."

Claire was taken aback by these contradictory remarks from Harriet's resolute speech. "But what about what you said about how we spend most of our days in the office? It seems to me that when you're good at what you spend most of your time on, you're more likely to be happy. I know that I've felt that way."

"Perhaps," Harriet said, as she turned towards Claire, "but I can only speak for myself. I've spent over thirty years in my career, forging my way to the top, and I've hated it the whole time."

"You can't be serious."

"It's true. Certainly there have been those thrilling days, especially those days when you close on a deal after weeks or even months of negotiating, but all in all, I've never really enjoyed it that much. I can go into all the details of why I hated it, but the bottom line is that there is this wide world out there, and I've spent most of it in an office room of sorts. It's damn depressing when you boil it down."

"Then why did you do it for so long?"

Harriet said, "It's life's cruel joke that I didn't realize it sooner. I tried for so long to convince myself that I enjoyed it, and then by the time I knew that I didn't, it was too late for me to change careers. I became too comfortable and the money was too good for me to start over elsewhere. But we're having this conversation because it's not too late for you."

Claire's constructed image of Harriet from the past month was now flung wide open. Until now she'd viewed her as an Amazonian warrior queen, a woman with iron will and limitless energy who could make anything happen through her hard-charging personality. But now Claire noticed the crow's feet around the edges of her brown eyes, the bitterness in her voice as she reflected on her career. No more a warrior queen, she seemed a battered warhorse at the end of service. Claire then remembered the older woman in the Cotswolds who had sat so peacefully in her farmhouse as she read her book. Maybe it had all been just a mirage. If even someone like Harriet had regrets at the end of her illustrious career, how could she expect to find that serenity that she thought she had witnessed?

She said to Harriet, "Maybe it's not too late. What would you have done instead?"

Harriet laughed. "I'm too old and tired to think of 'what ifs' now."

"I'm sure there was something."

Harriet paused and said, "I suppose growing up I'd always wanted to be an anthropologist. Maybe serve as a museum curator."

"A museum curator?" Claire imagined Harriet directing groups of school children through the halls of the British Museum as she gave lectures on the Greeks and Romans, and she couldn't help but laugh.

"I know," Harriet said, "it's so far removed from reality at this point I might as well have told you that I wanted to become a footballer in the Premier League." She stared down at her beer glass and said, "No, I'll retire soon. I want to make sure this family project is well on its way, and then I'm quitting for good. Looking back, what I've realized is that you don't always have to know your next steps in life, but at some point you have to figure out what matters to you. And once you've figured that out, you have to do everything you can to avoid the distractions and pursue them with everything you've got. You'll learn that you'll sometimes get cracks at these things later in life, but more often than not you only get a few chances or even just one chance. You have to seize it right then and there, or otherwise it's gone for good."

Claire nodded. Harriet spoke with such conviction, and it worried her that she wasn't quite sure she knew what mattered to her. She said to Harriet, "You talk as if you have regrets."

Harriet said, "I do. In this day and age you're not supposed to say that you have regrets, but I do. I wasn't one of those women who thought I had to marry—I was working too much to date well, and even the thought of being tied down with someone wasn't that appealing. But I'd always wanted a child, a boy perhaps. I went to an adoption agency and started the paperwork, but ultimately I decided that my work hours wouldn't allow me to be a proper mother. At that time I was rising in the ranks here at Wyman, so I wasn't ready to quit. There isn't a day that goes by when I don't regret that decision. Of course, I tell my family and friends that I have no such regrets of being a career woman."

Claire felt for Harriet. She wanted to say something to comfort her, but she found herself at a loss for words.

Harriet continued, "When we're working with the boys, I sometimes wonder what I would have been like as a parent. I'm quite fond of them."

"Jeffrey and Sam adore you as well. You would have been a magnificent mum." Claire herself was quite fond of the "boys".

"Hmm. They're quite different, aren't they?"

"Yes. Jeffrey will do well here. He's got all that energy and enthusiasm. I sometimes wonder about Sam. He's quieter for sure, and I sometimes wonder whether a corporate setting is the best place for him."

"On the contrary, Claire, I think in the long run Sam will do quite well. He's got a quiet strength, similar to what I see in you."

Claire blushed at the compliment and said nothing.

"In any event," Harriet said, "Promise me that when I'm gone that you'll take care of the boys."

"Please don't say that. I can't imagine our little family without you."

"Not yet, but everything comes to a close eventually," said Harriet.

Chapter 27

One Friday Claire received an envelope in her work mailbox. She opened the envelope and saw a pretty card with a simple note:

Happy one month anniversary. I have a surprise for you for this weekend. All I ask is that you pack your suitcase and have your passport ready by nine in the morning tomorrow.

Yours,

Lewis

Claire was ecstatic. She was still not used to the extravagance of some of Lewis's gifts, but a weekend trip to another country took it to another level. She remembered how earlier in the year she'd been in her flat alone while Maddie was whisked off to Paris by John. She was now the recipient of such a surprise, and that lonely night seemed a lifetime ago.

The next day Claire had just finished packing her suitcase when there was a ring at her door. She opened the door to find a car driver and his limousine waiting outside. The driver handed her a bouquet of flowers and said, "I was sent by Mr. Lewis Hardy to take you to the airport."

She accepted the flowers and got in the car. She'd never been inside a limousine before. The plush black leather felt cool to the touch, and she saw that there was a bottle of champagne on ice. The driver poured her a glass before closing the door and starting the car.

Claire had assumed that they would head to Heathrow, but several minutes into the car ride she noticed that it was headed in the opposite direction. She pressed the speaker button and asked, "Excuse me, but where are we headed?"

The driver said, "London City Airport, madam."

Claire was a bit surprised as she'd never taken a flight from there, but she settled back into her seat. The car arrived at the airport within an hour. The door of the limousine opened, and Claire stepped outside to see Lewis in front of her. He was wearing a long sleeve Oxford shirt with sky blue slacks and slip-on loafers without socks. Claire thought he looked more than dashing than ever—even if he looked as if he'd copied the wardrobe of a men's clothing catalog from top to bottom. She said to him, "Lewis, the limousine pick-up was a wonderful surprise. You've outdone yourself."

He smiled broadly and said to her, "Did you like it? It's just getting started."

"Do I like it? It seems like something out of a movie."

Lewis led her inside the terminal, and a man in a suit and tie greeted them. They followed him through the terminal, and Claire thought that it looked extremely small compared to the ones in Heathrow. She also saw no travelers around them, and just as she was about to make a remark about it, they were out of the terminal doors and on the airport tarmac. About a hundred paces ahead there was a small jet parked out in front of them.

Claire gasped. She put her hand to her mouth and asked, "Is that for us?"

Lewis laughed and said, "Yes, it's our chariot for the day."

"Oh my goodness! Do you own a private jet?"

He shook his head, "I'm afraid not. It's the Wyman family jet. John was kind enough to lend it to me for the weekend. It's a Gulfstream G-550. A top-of-the-line model even among private jets."

As Claire tried to wrap her head around the fact that she was about to ride a private jet, the pilot came over to greet them and led them inside the plane. They stepped up to the plane steps where a flight attendant in a navy uniform helped her up. They sat down in their plush seats, and the attendant handed them mimosas.

Claire was shocked. It was more than what she'd ever imagined in her life, and the trip hadn't even started. She turned to Lewis and said, "I still can't believe all of this. This is all so surreal. But are you going to tell me where we're headed?"

He grinned and said, "I was going to surprise you to the end, but do you really want to know?

"Yes, the anticipation might kill me."

"We're going to Amsterdam. Have you been there before?"

"Amsterdam! I love that city. I've been meaning to go back."

She'd been there seven years ago with some of her girl friends. They'd been on a tight budget then and had slummed it through hostels. Even so, she remembered it as a beautiful city of canals.

Lewis said, "Wait until you see the hotel."

Claire could only imagine what the hotel would look like as the plane took off. During the plane ride Lewis gave her a quick itinerary of the places he'd planned for her. Today would be spent people watching at the hotel veranda followed by dinner at one of his favorite restaurants. Tomorrow, brunch in the Jordaan neighborhood and a visit to the Van Gogh Museum. She thought it all sounded wonderful, and she looked out the window as the plane took off.

The plane ride lasted less than an hour, and before she knew it, they were already at Airport Schiphol. They stepped off the plane and were greeted by a customs agent who quickly cleared them and led them to the airport's private jet terminal. Inside, they were approached by a genteel, older man with silver hair. Lewis hugged him and said, "Erik! So good to see you again."

He responded with a Dutch accent, "Good to see you too, Mr. Hardy. And who is this lovely lady?"

Claire extended her hand and said, "Claire Moore."

He kissed her hand and said, "Welcome to Amsterdam, Miss Moore."

Erik collected their bags, and they headed out the terminal and to another limousine. Inside the car, Lewis said, "Erik has been my driver here in Amsterdam for the last twelve years."

"Your driver here? How often do you come here?"

"Maybe three to four times a year. It's one of my favorite cities."

"How did you first meet Erik?"

"There's a story behind it. The first time I came to Amsterdam I was just an associate buyer at M&S. I was here on a business trip, and I got lost in the city. Erik saw me stumbling around, asking for directions, and he took pity and took me around in his car. He's been my driver ever since."

Erik chimed in from the front seat, "And he's been very good to me over those years, Miss Moore. He's a good man, and I'm lucky to have found him."

Lewis laughed and said from the back seat, "I'm already paying you, so you don't have to lay it on so thick."

Claire smiled, and said to Erik, "From what I gather from the story, I think he was the lucky one to have found you."

They left the airport and headed toward Amsterdam. After clearing through some traffic on the highway, they waded into the main part of the city. Claire looked out the window as she saw the thousands of cyclists whizzing past the streets of the canals. It was an unusually warm October day, and the cafés were filled with people sitting outside with their drinks in hand.

The car stopped in front of a large building, and she and Lewis stepped out. Claire read the sign of the building: Intercontinental Amstel Hotel.

Claire observed the exterior of the hotel. The sheer opulence of the building astounded her. Every brick, window, and column of this magnificent hotel looked as if it was in pristine condition, and together they meshed intricately to form a beautiful palace straight out of the 19th century. Claire stared with her mouth agape as Erik took their bags out of the car, and Lewis grabbed her hand and said, "Come on, Claire, wait until you see the inside."

The lavish grandeur of the hotel was amplified inside. The lobby was a white hall with a grand staircase adorned with black carpet with golden flowers. Overhead a chandelier shimmered with light and crystal. Claire thought the scene was fit for the reception of kings and queens.

When they entered the lobby, the concierge greeted them and said to Lewis, "Mr. Hardy, so good to see you again, sir. Here are your keys to the Royal Suite."

Claire raised her eyebrows upon hearing that they were staying in a suite. Each turn of this trip was becoming more unbelievable, and she couldn't imagine what the suite would look like. When they stepped inside their room, Claire's wonderment of the hotel was complete. The suite had high ceilings with hardwood floors covered in ornate rugs. Ceiling-to-floor windows dressed with golden curtains were pulled back to reveal the Amstel river outside. Antique chairs and dressers were tastefully arranged alongside tables and paintings in the living room, and in the dining room sat a long dining table with a chandelier hanging over it. She walked into the bedroom and bathroom and saw more of the resplendent decor: exquisite paintings, ornamental faucets, and a king bed shrouded in a golden canopy.

Once Lewis was finished giving her the grand tour inside, he led her out to the balcony of their suite. The afternoon light touched down upon the river. Sailboats and river barges glided across the water as the specks of white light peeking beneath them reflected back and blinded Claire. Across the river she could see canal house buildings and other hotels built in the traditional Dutch architectural style. Near them she could make out tourists sitting underneath the shade of umbrellas of the cafés and enjoying the warm sun. And standing right in front of her on this balcony was her handsome man, who despite his busy schedule, had taken the time to arrange all of this for her.

"It's beautiful, isn't it?" he said. "If you're ready, we can head down to the balcony and sit on the veranda."

She didn't answer him right away. She remained deeply moved by this perfect effort that he had put in for her.

"Come here," she said quietly, as she pulled his hand and led him back to the bedroom.

Once in the bedroom, she sat down on the edge of the bed and waited for him. He took the cue and leaned into her, and she pulled him over her body as they settled on to their spacious bed.

Chapter 28

Lewis and Claire left the bedroom an hour later and headed down to the hotel's veranda. It was situated over the banks of the Amstel River, and from their table they could see the busy river traffic up close. Guided tour boats packed with tourists and rowboats with two or three people crisscrossed the river, and Claire waved to the boats occasionally between sips of her beer. She let out a content sigh and said, "I could get used to this."

Lewis feigned a concerned face and said, "Uh oh. Even my ridiculous salary wouldn't be able to support such a lifestyle continuously."

She teased, "Perhaps I should be dating John Wyman instead then."

"You'd have to settle for being his mistress, as he was taken over forty years ago."

They laughed and drank more of their beer. Lewis then spread his arms out and said, "Just look at this city, Claire. It's a perfect city if there ever was one. Its streets are spotless, bikes are the primary mode of transportation, and its people are tolerant and open-minded. It's the model of what I'd like Wyman to aspire to become."

"Still thinking about work, aren't you?"

He replied, "Always."

She said to him, "You know I'm a fan of your family experiment, but can I ask you something?"

"Please do."

"How does the company deal with the tasks and projects that no one wants to do? Using your city analogy, a city deals with its rubbish by hiring people to pick it up. But what family units at Wyman will want to deal with undesirable work?"

His eyes brightened as he said, "That's a very good question. I don't have the specific answer, but it'll be up to the family units to figure it out. Perhaps families will decide that the groups that take on these tasks should be paid more. Or maybe it'll be decided that we'll hire people outside the company to take on these tasks. That's the beauty of this new model; it's unpredictable, but determined by the employees in the decision-making. Maybe some of these families will even volunteer to take on these chores."

"Volunteer? You're joking."

"You have to stop thinking about it as a company but more as a city. When you look at cities, families volunteer out of civic duty all the time, and it's because they care about where they live and the people around them. But people spend more time at work, so why shouldn't the same espirit de corps be felt in the office?"

Claire said, "But the city services are run for the people who live in them, and the officials are elected to serve them. At Wyman, huge portions of profits are going to the Wyman family and senior leaders like you."

Lewis smiled and said, "Exactly. And I'll let you in on a little secret that hasn't been announced yet. I've convinced the Wymans that the management of profits should also be decided by the family groups. Maybe the distribution will be decided by an elected group of family units or by general vote, but it'll no longer be a top down decision.

She was very surprised to hear this. "How in the world did you trick the Wymans to agree to this?"

He said, "There was no trickery involved. The Wymans have all the money they could ever want, and they'd still own the company. What they're looking for now is the continuation of their legacy. They're aligned with my vision. If we succeed, the Wyman name will be remembered for more than just retail."

Claire frowned and said, "But there's that big word 'if'. I'm worried that you won't be given the time needed to see your vision met. You've been at the company for six months now, and we've just now split into our family groups."

He responded, "Don't worry about me. I spend enough nights thinking about this mad plan that I've put into motion. Besides, I have the Wymans' full support."

She didn't press the conversation, but she did worry, for his sake. There were still many questions surrounding this family plan, and it seemed that Lewis was coming up with solutions on the fly. It seemed that he was correct in that he had the Wymans' backing, but she also knew that the company was going to have to start bearing the fruits of this new plan.

They finished their beers, and after people watching a little longer, headed back to their suite to get ready for dinner. She wore a sleeveless black dress, and he put on a checkered shirt and khakis. Their restaurant for the evening was Indrapura, an Indonesian restaurant that was a ten minute walk from the hotel. They arrived at the restaurant at seven o'clock and were seated right away. It was not a lavish restaurant, but instead it was cozy and decorated with care. Claire particularly liked the potted plants that hung from the ceilings.

When they sat down at their table he asked her if she'd had Indonesian food before. When she responded that she had not, he said, "You're in for a treat. The rijsttafel here is to die for."

"What is the rijsttafel?"

"It means 'rice table'. They bring all kinds of sampling dishes at once, and you can try a little bit of everything."

They ordered the Indrapudra rijstaffel, and fifteen minutes later they were bombarded with an assortment of small dishes; lobster claws dipped in oyster sauce, green beans with shrimp, mango salad in peanut dressing, spiced beef with coconut sauce, and soybean cakes were just a sample of the feast that was laid before them.

Seeing this scrumptious spread in front of her, Claire remembered the ideal man she'd wanted out of the One Match pairing and began to laugh.

Lewis gave her a confused look and said, "What's wrong?"

"Nothing's wrong," she said. "I was just thinking about how I've always wanted to find someone with whom I can travel and go try food in exotic restaurants. You've somehow literally made my dreams come true."

He held her hands and said, "You've done the same for me, Claire."

They dug into the food, and she thought it was one of the best meals she'd ever had in her life. She walked back to the hotel in a state of contentment. When they reached the lobby, she thought they would head back to their suite for a quiet evening, but Lewis led her away to the river side of the hotel.

Curious, she followed him out to the pier of the hotel, where there was a boat waiting for them. Seeing her confusion, he said to her, "This is the surprise portion of the itinerary. I thought we might take an evening boat ride."

The idea of a boat ride sounded lovely. She took his hand as he led her onto the boat and inside its cabin. The cabin provided heated shelter from the now cool air outside, but its large glass windows allowed her to see the view all around. The interior consisted of wood flooring and a wooden bench with seat cushions. There was a bottle of champagne on the bench, and Lewis poured her a glass as the captain set sail from his enclosed area of the boat.

They sailed up the Amstel River and swiveled into one of the canals. Yellow lights from restaurants and hotels glowed all around them as the boat glided through the waves. Lewis pointed out different landmarks along the way and provided quick history lessons. "Did you know that the houses here are so skinny because the property tax was based on the width of the house? If you go inside them, they're so narrow, but many of them are quite beautiful in the interior."

Claire sipped her champagne and admired Lewis's considerable knowledge of the city. She leaned into him and enjoyed the view outside. Soon the boat stopped, and Lewis pointed to the window. "Look out there, Claire."

She looked outside and saw several illuminated bridges straight ahead. The twinkling lights accentuated the striking view of these bridges. As she continued to stare, he said from behind her, "We're in Reguliersgracht, where you can see seven bridges at once."

"It's beautiful," she said. She brought out her phone and tried to take some pictures even in the dark.

She then turned around to see Lewis on one knee and with a diamond ring in his hand.

She was caught off guard and could only stutter, "Lewis, what are you doing?"

He said to her, "I was going to wait until the new year to propose to you, but the moment just feels right. Claire, ever since I first met you, I knew you were the one. The last few weeks have only confirmed what I'd known from the start. Will you marry me?"

Claire couldn't fully comprehend what was happening. Her mind was spinning as she tried to absorb the fact that Lewis Hardy was on his knee proposing to her this very moment. She said, "But we've dated for such a short time. Are you sure? What if you end up changing your mind later?"

"I'm sure, Claire. I've never been surer of anything in my life, and I've always been right when I've followed my heart."

Claire looked at Lewis, the way his intense blue eyes waited with calm patience for her answer, and she felt comforted in his surety.

"Yes," she whispered, "yes, I'll marry you."

He slipped the ring on her finger, and then kissed her. Lewis then gestured to the captain, and the captain opened his door and said a quick congratulations to the both of them. Lewis poured another round of champagne for all three of them and implored the captain to take a glass, of which he took a small sip after much persuasion.

Claire remained in a daze as she examined her ring. She was finally getting married. After all her miserable dating and failed relationships, she had ended up with the most extraordinary man she'd ever met. She couldn't wait to tell her parents and friends. Her friends would be overjoyed. Her mother in particular would be so happy. All of that fretting and nagging from her would surely disappear now. Claire looked across the thoughtful and caring man sitting across from her, and she thought she was dreaming this scene in her sleep.

Their boat sailed through the canals and eventually slipped out into the port waters north of the waterways. The waves were choppier here, and the boat felt tiny in this open expanse. Claire felt a little frightened as the boat rocked back and forth, and she nestled up to Lewis for comfort. He held her and pointed out different landmarks such as the Central Station in the south. He then pointed in the opposite direction and said, "Look there. The EYE film museum."

Even in the darkness of the night Claire could see the contours of the white building. Its aerodynamic look resembled a sleek spaceship docked briefly in this city of water and light. She didn't know much about architecture, but she appreciated its creativity, the modernity of its design juxtaposed with the beautiful canal houses that had been preserved over the centuries. It was a majestic city, and she could understand why Lewis would love it so much.

Claire was impressed that he'd been able to pinpoint this monument from afar, but she knew that she shouldn't be surprised by now. Lewis's assured, internal map of the city even in darkness relieved her of her fear. The swirling waters around them no longer felt like the terrible sea seeking the destruction of their boat. As her fears subsided, Claire felt the world open up to her, with all its wondrous possibilities laid bare like pearls unearthed. She leaned into his chest as she continued to look out to the horizon of the city's yellow lights. She had finally found her partner. So this was what it felt like to be with someone you loved. To feel protected as you traveled through the dark waters unscathed. To feel comforted, unafraid. Strangely, more than any other feeling, in this very moment she felt a sense of rest—the kind of rest in which she could surrender her entire trust to someone else and feel at complete ease. No longer on her own, she was home at last.

Chapter 29

Claire woke up the next day in her hotel bed by herself. She rolled over to see a note on Lewis's side of the bed that said that he was at the pool for a quick swim. She used that time to call her friends and family about the engagement news, and she was showered with a chorus of congratulatory shrieks and impatient requests for details of the engagement.

A short while later Lewis came back from the swimming pool with a robe on and his hair still damp. He smiled and said, "Good morning, my fiancée."

Claire smiled back and said, "'Fiancée'. I feel like this is all still a dream."

He went up to her and kissed her. He then pulled back the gold curtains and said, "It's another beautiful day outside. Let's have brunch, shall we?"

They went down to the lobby where the concierge was waiting for them with two bicycles. They hopped on the bicycles, and she followed him to the Jordaan area in the northwest side of the city. Here the mood was quieter and away from the tourists, and they sat in the garden area of a small café that looked out to the Brouwersgracht Canal. As Claire nibbled on her smoked salmon and fruit and discussed with Lewis some early thoughts about wedding plans, she watched the bicyclists riding by at leisurely paces. There were riders and bicycles of all shapes and sizes—tandem bicycles, kids on tricycles, old-fashioned bikes with large handles. Her favorite was a bicycle in which a father carried three little children in a large basket attached to the front.

When they finished their brunch, they rode down past the canals to Vondelpark at the south of the city. At different parts of the ride, Claire pumped the pedals furiously to gather speed as she rode through the streets. She felt like a little girl again, happy and carefree as she sped past cars and pedestrians as Lewis kept pace. They reached the park after a ten minute ride. It was crowded with families and friends and couples enjoying the Sunday afternoon sun on the park's immaculate green lawns. Lewis said to her, "This is my favorite park in all the world. I've often come here by myself to people watch."

She said to him, "It's very nice." It was nice, but she thought that no park could best Hampstead Heath for her affections.

They rode through the paths of the park and then headed over to the Van Gogh Museum. When they arrived at the museum, there was a long queue lined up around the street, but the concierge had procured them tickets in advance. Claire felt a tinge of guilt as she and Lewis cut past the envious crowd.

Inside the museum Claire took her time observing the paintings. Van Gogh was one of her favorite artists, and she liked his paintings of the countryside and its laborers the best.

As she stared at *The Potato Eaters*, Lewis came up behind her and said, "It's a beautiful painting, isn't it?"

She looked at the weary peasants huddled over the morsels of potatoes in the dimly-lit room. "I can feel his great compassion for the people in the painting," she said, "but it makes me sad."

Lewis nodded. "Yes, in some ways it is a sad painting. But to me, it provides hope. Look at it carefully. Even in their poverty, their love and devotion to each other is pure. They would be hungry together rather than starve their souls on their own. When a group of people have such love, they are unbreakable."

She looked at him and could see the faraway dreaming look in his eyes. "You're relating this to your family plan at Wyman."

He gave a sheepish grin as he said, "Yes, you're right. You see, at its core, my family project for the company is about love. To foster love first within the family units, and then to link every family with each other so that this company may have a unifying strength that cannot be broken. I believe with every ounce of my being that if we can achieve this feat that a revolution would occur the world over. We will banish the notion of work as drudgery, and instead reclaim it as something noble and honest—a labor of love so to speak. People want to work—it's etched into the DNA of our existence—and they want to work with people they love. Of course, it's something I can't say out loud, because people won't understand it and will think I belong in a mental asylum, but I think you must understand, especially as we stand before this work of art."

Claire saw the way that Lewis spoke with such conviction and passion, and she understood for the first time the vast ambition of his goal. She understood now that this project was a missional endeavor that would consume him for the rest of his life. It was exhilarating to know that she would be joined with him as he pursued this purpose, and she was inspired but also a little worried of the mighty weight it might play in their lives.

She observed the painting more closely and said, "I think he must have been a great human being to paint with such compassion."

Lewis replied, "The man was brilliant. Poor fellow, to die with such suffering."

"In your family model for Wyman, how will you allow for such genius? The mad, solitary figure who prefers to toil away on his own?"

Lewis looked at her in surprise, and after a pause said, "You know, I hadn't thought of that. I don't have the slightest idea. Maybe we will have to make allowances for such individuals to reside in our company."

"Yes, it'd be a shame to drive away these people."

Lewis said, "But you know, even they are never truly alone. Even Van Gogh had his brother Theo to lean on over the years."

"Yes, that's true. Maybe for such employees in the company you'll need supporters rather than partners who can serve as encouragement or even make sure that they eat."

As she said those words, Claire thought of Becks and how Ashleigh had been with her as Becks labored to transform the pub. In the last few weeks Claire had thought intermittently about Becks, wondering how she was doing at the pub, but during the weekend she'd not entered her mind. She thought about how Becks had encouraged her to set out and start her own analytics company, saying that she believed in Claire's ability to make it happen. Would Becks have served as her Theo if Claire had taken on such an enterprise? But then again, it was all a moot point now.

Lewis interrupted her thought by saying, "I think these are all interesting ideas. Maybe you can help me think through them a little more in the upcoming days."

She replied, "If you'd like me to I will."

She continued on the tour of the paintings. When she got to *Wheatfield under Thunderclouds*, she stopped in her tracks. The green fields in the painting reminded her of the green hills of the Cotswolds. She thought of Will this time, and her hands started to tremble.

Lewis sensed that something was wrong and said, "What's wrong, Claire?"

"Nothing," she said. "I think I just need to sit down for a little bit."

Lewis sat next to her and held her as she tried to steady herself. "I'm all right," she said. "I think I just needed to gather myself a bit."

She ignored Lewis's concerned glances. Once she was able to stop her trembling, they continued touring the museum for another hour before riding their bikes back to the hotel.

At the hotel they began winding down their trip. They packed their belongings and spent a final moment on the balcony watching the boats once more. Erik arrived to pick them up a couple of hours later, and they were back at the Amsterdam Airport Schiphol to conclude their weekend.

When they were ushered back into their private jet, Claire sat down on her plane seat and looked out the window.

Lewis said, "It's a pity that it had to end, isn't it?"

Claire gave him a kiss and said, "Yes, but it was a divine weekend."

"Just think, Claire, we'll have many such weekends together for the rest of our lives."

His words triggered an instant feeling that bothered her. A voice inside her head told her that she didn't know this man at all. They'd only been dating for a month, and everything had happened so fast. She hadn't had the time to absorb it all. And he was so busy with his work plans that she wondered if he even knew her. She was now sitting in this private jet with him, and while it was spectacular in its own right along with the rest of the weekend, it was all so removed from who she was. Rather than getting to know each other better, it seemed as if the majority of their conversations during the weekend had been spent talking about his vision for the company. It was a pattern not too different from their previous dates.

She took a deep breath and told herself to calm down. She was only feeling normal jitters of realizing that she was finally getting married. Surely everyone must feel that they could know a person better before the final enjoinment. And yes, Lewis was preoccupied with the launch of the family model, but the intensity of his workload was bound to decrease with the project now well under way.

Nevertheless, Claire felt compelled to say something to alleviate this unsettling feeling. "Lewis," she said, "this engagement weekend was more than I could have ever hoped for, but I'm hoping that for our wedding it could be something simpler."

"Was it a little too much? I can assure you that this weekend was not representative of my typical lifestyle."

"No, this weekend was perfect, and I honestly mean that. It's just that when it comes to our wedding, my family's a rather ordinary family from Watford, and I don't think a lavish wedding would make them feel comfortable. And I'll remain forever astounded from this weekend, but deep inside, I'm not sure if a simpler wedding would really fit who I am as well."

Lewis gave her an affectionate glance and said, "That's what I love about you. You have to remember that I was just a boy from Kilburn once upon a time as well. If you don't want an extravagant wedding, we'll tone it down, but I want to ensure that it exudes the elegance that befits you."

Claire returned his smile, and feeling a bit better, she said, "I suppose I have to allow for some concessions. It happens once in a lifetime after all."

Feeling a bit better by his assurance, she leaned back in her seat and prepared for a quick nap as the plane started the ascent into the sky.

Chapter 30

November rolled in after the trip to Amsterdam, and Claire's focus shifted back to work. The majority of the company were busy preparing for the upcoming holiday season, but Claire's work family focused on prospecting for companies and deals for the upcoming years.

One day, Harriet got off the phone and said to Claire, "I've got something interesting."

Claire looked up from her monitor screen and turned to Harriet.

"I have several distributor contacts who bring in new product leads," said Harriet, "but the very best is Ned Horton. He just called, and he was very excited about a new product he wants us to look at. He'll be coming in next Friday with the product and some of the company representatives. He's always talking up his clients' offerings, but I've never heard him this excited before."

"That's brilliant. What's the product?"

Harriet shrugged. "That's the strange part. For some products he can't share until we sign the NDAs, but the funny thing about this lead was that he wouldn't even share the company bio that he was representing."

Claire was surprised by the lack of information. She asked, "How in the world are we going to prepare for the meeting then?"

Harriet said, "We'll just have to be on our toes. Let's get the boys to prep the facts sheets about Wyman, and we'll have to inform our logistics and marketing partners that they're going to have to be ready to talk about Wyman's advantages in their respective areas."

The three family groups followed Harriet's recommendation and spent time preparing presentations on the benefits of selling through Wyman. In their prep meetings they all took turns guessing as to what the mysterious product might be. Marcus, one of the family leads of the logistics team, thought that it could be some kind of new kids' toy given Ned's relationship with other toy vendors in the past. Amy, one of the two senior leads from the marketing group, wondered if it might be a new tablet or phone with bells and whistles that had yet to be seen in the market. Jeffrey and Sam had all kinds of wild ideas ranging from hover boards to jet packs. Claire herself couldn't even begin to imagine what might be presented, and she was glad that no one asked her to take a guess.

The day of the big meeting soon arrived, and all twelve members representing each of the three families filtered into a conference room. The junior associates were gently reminded to listen but remain quiet unless specific questions were directed at them. As they all sat in dizzy anticipation, Harriet left the room to fetch their guests.

She arrived back into the room five minutes later with just one man, which surprised Claire, and by the looks of the others, everyone else as well. The man was tall but walked with a stoop in his shoulders. He wore an ill-fitting brown suit that was noticeably out of fashion, and his silver hair was unkempt and shaggy around the ears. He was an older man, probably in his sixties based on his prominent wrinkles, but he looked energetic and sharp. He chatted amicably with Harriet as they entered the room, and Claire assumed that he was Ned Horton by their comfortable rapport. Sure enough, Harried introduced Ned to all the Wyman members sitting at the conference table, and he reached over and shook everyone's hands in a relaxed and friendly manner.

After the pleasantries were over, Harriet sat down across from Ned and said, "Well, this is a bit unusual, Ned. Where are your clients?"

Everyone laughed at Harriet's direct questioning, and Ned joined in with a hearty laugh of his own.

"Harriet, I missed you, too. Mind if I have a glass of water? I'm quite knackered from all the traveling."

"Let's get to the point instead. Do you have a client, and more importantly, do you have a product?"

Ned sat back in his chair and smiled. "What if I told you it was the most exciting client I've ever brought to you, and with it, the most exciting product as well?"

"Well, get on with it then."

"You wouldn't want me to present on a parched throat, would you, Harriet?"

Claire could see that Ned's coy exchanges were getting to Harriet. She looked as if she might hurl a chair out the conference window, but instead she calmly said, "Sam, why don't you fetch Mr. Horton here a glass?"

Sam obeyed her orders, and left the conference room. While they waited for him, Ned said nothing, and Harriet returned the silence. Claire observed the two of them in complete fascination. She assumed that they had already engaged in some unspoken game of negotiations before the product had even been unveiled. If so, she thought that she had completely underestimated Ned. At first glance she had taken him to be a slovenly, avuncular man who would capitulate to Harriet's aggressive demeanor, but she saw that he carried himself with a calmness and poise that was not easily perturbed.

After what felt like hours, Sam came back with a glass of water. Ned thanked him, and took a small sip. Seemingly satisfied with the situation, he then reached into his briefcase and pulled out a black, cylindrical object that was no larger than a hockey puck.

"This small object," he said, "is the future of the home."

Harriet's face was blank, betraying no hint of surprise or disappointment. The rest of them followed her lead and said nothing.

Ned continued, "It's a smart home device. You can use it to control your home in every single way imaginable. You can set it up so that you can turn on and off the lights in your home, adjust the temperature settings, turn on the television and stereo, and even order pizza from your flat."

He then proceeded into a demo of the product. He started off by saying, "Play me an Adele song." In less than a second the smart home device started playing "Someone Like You." He then asked for a news update, and a voice from the device provided a short summary of today's headlines.

The group of Wyman employees all looked at each other. Yes, the capabilities were impressive, but this smart home device didn't seem all that different from the voice recognition devices already in the market. Either they were missing something, or Ned Horton was pulling their leg. As if reading their minds, Harriet cut off Ned as he started to talk about the speaker specs of the device and said, "Enough of this bullshit, Ned. I know you didn't come all the way here to show me a knock-off of other smart home devices. If you don't bedazzle me in the next five minutes, I'm giving you the boot."

Ned stopped his presentation. His lips then curled up into a smile as he said, "You're the very best, Harriet, but patience was never your forte."

"Ned, I have the highest admiration for you, I really do, but I'm about two seconds away from kicking you out of this room."

"Very well. Here's something your other devices can't do."

He pulled out a small box and set it on the table. He opened the box and spread out flesh-colored strips across the table. He then distributed to them to all the Wyman members at the table and instructed them to put them on their temples. They all complied, and once they were affixed on their heads, Ned said, "Now Harriet, think of a song that you want the device to play."

Within seconds, the device was playing Elton John's "Rocket Man". Harriet gasped, and they all realized from her frozen expression that the song was precisely what Harriet had silently picked in her mind.

Before Claire could comprehend the significance of this feat, Ned then pointed to her and said, "Why don't you pick a song?"

The song "Imagine" popped into her mind, and the device switched to playing John Lennon's iconic song. Ned chuckled and said, "It's an appropriate choice."

As the others sat in awe, Ned said, "As you can see, this smart home device is not just a knockoff of other smart home products. It's a device that can be controlled by your thoughts. It's called One Home. It uses the same technology used in the dating service One Match. And that's because my client is Jorgen Magnussen, the creator of One Match. With the launch of One Home, he intends to change the company name from One Match to simply 'One'."

It was now Claire's turn to gasp. Of course. She pulled off the strip from her head and examined it. The design of the strip looked slightly different—it was a much smaller patch than the original One Match patch—but how could she have missed that it was the same technology that had read her mind and paired her with Becks?

Jeffrey, forgetting Harriet's instructions to stay quiet, blurted out, "Have you met Jorgen? What's he like?"

Harriet gave him a dirty look, but Ned smiled at him and said, "No, I haven't. Bit of a recluse, I must say. All our communication has been through email, and he sent me the device via the post. I dared hope that he might come out today, but that would have been hoping for too much."

Claire looked at the Wyman members at the table, and they were all still in a state of shock of what they'd just witnessed. Ned was obviously delighting in their astonishment as he explained, "One Home is going to revolutionize our lives. Just think; you'll be able to turn on the microwave, run the dishwasher, turn on the TV, or order groceries all on the blink of a thought. There will be no turning back once One Home is launched. This will be a kind of quantum leap in history, not unlike the buggy to the automobile, the typewriter to the computer. And now, humans to gods."

Claire flinched at Ned's last sweeping statement, but Harriet acted as if she was unimpressed. She replied, "But you'll have to be wearing the strip the whole time to control the device."

Claire could see that Harriet was still visibly shaken, but she was trying her best to display a stoic response after her initial amazement.

Ned shrugged. "The patch is the size of a button. Do you even notice that you're wearing it?"

Claire admitted to herself that the patch was hardly noticeable, and judging by Harriet's silence, she didn't disagree either.

Harriet continued the discussion in the practicalities. "How much will it retail for?"

Ned clasped his hands and said, "That's the best part. £200 when it comes out in two years. It'll be a device for every home."

"Two years? That's still quite a ways away. What if competitors come out with something before then?"

"I doubt that Jorgen's worried about any competitors for a mind recognition device."

"Has he filed for patents?"

"No, it'll be kept as a trade secret."

"What about regulatory approvals?"

"There'll be concerns in both the EU and the US, but the strategy will be to argue that it's the same technology as One Match. If he received approval for One Match, I don't see why One Home approvals wouldn't follow."

"What other retailers are you talking to?"

"So far, just you, Harriet. But I've got a UK roadshow with Biga, Tesco, M&S, Amazon, Harrods, Selfridges, and some other retailers set up in the next week or so. The US retailers and some of the other countries will follow after that."

Harriet simply nodded at all the information as Claire and the others hurried to write down all the information. She then said to Ned, "Would you mind stepping out to the kitchen for a cup of tea? We would like to spend some time amongst ourselves discussing this product."

Ned got up and said, "By all means. Take as long as you need. I'm sure you'll have quite a bit to discuss."

Chapter 31

As soon as Ned left the conference room, all twelve attendees began talking at once.

"Oh my god—was that for real?"

"£200 retail. We're going to sell millions of that device ourselves. It's going to be the next iPhone."

"That device can read your mind! Assuming that it even passes all the regulatory agencies, we should think about the moral implications of selling such an item."

"Are you joking? We're not the moral police. And besides, One Match has been reading people's minds for nearly a year now."

Harriet raised her hands to quiet the chatter, and she said "Let's all calm down for a moment before we collectively wet ourselves. What we witnessed was a demo of a prototype that's still two years away from hitting the market. They've got some work to do, and we've got some work to do. This will be a protracted process for the next two years, so let's take it one step at a time."

Amy replied, "You're the voice of reason as always, Harriet. Speaking on behalf of our little marketing family, we're willing to follow your lead on this matter."

Harriet said, "Good. This is the first step of the dance, and Ned knows the dance very well. When he comes back in the room, we will make it clear that we're interested in carrying One Home, but let's not go overboard and call it the next iPhone."

Claire saw Marcus turn a shade of red as he'd been the one who had made the iPhone comment.

Jamie, Amy's other senior family member on the marketing team, replied, "That's fine. We can start off by offering a full standalone kiosk in the electronics department along with AAA product exposure in our holiday catalog and our online merchandise spaces. Should be an appetizing proposal for a vendor that's never had a retail product before."

Harriet said, "Excellent. As for the contract terms, I'll offer the 60 day payment terms and standard co-op and damage allowances."

Marcus interrupted her and said, "On the logistics side we also want to propose FOB terms."

Harriet frowned. "FOB? Let's not muddy up the contract. That's something we discuss with our vendors after we've established some kind of a relationship."

Marcus's senior logistics partner Stephen shook his head and said, "We're trying to expand our FOB program in a big way, and we want One Home in it. This product is going to have spectacular sales, and we'll be damned if it's not included in FOB."

"We don't even know if it's going to be manufactured overseas! It could very well be produced in London for all we know." Harriet's eyes were shining and her teeth were clenched as if she was ready to get into a fist fight with both the logistic leads.

Marcus said, "Then why don't we at least find out?"

Harriet said nothing for a while, but then finally relented. "Fine. But let me introduce the topic in the proper point in the conversation."

While the others continued to talk, Sam whispered to Claire, "What's FOB?"

She whispered back to him, "It stands for 'freight on board'. It means that we go pick up the product from their warehouses rather than having them ship it to us. I heard that the logistics teams think they can create some large supply chain savings by expanding this program."

Claire sat at the table and felt something was off. She wasn't sure if she was comfortable with the mind recognition capabilities of One Home, but based on her own experience with One Match she had an intuitive feeling that One Home would be a tremendous success. Selling the item would certainly create a nice spike in sales, but if their main competitors were also carrying the item, there'd be no gain in market share.

She cleared her throat, and all the others turned to her. Seeing the other eleven pairs of eyes staring back at her expectantly, she suddenly thought her idea could be very stupid, but she said, "What if we offered to be the exclusive retailer for One Home?"

Jamie said, "Ridiculous. It's likely going to cost us a fortune."

Marcus chimed in, "It's also too risky. It's a manufacturer introducing their first product in retail."

Harriet raised a finger to her lips and said, "Please. I want to hear what my partner has to say." She turned to Claire and said, "Go on, Claire, please tell us more about what you're thinking."

Encouraged by Harriet's support, she ventured, "Well, I believe that if One Home is able to deliver on its promised capabilities, it would be a huge success. It'll raise revenues for us and everyone will be happy, but other retailers would sell loads of it as well, and maybe more than us. Sales and profits are nice, but we won't be any closer to the vision that Lewis laid out for us in the All Hands—the vision that Wyman could be restored as the palace of dreams. If we could start securing exclusives on amazing products, customers might start to believe again that Wyman is a special place of wonderment. One Home could be that catalyst product for us."

The others were silent. Claire wasn't sure what they were thinking of her idea. Finally, Harriet said, "Claire has reminded me of what we once had and lost here at Wyman. We had boldness once. We believed in our ability to shape the tastes of our times, and we bet big on the products and vendors that others wouldn't touch. Somewhere along the way we became timid, stopped thinking big. We used to carry exclusives all the time, but we've now become me-too followers. She's right. If we are to begin our climb out of the hole that we've dug for ourselves over the years, we need to start thinking big again, and what better start than a device that can read your mind?"

Marcus iterated, "But this vendor has never made a product before. We don't know if they can deal with the supply chain logistics of delivering thousands, and maybe even millions, of units at breakneck speeds for the holidays."

Harriet snorted, "You're the one who wanted to conduct an FOB deal for its sales potential."

"That's when we're one of many retailers carrying the product. If we're exclusive partners and we flop on this item because they can't make enough or if people are spooked by it or whatever, we'll be the laughingstock of all of Britain."

Amy said, "I'm afraid that I agree with our supply chain partners, Harriet. It's too much of a risk."

Claire looked over at Harriet. When she'd first proposed the idea she'd felt so sure of it, but now that all the other senior partners provided feedback, she felt the doubt creep in her own mind. She thought about One Home and One Match and everything that had happened after she'd decided to put on the patch that one fateful day. She knew in the bottom of her heart that One Match had not made an error when it had set her up with Becks. She knew that the technology was extraordinary, and that they could not miss out on the chance to capitalize on the opportunity.

She said to the group, "It's not true that the vendor has never had a product. We can't discard the fact that One Match is the most popular dating service in the world right now. Millions of the One Match device have been shipped out and used by people seeking companions, and we haven't read anything about shipment delays of the patch or it malfunctioning. To the contrary, more and more people are signing up for it each day because it works. Besides the staggering numbers you read about in the papers, I've had friends who've struggled for years to find a partner find their soul mates through One Match. It's not a large leap of faith to believe that the same innovator who created One Match could succeed with One Home."

Claire knew she was flushed in her cheeks. Even though she was a senior partner of one of the three groups, she still felt as if she was a junior member in comparison to the other senior partners who'd had years of experience. She couldn't imagine what they must be thinking of her.

After another round of unbearable silence, Jamie said, "One Match is fine and all, but we don't really know what's going on behind the curtain. When it's pairing couples as a dating service, people believe the technology is reading their minds when in fact it could have been a much simpler algorithm. With One Home, when people think that a light is being turned on, the lights have to be turned on every single time—there's no faking it."

Harriet replied, "And what do you supposed we just witnessed when it correctly guessed the exact songs that Claire and I were thinking of? Do you think that it got lucky? Or better yet, do you think that we're in cahoots with Ned Horton to pull off some silly joke on the rest of you?"

Jamie sat there and said nothing. No one else dared to mutter a word either.

Harriet continued, "Look, it's okay to be scared. But when the opportunity comes along, you have to pounce on it as if your life depends on it." She then pointed to the door and said, "If anyone or any team does not want to be associated with this deal anymore, you can leave right now. No one will blame you, and there'll be no shame if you don't believe in this product. But if you want to stay, we're going all in with this deal. One Home will either be Wyman's Folly or its Great Savior."

Claire looked over at the marketing and logistics family members, but no one from either side budged from their seats. She breathed a sigh of relief.

Harriet said, "Good. When we bring Ned back in, we're going to start off by discussing the regular terms and merchandising proposals. Jamie and

Amy will describe both the offline and online merchandising details. I'll then ask him to consider an exclusive agreement, and Claire can direct us in leading us through the discussion. Finally, we can bring up the FOB program as a potential inclusion in an exclusive deal. Obviously, we'll turn to Marcus and Stephen to walk Ned through the details here."

The other senior leaders didn't raise any objections, so Harriet asked Jeffrey to fetch Ned and bring him in. Claire couldn't believe that Harriet had asked her to direct the conversations about exclusivity. After all the previous years in which she had crunched the numbers in the background to provide for the dealmakers of Wyman, she was getting her chance to be front and center. She felt her stomach churning with nervous excitement, but she took a few deep breaths and told herself that she was ready.

Chapter 32

Jeffrey brought Ned back into the conference room. Ned drank his tea from the white mug he brought in from the kitchen. He asked, "So have we reached a verdict?"

Harriet replied, "Yes, we have. We'd like to be one of the retailers to carry One Home."

"Excellent."

"The terms will be standard. 2% for co-op, 2% for damage, and net 60 payout."

"How about net 45?"

"Net 60, but we'll give One Home AAA merchandising treatment that Amy and Jamie can speak about now."

Taking this cue, Amy nodded and said, "Yes, as Harriet mentions, we're prepared to market One Home as one of our premier products. In our stores we'll set up a dedicated kiosk in our electronics departments with an employee fully dedicated to demoing and answering questions about the product. During the holidays it will be one of our select items showcased in our store windows, and it will be on the cover of our annual holiday catalog."

Jamie added, "As for our online merchandising, we will run a top banner campaign on our homepage at 10% rotation, and at 20% rotation on our electronics page. We will also wage a full email campaign that includes premium promo spots in our Black Friday and Cyber Monday callouts. In short, we will be throwing the kitchen sink to ensure that One Home is on top of mind for all our customers during that holiday period."

Ned replied, "This is fantastic. I know that Jorgen will be pleased to hear the news."

Before Harriet could continue, Marcus stepped in and said, "We'd like to also talk about FOB terms."

All the eyes at the table turned to Marcus. Claire was shocked. Marcus was going off script. Harriet was now supposed to propose an exclusive arrangement, but Marcus apparently decided that he wasn't going to wait his turn. Claire saw that Harriet was throwing Marcus the nastiest look she'd ever seen, but Marcus avoided her gaze of death.

Harriet began to say, "Before we discuss FOB terms—"

Marcus cut her off and said, "At Wyman we are partnering with our vendors on our burgeoning FOB program. We pick up the goods from your source location to save you on the costs of shipping the items to our warehouses, and in return our vendors provide us with a discount on the cost of the goods—it's a win-win situation."

Ned furrowed his bushy brows and said, "I know what FOB is." He turned to Harriet and said, "I suppose I could bring this up with Jorgen, but I don't even know where he's having the product manufactured. I'll have to find out if he also wants the location known. Is this all necessary for the initial launch?"

Harriet said, "Well, I was just about to say—"

But again, Marcus interjected, "Yes, we believe that FOB is necessary, especially when the stakes are so high. This is not just a cost play for us. If we're betting so big on a product for an unproven manufacturer, we need assurance that the product will make it to our stores in time, and the only way to do that is to pick up the units ourselves."

Ned said, "You imply a lack of trust in our ability to deliver our units. You needn't worry about that. Jorgen has shipped more One Match patches in the last three months than what Wyman's top-selling product sold all of last year."

"Yes," Marcus said, "but delivering a blockbuster holiday launch through a retailer is a completely different beast altogether. You've got to have tight coordination with your retail partners to deliver the product just in time and then schedule the incremental units appropriately so that we don't run into capacity issues."

Ned unexpectedly got up from his seat at the table. He said, "Harriet, call me when your trust issues have been worked out. In the meantime, I'll be talking to retailers who don't have such a problem."

He started to pack One Home into his bag. Claire and the others turned to Harriet, but Harriet didn't say anything and continued to give Marcus the slow burn. Christ, thought Claire, in this pivotal moment Harriet was about to let One Home slip away because she was so incensed at Marcus. Claire felt that she had to do something.

"Wait," she said to Ned as he reached for the conference room door. "Mr. Horton, what if we told you that the FOB terms were part of our ask for an exclusive with One Home?"

Ned stopped from opening the door and turned to Claire. He said, "I'm listening."

"What my partner Marcus forgot to mention in his excitement to talk about the FOB terms was that we believe in One Home so much that we would like to propose that Wyman be the exclusive retailer for this product, either for a temporary duration or as a permanent partnership."

"An exclusive? It's been years since Wyman has pursued an exclusive with any of my products."

"Please, Mr. Horton, if you'd be willing to sit down again, I'd like to share our proposal."

Ned picked up his bag, and instead of walking out of the conference room, he walked back over to his original seat and sat down. The other Wyman employees all looked at Claire. It was her show now, and she ignored the feelings of timidity that were bubbling inside her. She tried to channel Lewis's confidence when he stepped on the stage for the All Hands meeting several months ago.

"Mr. Horton, what is the purpose of One Home? If one were to ask me after your astounding demo today, I would say that One Home's purpose is to help people find happiness in the home life. That is at the heart of One Home, isn't it? To further simplify the home life so that we can find a measure of peace and happiness at home. And dare I say, the ultimate pursuit of One will be to provide complete happiness in all aspects of our lives through its technology. I imagine someday that the technology will be incorporated into all our lives—in coffee shops, restaurants, our cars, our schools and our workplace—so that all of our experiences will be streamlined and effortless in our quest to find happiness."

Ned smiled and replied, "It's almost as if you've been in some of the phone conversations between Jorgen and myself. And please, call me Ned."

Encouraged by this response, Claire continued, "I have not eavesdropped on any conversations, but I believe in One Home with all my heart. I've had close friends who have used One Match to find happiness in their relationships, and if the technology is half as good in One Home, it will be a landmark innovation that will be recorded in the history books.

"Therefore, we want to do something we've never done before at Wyman. If we were to receive an exclusive, all the halls of Wyman's first floor will integrate One Home in some shape or form. We'd have to work out the details with our merchandising teams, but what I imagine is that the floor will be transformed into a large replica of a home. We will have a living room, a master bedroom, a children's room, kitchen, and entertainment room. These rooms will be decorated tastefully with the finest wares that Wyman has to offer for each of these living spaces.

However, the main showcase item in each room will be One Home. There will be a sales representative for each room who will pass out the One Home patches and give tutorials and demos on the uses of One Home in each of the settings. Our customers will be able to try it directly in each room and receive a truly immersive experience of using One Home in their homes. And by making it an exclusive, there will be crowds lining up around the block to get into the stores and try out this mysterious device. It will cause such mayhem and madness that the internet and the papers will be abuzz about One Home for months on end. It will be an unveiling reminiscent of olden days, when people of all walks of life, rich and poor, old and young, gathered en masse at department stores to witness the ushering in of new technologies and fashions. Wyman may have lost its way a bit over the years, but I know that it's still in our bones to be able to stage the kind of spectacles that no one else can."

Claire's hands were shaking after she finished her pitch. She had come up with the lines of her speech on the spot, and she had no idea if it'd even be possible to follow-up on her idea of a home setup for the entire first floor of every store.

As if reading her mind, Ned said, "Your proposal is brilliant but ambitious. Will you really get the necessary approvals for this?"

Harriet said, "If you provide us with the exclusive and a finished product with all the regulatory approvals, we will deliver on Claire's vision."

Ned leaned back and said, "That's fine. I'd need to talk to Jorgen about his terms for an exclusive, but I am very keen on Claire's idea, and I'll do everything I can on my part to make a deal happen."

Harriet said, "Then until we negotiate a deal, my request is that you cancel your meetings with your other retail partners."

"That's nonsense. I owe it to my client to see who can provide the best terms."

"No, if you show One Home to our competitors the deal is off. If we're going to do a grand unveil, we'd want to keep the existence of the product as secret as possible. You know that only Wyman has the physical presence and the brand and scope to deliver the kind of launch that Claire was talking about. And speaking of Claire, you have in her a passionate champion who will see the product all the way through to a smashing success."

Ned rubbed his chin in deep thought but finally said, "You drive a hard bargain, Harriet, but I suppose that I can hold off until we see how our negotiations for the exclusive turn out. If nothing else, Claire has sold me that Wyman understands the enormous potential of One Home."

He picked up his belongings and this time he shook hands with every member of the conference table before he headed out. He paused when he came up to Claire, and he said, "You have greatness in you. I respect it when I see it."

Claire turned scarlet at the compliment, and she said, "You're very kind, but our proposal was a group effort."

He chortled and said, "Ha. You're not so great at lying."

Harriet and he walked out of the conference room, and when Harriet walked back in a couple of minutes later, Claire could see that she was still angry.

Harriet turned to Marcus and said, "You nearly fucked this whole thing up by going rogue. If Claire hadn't rescued us, we would have lost one of the defining products in history."

Marcus shouted back at her, "You can't talk to me to like that. We're equal partners in this new family system. We'd agreed to bring up FOB, and I simply stepped in because you weren't bringing it up as promised."

"We'd agreed that I'd bring it up after the proposal of the exclusive! You didn't listen to me!" Harriet clenched her fists, and Claire was worried that she might assault Marcus.

Amy stepped in and said, "Please, restrain yourselves, especially in front of our junior partners. Everything worked out in the end. Let's celebrate the fact that we may end up with an exclusive item in our hands that could turn things around for this company." She turned to Claire and said, "You were absolutely marvelous. I have to admit, Claire, I didn't know that you were such a brilliant pitch person. You should come to some of our marketing pitches to our vendors."

Jamie added, "I couldn't agree more with my colleague. You saved our hides in there."

Claire said, "That's kind of you, but I think I'll stick with the number crunching in our biz dev group. I don't know what came over me. I guess I just really believe in the product."

Marcus shook his head and said, "This is all so reckless. We saw a ten minute demo of the product and now we're gambling the future of Wyman on this one product." He turned to Stephen and said, "You might be willing to partner in this nonsense, but I certainly don't want to be blamed when this leads to total disaster." With that, he stormed out of the conference room.

Harriet muttered, "Good riddance. We don't need him anyway."

Stephen sighed. "Let's just give him a moment. We can't run all the details of our logistics operations without him; after all, he's my senior partner in our family group. Marcus needs to cool down a little bit, and I'm sure he'll come around."

"Fine," Harriet said, "in the meantime, let's all go grab a pint to celebrate Claire's achievement today. First round will be on me."

Claire protested, "But I haven't done anything. We don't even know if the terms of the exclusive will be too high for us."

Harriet waved her hand and said, "Minor details. I've worked with Ned for a long time in this business, and if he wants something to work, we'll make it work. And trust me, you've convinced him that he wants to make this deal."

Claire still felt that they were celebrating a victory too soon, but she decided to trust Harriet. All eleven of them met at the lobby ten minutes later, and headed off towards the Shakespeare for some drinks.

Later that evening, Claire recounted the entire story to Lewis in her flat as they lay in bed. After she was finished, Lewis said, "I'm just so proud of you, Claire. Harriet gave me a quick rundown of what happened before I came here, and she told me what a magnificent speech you gave to sway Ned."

"I was just trying to channel some of your passion for Wyman. You don't think I went too far in what I promised him we can do?"

Lewis shook his head. "Not at all. I think it's a brilliant idea. It's these kinds of ideas that will turn this company around."

"Marcus didn't seem to think so. He walked out of our meeting, and I'm not sure where we're at with our logistics team."

"Harriet told me about Marcus. I talked to Marcus afterwards and let him know very clearly that he and his team will support this project."

"What was his response?"

Lewis sighed and said, "He wasn't too thrilled about it, but he doesn't have a choice. But enough about Marcus. This device—I wish I could have seen it in person. To think that it can read your mind...it's extraordinary but frightening to some degree."

Claire nodded and said, "Yes it is. We were all in such a rush to secure the item during the meeting today, but do you think we should even be selling it?"

Lewis was silent for a while before saying, "It's a good question. We may be unleashing Pandora's Box with this item. But if we don't do it, one of our competitors will. I'm not to judge if this technology will be good or bad for mankind. That is something for our politicians and philosophers to debate. All I know is that this is where we're headed, and we can choose to flow with the course of history or be left behind."

Claire thought that she disagreed with Lewis. He seemed resigned to an inevitability, but she wondered if Wyman had a larger role in determining which products would be safe for their customers. At the same time, she understood that Wyman no longer held the clout that it once did, and Lewis was likely correct in that the other retailers would carry the item. She wasn't sure what the right answer was, and since it was late, she decided to not press the subject and went to sleep.

Chapter 33

The Christmas holidays arrived soon after the One Home meeting. In late December Lewis took her to Ottolenghi in Islington. The restaurant was intimate, and its white, elegant decor was dimly lit by soft candle lights. They feasted on roasted aubergine with tahini yogurt, poached quail, puffed kale mixed with crispy tofu, and washed it down with a bottle of La Souteronne red. As they were finishing up their meal, Claire looked out the window and saw that it was snowing. She pointed and said, "Look, Lewis, it's snowing outside."

He looked out and said, "I can't remember the last time it snowed in London before Christmas."

"I don't remember either." Claire felt a resonant peace as she sipped her wine and continued to watch the snowflakes cast a blue hue in the night. For the first time in a long time Claire felt as if her life had a sense of direction, and she enjoyed this moment of stillness before the busyness of the holidays and wedding preparations afterwards.

When they went outside, the snow continued to fall, coming down now in heavy bunches that covered the glow of the street lamps. Claire held Lewis's hand as they walked down the ghostly road back to his car.

Later that night, Claire had a dream. She was at the sun room of the Silver Bells cottage late at night. There was a woman who stood by the bay window. She wore a silver robe, and the light of the moon stretched the shadows of the window panes across her face. Curious, Claire walked over closer to the woman, and she saw that it was Becks. Becks turned around to face her. While the silver robe covered her, Claire could see from the outline of her shape that she was just wearing the robe and nothing else.

Becks smiled at her but said nothing. Claire was about to say something, but Becks put her finger to her lips to signal silence. She then walked over to a nearby bed and beckoned Claire over. Claire came and laid down next to her. With their faces close to each other, Becks reached out and held Claire's face in her hand. Claire observed how loosely the robe clung to Becks. As Becks looked at her coyly, Claire slipped the robe off of her shoulder.

Before she could see what was underneath the robe, Claire woke up. She felt a tingling sensation as she recollected every frame of the dream. She didn't know what to make of the dream, but it had been wonderful to see Becks so vividly again. She wondered what Becks was up to during the holidays.

Claire spent Christmas at her parents' home in Watford, and Lewis swung by Christmas day to greet her and her family. Much to her chagrin, there was much fawning over him by her parents and her relatives, but Lewis was a good sport about it and charmed all of them with his impeccable manners and his generous compliments of her mother's cooking. During this time, the image of Becks in her silver robe came to Claire periodically. At first she tried to push it aside but eventually gave up. Remembering Becks in the dream brought up other memories of their conversations and that wonderful weekend. She knew that she missed Becks. A couple of months of dating Lewis had passed, and even now they lacked the intimacy she'd shared with her. It was starting to worry her now, but she hadn't told anyone yet, not even Maddie. She thought about calling Becks and wishing her a happy Christmas, but she dared not, as she was afraid that hearing her voice would only increase her longing for her.

Christmas went and New Year's Eve came, and Claire and Lewis celebrated the evening with a lavish party at the Blue Room of the Whitford Hotel. It was a delayed engagement party of sorts, and this time it was Claire's turn to be introduced to Lewis's many family and friends. Lewis had picked out a flowing, red Versace dress for Claire to wear, and she felt a little self-conscious and overwhelmed as she greeted famous businessmen and statesmen and their wives in her voluminous gown. Her one respite was that Lewis's parents were kind people who greeted her with enthusiasm. His father was a balding stout man, and he kissed her hand and expressed his pleasure in meeting her. His mother gave her a warm hug and told her that she was thrilled to finally have a daughter. Claire was relieved that his parents were not stuffy at all, and her mood brightened further when she saw her friends Maddie and Lucy enter the party.

Lewis had rented out the entire room, and it was a grand hall that brought back memories of the lobby at the Amstel Amsterdam Hotel. Like that lobby, there was a monumental staircase at the back of the room, and crystal chandeliers hanging from its high ceilings. Flickering candle light contrasted the strobe lights that poured over the room from the light fixtures above. Bartenders in tuxedos were busy mixing drinks in the west end of the room as servers in their own penguin suits passed out salmon and yellow tuna sashimi. A live samba band played music for a crowd of guests dancing on the dance floor, and other guests looked out into the spectacular view of the River Thames as fireworks lined up the night sky.

During a break from greeting guests, Lewis and Claire sat down on one of the couches with Maddie and Lucy. After some chit chat, Lewis asked, "Claire, have you given more thought to our wedding venue?"

She said, "No, I'm afraid I haven't. I just know that I'd like it in Watford, or maybe in London, and nothing more. Did you have something in mind?"

He smiled and said, "Either place would be fine, and I understand that Watford is your hometown, but I was thinking about Yorkshire."

"Yorkshire?"

"Yes, it's becoming a destination for visitors around the globe when they visit the UK, and for good reason. I was there last summer and was astounded by some of the locations there." He opened his breast pocket from his suit and handed her a brochure. "This is Ripley Castle. It's a seven hundred year-old castle with exquisite views of the countryside. I called them this morning, and they have a weekend in June if we move on it now."

Claire looked over the pamphlet with her friends. Lucy said, "Claire, you'd be mad not to have it here. Look at this castle. It'll be the most perfect wedding."

Claire agreed, "It is very beautiful. But I think my parents were set on having it in Watford. I think my mum has invited the whole town."

"Yes, I had a chat with your mother as well. I showed her the pictures, and she agreed to have it there if I would pay for all her guests to travel and stay in Yorkshire, to which I happily obliged," said Lewis.

Claire said, "You did? That mother of mine has no shame. That's very generous of you, but I'd have hoped you would consult me on the matter."

"Yes, which is what I'm doing now. If you'd rather have it in Watford, I can pick up the phone first thing tomorrow and change the plans."

Claire saw Lucy's pleading look and pictured how thrilled her mother must be at the prospect of her getting married in such a location. She said, "I don't know. It looks very lavish and expensive, and I thought we'd agreed it'd be a simpler wedding."

Lewis replied, "I can assure you that as costs go, it's actually quite reasonable and in line with your idea of keeping down the excess. That's what's so exciting about the venue; it'll be a very elegant wedding without being over the top."

He could be so persuasive, and she felt herself giving in. "That's fine then. We can have it at Ripley Castle."

As Lucy gave her a large grin, Lewis said, "Oh, and I also told your mother that I'd like to pay for the entire wedding, including your wedding dress."

"Lewis, you don't have to."

"Claire, I insist. It'll be the most important day of our lives, and I don't want to spare any expenses. I was thinking that £10,000 should be a sufficient sum for your dress, but please tell me if that's not enough."

Both Maddie's and Lucy's eyes enlarged concurrently at the figure. In disbelief herself, Claire said, "No, I think that's plenty enough."

"Perfect," Lewis said. "I'm sure you'll want to pick out your wedding dress yourself, but I have heard from friends that Halle Hardy Couture always has excellent service."

Barely containing herself, Lucy said, "Halle Hardy! That's the most prestigious wedding boutique in London. All the celebrities shop there."

Claire said politely to Lewis, "I'll check out that shop per your suggestion."

"Brilliant. If you'll excuse me, ladies, I must continue my role tonight as the host of the party. Claire, darling, perhaps when you're ready you'll rejoin me as well."

"Of course, Lewis."

The three of them watched Lewis disappear into the crowd. Lucy said, "Christ. Look at him in his tuxedo. He looks like James Bond's hotter brother. You're marrying the perfect man. Would it be possible to rent him for parties?"

Maddie said, "He sure seems to know what he wants for the wedding, doesn't he?"

Claire narrowed her eyes and replied, "Yes, it can be a bit overwhelming. Sometimes it seems like he's two paces ahead of me."

Maddie asked, "What do you mean?"

Claire sighed. "Oh, I don't know. It's like he's got a plan for us for every step before I've even started thinking about it, and I'm always trying to play catch up."

"Boo hoo, Claire," Lucy said. "Must be so tough to have a man who can predict your every need and take care of it."

Claire laughed and said nothing more as she thought Lucy might have a point, but she noticed that Maddie continued to look at her with a bit of a concern. She didn't want to get into a lengthy discussion about her apprehensions of her impending marriage, so she excused herself to get a drink. After picking up a martini, she walked over to the room's expansive windows.

As she peered out to watch the fireworks illuminate the dark river, a voice said to her, "It's quite a scene, isn't it?" Claire looked over and saw that it was Harriet in an elegant gray dress.

"Harriet," Claire said, "it's so good to see you. I'm glad that you made it."

Harriet motioned to the river and said, "In my younger days I used to walk along these banks all the time. Watching all the tourists, daydreaming of how I might make something of myself in this vast city. It's ironic that I now look back at those days as some of the happiest days of my life."

"Mmm. I like to come out to the river, too. Usually to catch a play at the Globe or to go to the Tate Modern, though, and not to watch the tourists. They can be overbearing."

Harriet turned to look out the window again and said, "They affirm to us that we live in a city that still matters."

They stared out to the river together for a while, and then Claire said to her, "Have you heard back from Ned? Do we have a deal?"

Harriet replied, "Do you really want to be talking shop right now?"

"So you've heard back then. Please, what did he say?"

"Oh, alright." Harriet said. "There's not a deal in place, but it's looking good. Apparently Jorgen Magnussen liked the idea of a temporary exclusive, and Ned's convinced him that we'd be the best partners for the launch. They've agreed to halt all roadshows for now until a deal is agreed upon."

Claire knew that she should be happy at the news, but she couldn't help but fret that a contract wasn't signed yet. "How long do you think it'll take to get a contract in place?" she asked.

Harriet shrugged. "Each case is different, but it can take up to a couple of months—assuming that it goes through. We don't even have a figure from them yet, and then the bloody solicitors will muck things up a bit as we wrestle back and forth on all the details."

"I just wish we knew for certain. I know that we're still two years away, but there'll be so many tasks to coordinate across all of Wyman if we want to launch with the grand vision we sold Ned on."

Harriet put an arm around Claire's shoulder and said, "I understand your worries, but we will get the deal done, and this company will rally to unveil One Home like never before. In the meantime, let's forget about work and enjoy this celebration of yours."

She asked Harriet, "What do you think of One Home as a product? Do you think that it's good for society?"

Harriet shrugged her shoulders and said, "It's not for me to judge. My job is to determine if it'll make this company money."

Claire said, "You're just like Lewis. That's pretty much what he said."

"We've been in this business for a long time. Unless we know that an item will blatantly harm our customers, we have to leave it to them to decide for themselves. Otherwise you can convince yourself of the potential negative effects of every single item in our stores. You'd go mad. Lewis understands that."

On cue, Lewis came up to them and said, "Harriet, so lovely to see you."

Harriet nodded to him and said, "Congratulations, Lewis. You're marrying an excellent woman."

"Don't I know it." He turned to Claire and said, "I don't mean to spoil the conversation of work family members, but there are a few more guests that I'd like you to meet."

Harriet held up her cocktail and said, "Please, get going. I've got plenty of company."

Reluctantly, Claire went with Lewis to greet yet another set of dignitaries. As they walked away she turned back to look over her shoulder, and she saw that Harriet had resumed looking out the window to the abyss beyond.

Chapter 34

A week later, Claire stopped by Halle Hardy in Mayfair with Maddie. Claire tried on several dresses that her assigned consultant recommended. They were all exquisite presentations, but Claire felt uncomfortable and out of place. They took a lunch break at the store's private oyster bar, and as they slurped their oysters, Maddie said to Claire, "I still don't know why you didn't invite Lucy. She's going to murder the both of us when she finds out that we went dress shopping without her."

"I didn't invite her because there's something that I wanted to talk to you about alone."

"Oh?"

"I'm not sure if I want to get married to Lewis."

Maddie stopped in the middle of her swallowing and nearly choked. She recovered and whispered, "Are you serious? What's wrong? Did something happen? Did you two have a fight?"

"No, nothing's happened."

"What is it then? Is he terrible in bed? That's it, isn't it? I've read that sometimes amazing looking men are horrendous lovers."

"No, he's fine in bed," Claire replied.

"Then what is it? He's everything a woman dreams of. He's rich, handsome, charming, and he obviously dotes on you."

Claire paused and then said, "Yes, he checks off all the checkboxes, but something is missing. There's just a level of mutual comfort that's not quite all the way there. We're stiff around each other."

"That's just because you've known each other a couple of months. It takes time to get to know each other fully. I feel that John and I are still getting to know each other."

"But what about the fact that he'd pretty much decided on the wedding venue by the time he told me about it? Or that he picked out the dress for me to wear at the New Year's party? He does that kind of thing every now and then."

Maddie replied, "Those alpha males are always like that. I admit that it was a bit forward, but at least he knows what he wants. Better than winding up with someone who's indecisive and snivelly. If you look hard enough, you can always find negative faults about a person. No one's perfect, but Lewis sure seems to come close."

"But I think there are people you can be more comfortable with, ones with whom you can naturally banter and make decisions together without the other serving as the leader. Do you know that I've never joked with Lewis? Never teased him either." Claire thought about the countless times that she and Becks had mocked each other in their conversations.

"That's the problem? Go crack a joke tonight."

"You can't just be cheeky with someone at the drop of a hat. The timing has to be right, and you have to be comfortable with that person."

Maddie snorted, "That's just ridiculous. If I didn't know better I'd think you were making excuses because you had feelings for someone else."

Claire was silent.

Maddie looked around the room to make sure no one was watching them, and then she leaned in. "Christ, there is someone else, isn't there? It's okay. You can tell me."

Claire also looked around and then leaned in to say, "I think I may have feelings for Becks."

"For Becks?" Maddie stared at her with her mouth agape.

Claire nodded. "Yes, I've had a dream about her, and I've been thinking about her constantly since then."

"Was it sexual?"

"I don't know. Maybe. She was wearing nothing but a robe in the dream, but she was fully covered. I was taking it off but then I woke up."

"Then of course it was sexual!" Maddie said. "I don't believe this."

"I don't believe it myself. I thought at first my feelings were just because I was feeling guilty about breaking up with her, but now I know that I miss her."

"But are you sure?" Maddie asked. "What if you're having these feelings because that bloody One Match paired the two of you up? I should have never bought the service for you."

Claire replied, "And that's why I wanted to talk to you. You and John met through One Match, and now you're together. Did you ever wonder if you two would have loved each other if it weren't for its algorithms telling you so?"

Maddie ran her hands through her hair. "I don't know. I asked myself that question millions of times. We'll never know, will we? I just decided at the end that the act of loving someone is an active endeavor, and regardless of whether One Match was our initiator, we were the ones choosing to continue loving each other."

Claire dwelled a bit on what Maddie said. "Yes, that makes sense to me. I think at this point if I gave up Lewis for Becks, I'd actively be choosing Becks no matter that One Match paired us up initially."

"But it was such a short time. You knew her only for a few months, and you only met in person a couple of times after that first meeting."

"It was short, but everything fell into place right from the beginning, and we had so many conversations through our GChats and texts. I miss her terribly. I miss the way we used to grouse about simple things to each other. I miss the way she would playfully tease me and the way I would do the same to her. I miss her kindness, and the way she cared for me in Bourton. And her weekend in London was one of the best moments of my life."

Maddie said, "You and I've had great times together, but we're not lesbians in love. Are you sure that One Match isn't clouding your thinking?"

Claire shook her head. "No offense, but I've never wanted you to kiss me. I want that and more from Becks."

Maddie said nothing for a while. She then sighed and said, "You know, maybe you're on to something here."

"What do you mean?"

"I've been reading articles proclaiming the end of male dominance. The basic thesis is that men have been the domineering sex because their physical traits gave them an advantage in occupations involving physical labor. But those days are over now, and women are taking over in professions such as law, medicine, and elsewhere. Maybe we're smarter and more emotionally adapted than men, and if that's the case, why do we need men? We could eventually have a society ruled by women, and a few men will be kept in captivity to help us breed. You might be a pioneer in this movement."

"Stop being ridiculous. This isn't a joke. It's not that I'm swearing off men and choosing women. I just want to be with Becks."

Maddie asked, "Then what's stopping you?"

"We haven't talked in a couple of months. I can't just suddenly give her a call or show up at her doorstep in Bourton," Claire said. "And, I'm not sure if I'm ready to think of myself as a gay person. It changes things about one's identity, doesn't it?"

Maddie reached over and gave Claire a hug. "Oh, Claire," she said. "You'll always be my best friend, and I will always support you."

"But what should I do?" she asked.

Maddie said to her, "Maybe you should send her a letter via post. You always write beautiful letters, and no one can ignore a letter through the post."

"But what if she doesn't respond?"

"At least you'll know that you tried. But I think you'll find some way for her to get back to you."

Claire was grateful that her friend was supportive of her. She looked around and said "It does mean that we may be giving up a Halle Hardy wedding dress."

Maddie said, "I just want to see you be happy. If that means that we're giving up £10,000 wedding dresses and Yorkshire weddings, so be it. But we may have to head straight to a pub when we leave this shop to numb the pain of losing all of this."

Claire stared out the window of the store. "I just hope that she'll write back to me."

Chapter 35

Later that evening Claire sat down at her kitchen table to write her letter. For hours she squirmed in her seat, trying to come up with the right words to say. She wrote several drafts of her opening paragraph and threw them away into the rubbish bin because they sounded too formal. Finally, she tried to picture Becks, and she thought of seeing her in the Cotswolds. The scene pleased her, and she was able to pen her letter:

Dear Becks,

How are you? As I'm writing this letter, I'm picturing you at The Happy Clam. You are toiling away in that immaculate kitchen of yours, cooking up a storm of delicious food and directing your line cooks and servers as your hungry customers eagerly await their dishes. Of course, you are wearing your standard black T-shirt and blue jeans, but over your outfit you have a white apron with stew stains and blotches. Beads of sweat form on your forehead as you concentrate over your food with intense focus. You are in your element, and you are as lovely as anyone can be.

My memory of The Happy Clam seems as if it were ages ago. So much has happened since we last saw each other in London. For one thing, I'm getting married. Lewis Hardy proposed to me in October in Amsterdam. It came as a sudden surprise but I accepted his proposal. We are scheduled to be married on the third Saturday of June in Ripley Castle of Yorkshire. I hear that it's a beautiful setting. There is a lake and a deer park near the castle, and the building itself is supposed to be a picturesque setting for weddings. I've yet to find a wedding dress, but I suppose I have some time.

Despite the rolling wheels of the wedding march, however, if you would take me back, I would break off this engagement right now, and come to you. I know it must be a surprise for you to read this, but I am surer of this thought than I have ever been of anything in my life, and my only regret is that I didn't say it earlier to you when I had the chance. When I told you at the café on Finchley Road that I was dating Lewis, the wisest part of me knew that I was making a mistake, but I was too afraid to know it then. I was unsure of what it might mean to acknowledge that I was attracted to you, and I'm still unsure of what this means. You knew early in your life that you were attracted to the same sex; I don't even know at this point if I'm attracted to women or if it is you only.

Even with this unknown, my desire for you overcomes it. I love you and miss you. I miss talking the day away with you. I miss seeing you in your black shirts and your lovely dresses. I miss the way you understood me and the way I understood you. I miss you so much that you only have to reply back to this letter with the words, "I take you back", and I will be at Bourton on the first train over with suitcase in hand.

I will understand if you don't feel the same way about me anymore. Perhaps you've even found someone else. But I only ask that you respond to my letter so that I may know before I make the biggest decision of my life. Silence from you would be too much to bear, and at the very least, please write to me to let me know that you are well.

Yours,

Claire

After Claire sent out the letter to Becks, every day of waiting served as torture. She couldn't concentrate at the office, and she ran to her mailbox every day after work to to find no response. She thought of sending a follow-up email or text to Becks, and it took every bit of willpower to hold off from doing so. Finally, about a week after sending her letter, a small envelope addressed to Ms. Moore from Becks Kennedy arrived. Her hands trembling with anticipation, Claire tore upon the envelope and read the letter inside:

Dear Claire,

Thank you so much for writing me the beautiful letter. I was touched by it deeply, and in my vanity I've read it many times over. I would say congratulations to your engagement, but it seems that the content of your letter dictates that I take a different course.

Then let me start off by telling you that I miss you, too. I am not seeing anyone else, and my feelings for you have not changed since our last meeting. And if I'm being honest with you and myself, some part of me feels a pleasure in knowing that your affections for me have returned, or perhaps never left. Nearly all of me is aching to write the words that you've asked me to write: I take you back.

But the part of me that loves you at its highest and purest plane won't allow it. As you said yourself, there is still a part of you that fears what it means to love another woman. I wish I could tell you that it's a small change, but I would be lying to you. If we were to be together, your sense of yourself, and how your friends and family members view you might change. And if our relationship were to not work out, I could not live with the fact that you threw away what you had with Lewis. From everything that you told me about your desired qualities in a man and your descriptions of Lewis, I believe that he will bring you happiness and prosperity over the years. I cannot promise the same with us.

You must remember, too, that our relationship was born through machine and data. While it may be too extreme to say that it was tainted as a result, I remain at unease with this fact. You and I will never know how much we were swayed by this mysterious match maker. The world is changing rapidly. It's getting more difficult to understand the truth of ourselves. But I know that I want to love someone with clarity of mind, unclouded by the experiments of alchemists, and I know that you'd want the same for yourself.

Therefore, I cannot say yes, for if we were to try and fail, the burden of what you gave up for me under the influence of this science would be too much for me to bear. For what it's worth, you've changed me as well. Before I met you, I was sleepwalking through my life, casually dating and humming along with the daily beat of The Happy Clam. But you've sent coursing a new vein of energy through me, and I want to thank you for this injection of vitality. I'm making preparations to move to Thailand, and if all goes to plan, I will send you a postcard from there next year.

In closing, I wish you the very best. Don't think of me and only concentrate on your upcoming marriage to Lewis. Perhaps many years later when you are happy and content you will recall our short time together, and my apparition will be a source of a faraway and good memory. Until then, I wish you only happiness and joy in your journey ahead.

Love,

Becks

The first reading of Becks's response felt as if a quiet bomb had detonated. The shock of the rejection was only slightly blunted by the tenderness of Becks's words. For days afterward, Claire went through the motions of the day listlessly while trying to hide the numbing pain that reverberated in rolling waves. She read the letter many times over, trying to find some clue or hint that Becks was willing to change her mind if Claire tried to persuade her, but her verdict seemed clear and immovable.

After a couple of weeks Maddie asked her if she'd ever heard back from Becks. Claire lied and said that she'd not.

Maddie replied, "It's probably for the best. You were about to make such a sacrifice, but it all seems so ridiculous now, doesn't it?"

"Yes," Claire said. "I suppose it was all just very ridiculous."

"Well, I'm glad that this little hiccup has passed and you can go back to focusing on your wedding."

Claire didn't believe that she would ever get over "this little hiccup". She resolved to never tell anyone about the letters. The letters, and the short-lived relationship itself, were too dear to her even in the bitter ending, and she knew that no one else could understand what had happened and why it had mattered.

As for Lewis, she initially thought that she should call off the wedding. There were moments in the following weeks after the letters in which she thought that she would blurt out to him that she no longer wanted to get married, but she couldn't quite pull the trigger. She knew that he loved her, and as she delayed calling off the wedding, she eventually convinced herself that perhaps in due time she could love him—if not ever in the same way that she loved Becks. She decided that the wedding plans would continue.

Chapter 36

The winter and spring months of the new calendar year were a slog. There was a long task list of wedding preparations that she had to check off with Lewis. She finally picked out a dress, but there were guest invitations to be sent out, menus and cakes to be sampled, flowers to be arranged, photographers to be selected, and so on and so on. Claire had always dreamed of having a perfect wedding, but her reluctant outlook for the marriage made each task seem like an unbearable chore.

Her work life was not any easier. Harriet was the main lead in the negotiations with One, but Claire and all the other members of the project were very much involved. The talks dragged on for months as they and their legal counsel wrestled back and forth with Ned Horton and One's solicitors. The discussions first centered around the buy-in amount for the exclusive. Ned originally proposed two million units that Wyman would have to commit to purchasing, but eventually they reached a settlement of one and a half million units. Once the exclusive purchase quantity was settled, they revisited the vendor terms. When vendor terms were finalized, they then had to iron out the details of the FOB plans which required supply chain partners on both sides, and then discussions of merchandising for both online and the physical stores brought on another series of extensive talks. It was soon May, and Claire wondered if they'd ever finalize the details that had seemed like trivial concerns back in November.

A few weeks before the wedding day Claire was sitting at her cubicle when Harriet stormed over looking as angry as Claire had ever seen her. Harriet said to her, "We have to go to the phone booth room and call Lewis. Something's come up."

Claire followed her wordlessly to the room as Sam and Jeffrey looked on. When they entered the tiny room, Harriet turned on the speaker setting on the phone and began dialing. As soon as Lewis answered on the other line, she shouted, "That back-stabbing traitor Marcus! He's left us for Biga!"

Claire nearly gasped, but she heard Lewis calmly respond, "So I've heard. HR informed me this morning. We'll block him from starting anytime soon. He's got a non-compete clause."

"He's already told them about One Home. They've reached out to Ned about a counter-proposal to ours. They're proposing a commit of five million units in all their countries combined. Ned's team has stopped negotiations with our legal counsel. We're completely fucked and we're going to lose the deal!"

Spit flew in the room as Harriet raged on. Claire herself felt sick at the thought of losing the deal after the many months of exhaustive work that had been put into it. She'd known that Marcus had remained unhappy ever since the initial meeting with Ned, but she'd never imagined that he would skip over to a competitor and share information on the deal. Lewis kept trying to calm Harriet down to no avail. She repeatedly screamed about suing Marcus until he was penniless, and Lewis attempted to divert her attention back to the more urgent situation of losing One Home.

"Let's call Ned. I can talk to him. But we should come up with a plan on what we're going to pitch." Lewis then said, "Claire, if you don't mind, may I have a word with Harriet in private?"

"Of course." She wondered what couldn't be said to her as well, but she was also relieved to take a step back from digesting the bad news in the stuffy room. Claire went back to her desk and put on her headphones to do some work. But she soon heard voices coming from the direction of the phone room, so she took off her headphones. Sure enough, she could hear Harriet and Lewis talking. Claire looked over at the room and she could see that the door was slightly ajar. She'd closed it when she'd left the room, but the latch must have not clicked all the way. She looked around and saw that there was no one in the vicinity—Jeffrey and Sam must have gone away for lunch. She decided to walk over and close the door without attracting Harriet's attention, but before she could do so, she overheard Harriet say, "No, I won't do it."

"What other options do we have? We can offer various concessions, but we'll never match five million. You said yourself that we'll lose the deal."

"Lewis, you'll regret this later. Think of the impact to your family program. You told me yourself that you wanted it to be clean."

"Yes, but if we lose this deal, there won't be a family program to continue! Don't you understand this? Call Ned and do it."

Claire froze. She couldn't believe what she'd just heard. What were they trying to do with Ned and why would Lewis regret it later? She guessed that Lewis was demanding that Harriet either blackmail or bribe Ned. She felt her hands shaking, and her anxiety attack started up again. She began to tremble all over. However, she had the wherewithal to realize that she had to close the phone room door. With Harriet's back still turned away from the door, Claire quietly closed it without her noticing. Then with her anxiety spreading all over her, she hurried herself to the toilet. Once there, she sat down in a stall and tried to steady herself. She tried to convince herself that she'd just imagined the snippet of conversation she'd overheard, but she knew that it had been real. Lewis's curt and impatient orders to Harriet had sounded alien to his usual calm and collected demeanor, but there was no mistaking what had happened.

She sat on the toilet seat for at least an hour trying to gather herself and debating what to do next. On one hand she could pretend that she hadn't heard anything. This seemed like the most practical recourse, especially given that she wasn't supposed to have heard the conversation. On the other hand, she was marrying Lewis in a couple of weeks. She had to find out the truth, even if it meant admitting that she'd left the door ajar.

Claire took a deep breath and left the loo. When she walked back to the office room, she saw that Harriet was now sitting in her cubicle next to Claire's. She tapped Harriet and said quietly, "Do you mind if we step into one of the conference rooms for a quick chat?"

Harriet said, "Is it okay if we speak a little later? I'm just typing out an email that I need to send out."

Afraid that she might lose her nerve later, Claire whispered, "I accidentally overheard a portion of your conversation with Lewis."

Harriet stopped typing, and her face went pale. But she quickly recovered and stood up with Claire to step into a nearby meeting room. Once inside and the door shut, Claire explained what had happened.

She braced herself for one of Harriet's famous angry outbursts to finally be directed at her, but Harriet said, "Thanks for telling me, but I think you misheard what we discussed. Lewis was simply asking me to reach out to Ned as to what alternative solutions we could explore together."

Harriet displayed a nonchalant face, but Claire knew that she wasn't telling the truth. It was so tempting to accept Harriet's answer, but she knew that she couldn't let it go. Before Harriet could stand up to leave, Claire touched her hand and said, "I know what I heard. Please, Harriet. I'm marrying this man. I need to know what Lewis was ordering. I'm about to make the biggest decision of my life in a couple of weeks."

Harriet flinched but said nothing. Claire implored, "Please, Harriet. I need to know. As your partner, as your work family member, I'm asking for the truth."

Harriet maintained her stoic disposition, but she said, "Think long and carefully if you really want to know. It would make it so much easier for you if you didn't."

Claire nodded and said, "I want to know."

Harriet took a breath and leaned back into her chair. "I suppose you'll be finding out soon enough, anyway."

She then said, "About two months ago Ned threw in a new wrinkle to our deal. Apparently Jorgen has come up with a new use for his technology. He wants to use its brain-scanning capabilities to place people in jobs best suited for their skill set. It's called One Work. Given our grand experiment with our family program, he believes it's the perfect fit. One Work would not only pair up employees into families, it would also dictate their roles and functions."

It took a moment for Harriet's revelation to set in. Claire was relieved to hear that Lewis hadn't ordered Harriet to blackmail or bribe Ned, but the answer had turned out to be much different than she expected. She recalled that she'd half-joked to Lewis on their first date that he use One Match to pair Wyman employees, but she hadn't expected this solution to be at the cusp of reality.

Claire guessed, "And Lewis has been rejecting the proposal to this point. The whole point of the program is to free us to decide what we want to pursue as families. He even told me that his eventual plan is for employees to select their own family members."

"Precisely. But even Lewis knows that we can't lose One Home over to Biga."

"So what happened? Did you call Ned? I stopped listening after your talk with Lewis."

Harriet nodded. "I called Ned. We have to finalize the terms, but the deal is done. Lewis will be announcing the rollout of One Work after your wedding. All current employees will stay in their current family groups and projects, but new members will be evaluated by One Work."

Claire winced at what Harriet had to say. "How does letting a computer algorithm dictate your family group and your role even remotely resemble the family plan that we're carrying out right now? It's going to bastardize the whole thing."

"It's a fair question," Harriet said, "but once in these groups the members will have a fair degree of autonomy on which projects and programs to tackle. Besides, Jorgen's agreed that it'll be an experiment. If we find that the family groups picked by One Work are less productive than the current arrangements after one year of testing, we'll be free to shelve the project."

"I've seen One Match in action. I know it will win out, and Lewis's vision will be compromised. He's underestimating the power of the technology." Claire was tempted to blurt out that she had used One Match herself, but bit her tongue. She knew that a person had to have experienced One Match for herself to really understand its uncanny matching capabilities.

"And if it wins out, then perhaps it will further enhance the program. Whatever happens, we must do everything we can to hang onto the deal." Claire must have looked unconvinced because Harriet sighed. She then asked Claire, "How happy were you working here before Lewis instituted his family program?"

"Not very," Claire admitted.

"And now that you're part of a team, a genuine team, working hand-in-hand every day with people you care about, how happy are you now?"

Claire could see where this was going but answered truthfully, "It's the most fun I've ever had at work."

"That's what I thought," Harriet said, "and it's been the same for me. To work with you, Jeffrey, and Sam...it took me my whole career to find out that this is what truly matters. And I'm telling you right now, if we lose One Home and Biga sells millions, Lewis will surely get sacked, and this family experiment will die out in a whimper. And it's not just about Wyman. Think of the millions of people out there, clocking into work every day, living out the majority of their days in cubed desperation with only the picture frames of their loved ones to remind them of what they're suffering for. This system has failed us—the fundamental goodness of work has given way to cold transactions of labor for pay—and if things continue the way they are now, it will all get burned to the ground. Maybe not now, but eventually there will be a reckoning. It may be even sooner than we think. This is our only hope to right what we have lost along the way."

Claire said, "But everything is moving so quickly. The ramifications of integrating One Work could be massive, and we've not thought it through."

Harriet replied, "We have no time. We have to do what we have to do in order to keep the mission alive at all costs. The mission is everything."

Claire slumped in her seat. It felt to her that Lewis and Harriet were making decisions that were bound to have far-reaching consequences that just the two of them shouldn't be making in haste.

Harriet said to her, "Don't look so forlorn, Claire. I have to be honest with you. When Lewis first asked me to be your family partner, I was skeptical given how young and inexperienced you were. You have to forgive me. I thought I was having to serve as your nanny purely because of Lewis's attraction to you, but since our partnership has started you have impressed me over and over again. You remind me of when I was your age. You don't have my ambition, but your skills are more developed than mine were at the same juncture of your career. I'll be retiring soon, but I'll keep my promise to Lewis to train you, and when you're ready, you'll become a cornerstone of this mission here at Wyman, and perhaps even beyond."

The details of her pairing with Harriet stung her. Lewis and Harriet had always made it seem as if Harriet had been a willing partner to Claire from the get-go, but the truth was finally out. Claire became angry at the deception and said, "So you put up with me so that someday I could sit by Lewis's side as he rules Wyman? What if I didn't want to?"

"Don't pout. It's unfitting on you. You know as well as I do that Lewis has no intention of taking over Wyman. His goal is to decentralize the way we work. And he wanted me to develop your business acumen because he cares for you. He wants you to be involved with him as he seeks to change our work lives."

Claire said, "I'm different from you and him. I don't believe that you have to sacrifice your principles for your cause."

Harriet bristled and said, "Lewis and I aren't sacrificing our principles. We are experimenting while we keep the longer vision in mind. Besides, we have no other options. Do you have a better suggestion?"

Claire wanted to say something but couldn't come up with an answer. Lewis and Harriet were zealous in their goal to keep the family model alive, but she felt that Harriet wasn't exaggerating either when she said losing One Home would cost Lewis his job; having demoed the product firsthand, she remained convinced that it would be a smashing success for the retailer that won the deal. When Claire remained hopelessly silent, Harriet gave her a pat on her shoulder and left the conference room.

Chapter 37

In the days leading up to the wedding, Claire thought of approaching Lewis about her discovery of One Work but decided not to in the end. She understood that his mind was made up, and she didn't want to add additional stress to what he must be feeling. She still felt uneasy about the plan to merge it into the family program, but she was also distracted with all the last minute details that needed to close for her wedding.

On the Wednesday evening of the wedding week, Claire and her bridesmaids hopped on the train to Harrogate in North Yorkshire to begin the wedding festivities. They checked into the Majestic Hotel that evening and held a very tame hen party at Claire's request. The party consisted of a relaxed dinner in the hotel's restaurant followed by a few drinks at the bar. Lucy had a tad too much to drink by the night's end, but otherwise Claire was thankful that her friends had respected her wishes to keep her away from any final debauchery.

As Claire lay on her hotel bed that evening, she had another dream of Becks. There was no silver robe this time; instead, she and Claire were sitting at a bar of a crowded pub. They were both laughing and at one point Becks asked her if she and Lewis had any children yet. Claire replied that they hadn't, and it was because she had always held out hope that she would reunite with Becks.

Claire woke up in the morning with a start. She felt the dream was an omen that she was about to make a mistake. Before she could contemplate it further, her parade of bridesmaids knocked on her door to get her up and head towards Ripley Castle for a viewing. She got ready quickly, and they took the ten minute drive to the castle. They met with her wedding planner in front of the castle entrance, and they toured its grounds. Claire had visited the castle in March, but she realized that the backdrop of a summer day exposed the full glory of her venue. The circular lawn in front of the East Wing was perfectly manicured, and the wing itself offered clear views of the deer park and castle courtyard.

Lewis arrived the next day along with many family members of both sides. In Claire's family there was Aunt Gertrude, Uncle Stephen, Aunt Emily, Cousin Daniel, Cousin Michael and a slew of other relatives she'd not seen in ages. They came in waves on the train rides that Lewis had paid for, and soon the Majestic Hotel was filled with the chaotic hubbub of suitcases and hugs and conversations. Her work family of Harriet and the "boys" arrived too, and Claire was surprised to realize that they really felt as close to her as her blood relatives. She'd not talked to Harriet for several days after their conversation of their initial pairing, but she'd let her grudge go before the wedding, as she admitted to herself that if she'd been in Harriet's shoes her reaction may have been the same. Claire tried her best to greet everyone with a gracious air, but after a couple of hours of shaking hands and giving kisses on cheeks, she decided to steal away for a little while before her face cracked from her forced smiles.

She snuck out the back door of the hotel and walked to a pasture nearby. She took a stroll through the green lawn, and she thought of the enormity of her wedding ceremony the next day. She had continued to think of her new dream during the greetings at the hotel, and her despair of getting married had intensified during this time. She felt that she should call off the wedding, but with all the preparations that had gone into it, it felt like an impossibility.

As she thought about the wedding, she heard a rustling behind her and turned around. It was Maddie.

"Christ, you gave me a fright, Maddie," Claire said.

Maddie had a worried look and said to her, "Is everything all right, Claire? I saw you sneak away, and I thought I should chase after you. The wedding rehearsal is about to start, you know."

Claire replied, "Yes, everything's fine. I just needed a bit of fresh air, that's all."

"You've never been good at lying," said Maddie.

Claire took the bait and said, "Suppose that I think this wedding is a mistake."

"Are you thinking of Becks again?"

Claire nodded. "And what if I am?"

"Becks is gone—you told me yourself. You're only thinking of her because you're experiencing wedding jitters. It happens to all of us."

"But what if it's not just jitters? What if my instincts are correct?"

Maddie ignored her questions. Instead she extended her hand to Claire and said, "Take my hand and come back with me."

Claire paused and Maddie waited for her. "Please, Claire," she said.

Reluctantly, Claire took her hand, and they walked back to the hotel.

Shortly after their return, the wedding party headed up north to Ripley Castle for the rehearsal. Having served as a bridesmaid so many times in her life, Claire felt as if she could conduct the rehearsal on the wedding coordinator's behalf: Groom and best man at front. Parents come in. Flower girl. Bridesmaids and groomsmen come in. Ringbearer. Bride comes in with father. Biblical passages read. Homily given. Wedding vows exchanged. Kiss to the bride. Bride and groom leave the stage. Wedding party exits the stage.

Yes, she had it all memorized, and with each practiced step her feeling of dread increased. As she rehearsed giving her vows to Lewis, her declarations that she would love him in sickness and in health rang hollow to her ears. She wanted to yell out that everything had to stop right now, but the words were caught in her throat; her courage faltered at the sight of her parents sitting in the front row, finally approving of a choice she had made in her life. She hated that her parents held such sway, but she couldn't blame them. She knew that her desire to please extended out to a sphere beyond them, and her relatives, friends, colleagues, and Lewis were all part of that web that kept her bound to that desire. She was trapped, and all she could do was continue the motions of the rehearsal as she felt her fate fan out into an inevitable defeat.

Chapter 38

Once they finished the rehearsal at the castle, they all headed back to the Majestic hotel for the rehearsal dinner at the Majestic Restaurant. The bridesmaids groaned to Claire that she should have told them that the rehearsal dinner would be at the same location as their previous hen party, but it was the least of Claire's worries. She picked at her steak and vegetables and tried to look happy for Lewis and their guests.

After the meal was cleared, several close friends and family members provided toasts. Lewis's younger brother Richard displayed a slideshow with funny pictures of Lewis when he was a child. His mates from his uni days also regaled the crowd with embarrassing stories of Lewis when he'd been a student. One particularly funny story was when he'd botched a date by mistaking the girl for her twin sister.

Soon Lewis's father took the microphone. He said to the crowd, "Every father believes his son is special. I am no different. Even when Lewis was two years old, I thought he was such a precocious child. He was so scared of the dark that he'd beg me to sleep with him. I would lay next to him and hold him in my arms, and he would talk on and on, babbling words about who knows what. And I would pray in that darkness next to him, pray that he would grow up to be a man someday who was honest and good.

"My prayers have been answered a thousand times over throughout his life. I don't mean to embarrass Lewis, but all his life he's always been a good boy, and he has made us proud. Many of you know about his accomplishments in his career, but most of you don't know the generosity that he's displayed time after time. When Lewis and Richard were growing up we often couldn't afford second helpings of meat for the boys, and when Richard finished his portion Lewis always gave him his remaining portion, saying that he'd had his fill. He was that kind of older brother, and as Lewis grew up to be a man, he often donated anonymously to charities and helped those in need. I know for a fact that he's given away much of his salary to causes around the world, and while he'd like to keep it quiet, as his proud father, I'm afraid that I can't withhold my praise for fear that my chest would burst."

Both Lewis and Richard sat as if they wanted to steal away, but in the crowd there were only faces of admiration for both Lewis and his father. He continued, "As a father, you want two things for your son. You want him to grow up to be a better man than you, and you want him to have more than you. He's certainly grown up to be a better man than me, and he'd accomplished and attained more than I could have ever dreamed of except for one missing piece. His mother and I always assumed that he would find a wife earlier in life, but it now seems the wait was worth it. We've known Claire for just over six months now, and in that time she's proven to be everything we'd hoped for Lewis. Kind and considerate, she matches Lewis's humility, and we know that the two of them will work together to create a union that will be a blessing to each other and to those around them."

He turned to the two of them and holding his glass of champagne, he said, "So let us raise our glasses for Lewis and Claire. May they shine like lights in this world, and teach us all how to lead lives of grace and humility."

It was Claire's turn to be embarrassed. As the hands with glasses went up and the faces turned to her, she looked at Lewis and ached for him. For all his faults, for all his obsession with his family project and his need to control everything two steps ahead, he was still a good man; his father's generous speech only cast a brighter sheen on what was already a glowing portrait. She saw his adoring face turn to her, and she knew that he deserved a woman who loved him.

Lewis's father exited the stage, and it was Claire's side turn to roast and toast her. Her mother spoke of her joy in finally seeing Claire getting married, and to such a handsome catch at that. Lucy and Sarah gave quick speeches that were sweet and funny, and Lucy squeezed out her line about renting Lewis for parties and drew a large laughter from the crowd.

Maddie was to last person to give a toast. She took the stage and said, "I realize as the maid of honor that I'll be giving a speech tomorrow, but I also wanted to say some words today in this more intimate setting. I've known Claire pretty much my whole life. We first met when we were three years old when our mums organized a play date so that they could drink and get pissed together while we fought each other for the same toys. Since that fateful day, Claire has been my partner in crime, my confidante, and my best friend for over twenty-six years. She's been there for me through both the happy and dark days, through break-ups and travels and moves, and I'd like to think that I've done the same for her.

"And through the years I've witnessed with heartache and pain the troubles that my Claire, my beautiful and lovely Claire, experienced in finding her soul mate. How was it that such a lovely person inside and out struggled to find the right person? Just as a primer, there was Ned, the twitchy imbecile who insisted that Claire brush her teeth before they kissed each time. There was Rob, our favorite narcissist who used to stare at himself in the mirror for hours. Let's not even go into Will, and I believe there was even a Harold who pretended to be an underwear model before revealing his true physical identity, at which point Claire deduced that it was more likely that he would someday model women's knickers."

As the room roared with laughter, Maddie continued, but now fixated her gaze towards Claire. "So when it came to be that we went wedding dress shopping one day, and she told me that she had finally met her match, I was hopeful for Claire. She was adamant that this was different from all her previous matches, and from the look in her eyes, I knew that it was indeed different this time around."

Claire had been laughing along at the speech, but Maddie's last lines caught her off guard. They both knew very well that on that day Claire had expressed her longing for Becks. She looked again at Maddie, and as Maddie looked back at her with a trace of a wink, Claire realized that she knew exactly what she was saying and was not mixing up the conversation of that day.

"I don't know what the future holds, but I only wish for her ultimate happiness, and I will stand by her side, always, as she continues to navigate through all the trials and tribulations of her journey ahead. A toast, ladies and gentlemen, to my dear friend Claire."

Claire continued to stare at Maddie as the others raised their glasses and clapped. As soon as the dinner came to a close, Claire grabbed her and hurried her over into an empty conference room of the hotel and said, "What was the meaning of that speech?"

"I'm sorry, Claire. It's just that I've been observing you during the rehearsal and dinner, and you look so miserable. No one else seems to notice, but I see it. We can't have you marry him if you feel that it's the wrong thing to do," Maddie said.

Claire said, "I don't want to marry him, but I've lost Becks."

"Then go after her."

Claire shook her head no. "I can't. It's in the past now. She made it clear that it was over between us."

Maddie said, "Then at the very least, Claire, break it off with Lewis. Spare him and spare yourself."

"It will crush him. Remember how he broke off a previous engagement at the last moment? It will seem like some cruel joke if I did the same."

"Better now than later. You still have time. If you don't do this now, you'll regret it for the rest of your life. I'm so sorry, Claire. I didn't realize how much she meant to you, and now we're at this point."

Claire replied, "No, it wasn't your fault. It was always my choice, and now I have to do the right thing."

"So you'll break it off?"

Claire peered down to the corridor where Lewis's room was. She felt her hands shaking again and tried to ward off the anxiety that had plagued her sporadically in the past year. "Yes," Claire said and squeezed Maddie's hand. "I'll end it tonight. Wish me luck."

Chapter 39

Claire made her way down the corridor and knocked on Lewis's room. He opened the door, and she saw that there were several of his groomsmen, including their Amsterdam driver, Erik, in the room. Surprised by her visit, he smiled and said, "Claire, I didn't expect to see you now. We're just about to head off on our stag party. The boys have assured me that it won't be anything you'd disapprove of."

Claire returned the smile and said, "I hate to delay the night of depravity ahead, but do you mind if I speak to you in private for a few minutes?"

"Of course. Let's step into my brother's room."

He led her to the neighboring room and closed the door. "So what did you want to talk about?" he asked.

She looked at his expectant face, and she recalled the memories they'd shared since October. Amsterdam in particular stood out, and she remembered the way that she and Lewis had rode their bicycles through the streets of Jordaan, laughing and so full of joy at the promise of their new engagement. That postcard scene shone in her mind like a frayed relic from a bygone era. She took a deep breath and said, "Lewis, this is the worst thing I've done in my life, but I have to tell you that I can't marry you. I love another person."

She cringed as she waited for the response, but he continued to stand opposite of her without flinching, seemingly unperturbed. He then asked her, "Does he love you back?"

Claire was taken aback by the question but answered him, "No, the person doesn't love me back."

"Then I beg you to reconsider. I'm very much in love with you, and I think if you would allow yourself, in due time you could fall in love with me."

Claire looked out the window of the hotel room. It was still light out but the moon was rising. Traces of her dream of Becks in her silver robe flashed through her mind. She said, "Lewis, we're not many years apart, but we're at very different stages of our lives, you and I. At some point you figured out how to proceed about your life and formed a clear vision of what you wanted. You are like a sun king, and people like Erik orbit around you. Even a year ago I might have been happy to be one of your orbiting planets, but things have changed and I need an equal partner. All my life I've just meandered along, accepting the suggestions and paths laid before me. I studied finance because my father suggested it, I've dated men because they asked me out. But somewhere this last year I realized that there are certain things that I want in life of my own choosing, and I need someone who'll stumble along with me as I explore them. You're a man of many talents, but stumbling isn't one of them."

Lewis replied, "I may not hesitate when I make my decisions, but you're mistaken if you think I have some grand scheme of what I would like our life to be. If you wanted me to quit Wyman and stay home to watch our children someday so that you can continue your career, I would do it in an instant and not look back. Don't you see that I worship you?"

"But that's just it, Lewis. I'm not looking to be worshipped or rescued or protected or trained. I'm looking to live in equal footing with my partner through what this life has to offer."

He ran his hand through his hair in resigned exasperation. "Will you chase after him then?"

"No, I'm going to start over."

Lewis gave a sigh and said, "It's not lost on me that the ironic symmetry of what I put Cecilia through has now come to me in full circle."

Claire said, "And it was never my intent to lay this upon you. I wish I would have had the conviction and foresight to tell you months ago."

He held her hand and said, "Is there nothing that I can do to change your mind?"

Claire replied, "No, I'm afraid not." She paused, and then added, "And this person that I love is a woman."

"A woman?" He looked up at her in surprise.

"Yes, I was matched up with her through One Match before I met you."

"Through One Match? A woman? Why didn't you tell me before that you were gay?"

She shook her head and said, "I didn't think I was, and I don't even know now as to how I'd classify myself. I thought my feelings for her were gone when I met you, but apparently they were not. I'm so sorry, Lewis. If I could go back I would have done so many things differently, and above all, I would have never hurt you. I'm telling you now so that I can spare you of some greater pain later."

Lewis observed her as if recovering somewhat from his initial shock and trying to make sense of the confusing puzzle that lay in front of him. He said, "Where was it that we went wrong? Why didn't I see the signals so that I could have fixed it?"

She shook her head and replied, "There was nothing that you could have fixed. I was—am—just in love in with this woman."

Lewis said nothing and looked out the window for a while. He finally said, "This family model that I'm building for Wyman...I'm building families at work but unable to establish one for myself. To have that loving family like the one I grew up with—it's all I ever wanted, but more and more it seems like an illusion that's floating further out from shore. It feels foolish of me to think that I could build a revolution when I can't even start a family of my own."

She felt pity as she thought about his family mission and the compromise he was about to make with One Work. He was so consumed by his dream, but to her a family formed by One Work seemed so far removed from the group of people they had seen in *The Potato Eaters*. The thought occurred to her that in his quest to preserve the vision of the work family concept that he would lose the families themselves. But all she said was, "I believe that you will have a family someday. I just wasn't the woman."

Lewis said to her, "I was so sure that you were the one. I would have given up everything for you."

Sensing his resignation she said, "Within every inch of me, I believe you. You will make some lucky woman so happy, and she will do the same for you—I swear it."

He was deep in thought in some faraway place. She said, "As for this wedding, I know that quite a bit of money went into it. I'll pay you back for all of it. It may take years, but I promise that I'll pay you back every pence."

He gave her a rueful smile and said, "I appreciate the gesture, but I can't accept your offer. There's no need for both of us to suffer."

Even in his pain Lewis was good to her, and Claire felt the ache all over again. She asked, "Is there any final thing I can do for you?"

He mulled it over and said, "There is one small favor that you could do for me."

"Yes, anything."

"If you could walk with me back to my groomsmen with a cheerful expression and see me off to my stag party, and then leave back for London quietly tonight. I will explain to our guests as to what's happened tomorrow morning. I'm not sure if I'm ready to face the reality tonight."

Claire nodded. They walked back to his room arm-in-arm, and she gave him a long kiss in front of his stag party mates as they hooted and hollered. His brother Richard yelled out, "Crown the king! Crown the king!"

They put on him a crown made of toilet paper and changed him into the same ridiculous toga that they were all wearing. They then hoisted him on their shoulders as they headed out to the hallway. Richard, obviously quite drunk from pre-celebrations, said to the group, "The wenches in this pissing hole of a village won't know what hit them tonight!"

Playing her part, Claire yelled out after them, "Behave yourselves!"

Lewis looked back at her one final time at her as he was carried out, and she waved good-bye as he headed out the hotel.

Chapter 40

After Claire saw him off, she walked back to her own suite and packed her belongings. She peeked around the hallway to make sure that no one was looking, and slipped out of the hotel and hailed a taxi from a few blocks away. She took it to the train station and looked over the time table to see that she could still catch the nine o'clock train back to King's Cross station.

She sat down on one of the benches of the train station. Dusk was settling in, and deep into the purple sky she could see the moon up ahead. As she sat, she realized that it was about a year ago that she had sat at the train station in the Cotswolds with Becks. So much had happened since then, and yet, here she was again in her elliptic journey, alone and waiting for a train back to London.

She gauged her emotions and was surprised to find that beyond her feelings of guilt and shame for what she'd done, she felt refreshed and at peace. She knew for certain now that she'd made the right choice, and she was relieved that she'd not gone through the wedding for both their sakes.

The train arrived on time, and it was largely empty. Claire sat down next to a window and spread out her suitcase next to her, and an older man sat across from her. As the train pulled out of the station, the roving scenery unraveled before her eyes. Claire sat and watched as the sun faded behind the hills. The man said to her, "It's beautiful, isn't it?"

"Yes," she nodded. "It's all very beautiful."

She continued to watch until the sun was completely gone. She felt a cathartic release, as if she were a bird let out of her cage. The views brought memories of the Cotswolds and eventually Becks, and with this feeling in tow she pulled out her tablet and typed a letter:

Dear Becks,

I'm writing this email to you on a train going back to London from Yorkshire on the eve of my wedding day. I've broken off my wedding to Lewis. I can tell you all the details, but I'll just say that I realized that we weren't meant for each other. In the past I could have married him and been happy, but that seems like a lifetime ago.

The train is passing by meadows and fields that are fading into the dark as night approaches. Rivulets flow into the streams, and they in turn feed the mighty tributaries that pour into the river within me. I am filled with a lark's song as the beauty of what I see out the window reminds me of your home in the hills.

I dreamed of you. It was night and you were in a silver robe. You lay next to me and enveloped me. I woke up, shuddering from the warmth of your embrace. You've lingered in my mind ever since, and the memory of your face is the bloom of my every morning.

I once heard a vicar say that when a great and momentous event occurs in your life, that something has to change. You've had that impact in my life, and I have changed. Everything has changed. I am going back to London, and I will start over. I am afraid, but I am ready. Thank you for everything.

Yours,

Claire

Tears streaming down her face, Claire stared at the letter on her screen. Part of her wanted to send it out, but she wasn't quite sure what the purpose would be. Becks had moved on, and she needed to move on as well. She finally pressed the discard button. Claire then wrote out the following email from her work Outlook account instead:

Hello Harriet,

You told me a couple of weeks ago that you didn't know of a better way than the path that you and Lewis have chosen. I didn't know either at the time, but I now have an answer. I want to let you know that I'm resigning from Wyman and striking out on my own. It was an honor to work with you, but I've decided to move on to a new chapter in my life. I'm not sure what I'll do next, but I'll figure it out. I give you my word, however, that I will take care of Jeffrey and Sam.

Cheers,

Claire

She pressed the send button, shut her laptop, and settled into her seat. The moon shone out of the window, and as Claire closed her eyes to sleep, the first stanza of She Walks in Beauty blew gently into her oncoming sleep:

She walks in beauty, like the night

Of cloudless climes and starry skies;
And all that's best of dark and bright
Meet in her aspect and her eyes;
Thus mellowed to that tender light
Which heaven to gaudy day denies

One Year Later

Chapter 41

"I must say, Claire, that I think we can reduce our sessions to once a month. You've responded well to the medication, and you seem to be in good physical shape. What do you think?"

"I think I agree, Dr. Harris. You've been very helpful. I haven't felt the anxiety attacks the last two months, and I feel that I can walk down any street in London without worry."

"But I want you to be careful. You've been through a lot, and I wouldn't want to see a relapse."

Claire got up from the chair and shook Dr. Harris's hand. She said, "I can't believe it's been nine months since I came to you."

"Best of luck to you, Claire, and I'll see you in a month," he said.

Claire stepped outside the office and into the warm July day. She rode the Tube to Acton, and climbed up the stairs in a dodgy building between the Poundland and the chicken shop on Acton's High Street. She opened the door that had the words, "Moore Analytics" printed on it, and stepped into the small office space. The office had two desks, a drawer with a stack of folders and papers, and not much more beyond that. Sam was at his desk, typing away on his laptop with deep concentration.

He looked up when Claire entered and asked, "How did the session go?"

Claire smiled broadly and said, "It went well. We're reducing it to once a month."

"Brilliant." He reached into his mini fridge and pulled out two bottles of beer.

"Drinking on the job, are we?"

"Yes," Sam said, "but that was one of the promised perks of the job when I joined."

Claire accepted her bottle and said, "I suppose I made some regrettable promises to bring you over. Have you convinced Jeffrey to come over to us yet?"

Sam shook his head. "Chatted with him yesterday, and he's still enjoying Wyman for now. He likes our replacements in their new family, but he says it's not the same."

"He better not like them more than us. And tell him to stop wanking around and come over to us."

Sam said, "He might. Harriet's announced that she's going to retire after the launch of One Home this year, so Jeffrey will decide what he's going to do after that." Sam then added, "He said that Harriet says hello to you."

"Hmm." Claire hadn't spoken to Harriet since the breakup of her wedding. She was glad to know that Harriet didn't begrudge her for leaving Lewis and her so abruptly, but she didn't imagine that she'd be reaching out to Harriet anytime soon.

"Did I miss anything while I was out?" she asked.

"There were a couple of items. First, our software team in Romania had some questions on the requirements doc you sent them. Second, Mr. Kahn called again wondering if you can explain to him how to group his sales data into custom categories."

"For Christ's sake, I've explained it to him three times already. Would it be against the law to sack him as a client?"

"I don't know if it's legal or not," Sam said, "but he is one of just ten clients we have at the moment."

"Fine, I'll give him a call. What else?"

"I've received a notice that we've maxed out our third credit card. So including the loan from the bank, we currently have a burn rate of ten months to turn a profit."

"Bloody hell. Next."

"Your father called and said that if you came down to Watford, there's a chance that your mum might start talking to you again. He thinks it's worth a shot."

"Ha, fat chance."

Sam asked, "She's still not talking to you over the wedding?'

Claire said, "My mum can hold grudges. She was particularly smitten with Lewis. I've tried over and over to talk to her, but I'm at my wit's end. Anything else?"

"Maddie called to make sure that I remind you that your date will meet you at the Bibimbap Bistro at Fulham at seven this evening."

"Thanks. She's already texted me."

Sam stopped and said, "It's good that you're dating again."

Claire shrugged and said, "Probably nothing will come of it. Maddie's been bugging me for months now to start dating and meet her friend, so I finally agreed to get her off my back."

Sam continued, "You also received this postcard in the mail."

Claire took the postcard and looked it over. The front of the card showed a picture of a wooden boat moored to the white sand of a picturesque beach with the words "Thailand" going across the top. Claire turned the card over. It was blank except for the address to her old flat at Swiss Cottage; it'd arrived at the office because she'd requested to the post office to forward her mail to the office until she'd finished moving into her new flat in Acton.

"She's actually done it then," Claire muttered as she surveyed the front once more. In her sessions with Dr. Harris she'd brought up Becks, but over the months her relationship with Becks had felt like a distant memory. To receive a tangible postcard from her felt like an aberration in time.

"Hope you're well, Becks," she whispered.

Sam asked, "Who's it from?"

Claire looked up at Sam and said, "An old friend."

Chapter 42

Claire left the office at six and hurried over to Fulham on the District Line. She'd never been to Bibimbap Bistro, so she had a bit of a hard time finding it once she'd arrived in Fulham. It was ten minutes past seven when she finally found the tiny restaurant and entered.

The restaurant was noisy and crowded. A mostly Asian crowd of people were huddled around stone bowls of rice and vegetables. Claire's stomach growled at the sight of the bowls, and she scanned the place with greater urgency. Finally, she spotted the table with the red tulip.

She walked over and sat down at the table with her red tulip. The person at the table looked at her and shook her hand. "Hello, I'm Uday Patel."

"Claire Moore."

Uday was a clean shaven South Asian of medium build. He had handsome brown eyes and thick wavy black hair, and he wore a brown jacket over his pink dress shirt.

He replied, "Maddie's been raving about you for weeks, and it's finally nice to meet you in person. She was certainly correct about your beauty."

His compliment struck a wrong chord with her. She knew that the comment about her physical appearance was harmless enough, but it brought back rushing memories of the dating rituals she had experienced time after time. She suddenly felt tired. It was a mistake to try dating again right now. She wasn't ready. She said, "Thank you. It's been a while since I've dated, so you'll have to excuse me if I seem a little off."

He smiled and said, "That's perfectly fine. Maddie mentioned that your last break-up was difficult. She says that it's been a year."

Uday seemed like a nice enough man, but she continued to feel the fatigue and decided to end the date. "Yes, I was quite in love with her. To be honest, I'm not sure if I'm over her."

As she'd hoped, he gave a look of confusion and said, "It was a woman? For some reason Maddie made it seem as if your break-up was with a man."

"I broke off my engagement because I loved a woman."

"And she didn't love you back?"

"She decided that she couldn't be with me at the end," she replied. "But we ended in good terms. I just received a postcard from her from Thailand today." She felt detached as she told him the truth in matter-of-fact terms. She realized that even now there had been very few people to whom she'd told her affections for Becks. Maddie, Dr. Harris, and now this perfect stranger. She told him the truth because part of her wanted to scare him away, but another part of her just wanted to say the truth out loud to share her story.

Uday took a sip of his water and was silent for a while. He then cleared his throat and said, "Does this mean that you're bisexual?"

Claire said, "I don't know. Technically, yes. Does it bother you?"

"If I'm being honest, I think so. The thought never occurred to me that I might date a bisexual woman."

His honesty was a tiny bit endearing. Claire said, "That's all right, I understand. But I don't think of myself in terms of being 'bisexual' or 'heterosexual'. I used One Match when I was paired up with her. It scanned my brain once, and after analyzing the networks of firing neurons, decided that I was a match with a person whose patterns seemed compatible with mine. It just happened that it was a woman. If we see ourselves as compatible collections of cells, our sex seems a bit irrelevant, doesn't it?"

Uday took another drink from his water glass and looked deep in thought. "Perhaps," he said, "but I like to think we're more than just a collection of cells. Something more spiritual."

"You mean that maybe we have souls?"

"Yes."

"What do souls care of the sex of someone? Don't you think that it has more to do with biology—humanity's need to procreate? But given the current population state of the world, and the inevitability that babies will be born in incubators in the near future, maybe this physiological concern is over, and it's just a matter of unwinding thousands of years of social dogma that was built around this need."

Uday surmised, "Babies in incubators? God, you're a bleak woman. Maddie never mentioned that part." He gave her a smile as he said this, and she smiled despite herself.

"Do you disagree?"

"I understand where you're coming from, but like you said, I have years of social teachings ingrained into me. I can grasp your points conceptually, but at a practical level, it's difficult for me to overcome it."

"I appreciate your honesty," Claire said. "It took a long time for me to embrace it, so I don't begrudge you. Feel free to leave whenever you'd like; I'll still be ordering my bibimbap because I'm famished." Even as she said this, she realized that her stance on this date of hers had softened. He seemed contemplative of what she had to say while admitting his discomfort at the same time.

He didn't leave the table. Instead, he asked her, "Did you remain friends with this woman after the end of your relationship?"

"No, the parting was benign, but we didn't stay in touch."

"Then why did she send you a postcard? Seems a bit odd, doesn't it?"

Claire reflected on the postcard. She said, "What is it that you're getting at?"

"I don't know what your relationship was like, and I don't pretend to be a psychologist, but perhaps she's reaching out to you. I wouldn't send a postcard to a past girlfriend unless something remained."

"I doubt it. She made it quite clear in our last meeting and in a subsequent letter that nothing would come of us."

"People change their minds. You can always find out."

"But she's all the way in Thailand, and god knows where in that country."

"I went to Thailand last year. Easy plane ride. Finished a whole season of *Breaking Bad* on the trip, and then we landed."

She felt a flicker of excitement at the thought of traveling to Thailand to see Becks. She said to him, "Why are you urging me? We're complete strangers. What does it matter to you if she's changed her mind?"

Uday leaned back in his chair and said, "I do believe in the concept of the soul. I also believe in soul mates. You should run after her. And if you don't mind, I think I will stay for the bibimbap. You're not the only one who's hungry."

Chapter 43

Claire did not get on a plane ride to Thailand. She'd briefly thought of buying the plane ticket after her dinner with Uday, but the moment passed, and with it, the impulse to pull the trigger.

Instead, a few days later when she was sitting bored in her flat, she found herself texting Uday, "When can we meet again?" He responded to her a few minutes later, "How about tonight?"

They met an hour later at the Brewdog pub at Shepherd's Bush. As they drank their ciders together, he didn't ask about Becks or why she'd asked him out again. She sensed that he knew that she simply wanted company, and she appreciated him not mentioning the matters of their first meeting. They talked about their favorite spots in London, British politics, their work, and a hodge podge of other topics. When the bartender asked for last calls, Claire was surprised by how quickly the time had flown by. When they stepped out of the pub, Uday walked her to the nearest Tube stop, and simply bid her goodnight.

Claire waited for several days to receive a text or call from Uday, but when there was nothing from him, she swallowed her pride and sent another text asking him out for dinner. They met this time at the Indian restaurant Guglee in her old neighborhood of Swiss Cottage. Claire again had a wonderful time as they talked about more personal matters of their family and their childhood upbringings. Uday had grown up in the small city of Anand in the Gujarat state of India until his family immigrated to Brighton when he was nine. His parents owned a small curry shop by the beach pier, and much of Uday's summers were spent attending the cash register while the other kids frolicked on the beach. He didn't mind, however, as he spent the days reading books he'd checked out from the library. He enjoyed all genres, but in particularly he devoured history books. He eventually studied law at Oxford and became a barrister at the same law firm that Maddie worked at. It was a classic immigrant success story, and while Uday didn't boast of his efforts in getting to his current position, Claire admired the resolve of both him and his parents that got him to such standing.

After dinner Uday walked her to the Tube stop again and was about to split off when Claire said, "Wait. When are you going to ask me out again?"

"I'm not quite sure what we're doing. I thought you were in love with another woman," he said.

It was a fair point. She winced at their initial conversation at the Bibimbap Bistro when she'd made attempts to scare him away. Claire wondered if she really was ready to start dating again, but she reminded herself that it had now been a year. "Suppose I told you that I'm ready to move on. With you."

Claire waited for a reply as Uday seemed to study her with careful consideration. "Perhaps we can have dinner tomorrow at seven," he finally said.

"Yes, I'd like that." He didn't make a move to kiss or even hug her, and instead, he gave her a quick nod and walked away. She was slightly disappointed but also intrigued by his pointed distance from her.

The next day when Claire walked into her office, Sam said to her, "Mr. Kahn's on the call for you."

"Oh, good lord." She put the call on speaker, and said, "Hello, Mr. Kahn. What can I do for you?"

"Claire," he said, "I finally figured out how to download the data to a .csv file, but I still don't understand how to use this Excel program that you told me about. Can you help me with it? You'll need to walk me through it step-by-step because you know I'm not good with these computers."

Claire looked over at Sam, and she could see that he was biting his lip to prevent from laughing. Trying to teach Mr. Kahn how to even use the basics of Excel was going to take hours. She felt a massive headache settling upon her already, but she gritted her teeth and said, "Yes, Mr. Kahn, I'd be happy to walk you through the steps."

Three hours later, Mr. Kahn finally let the two of them go after getting his data onto Excel and manipulated into simple pivot tables. Claire and Sam sat exhausted by their computers. Sam then cleared his throat as if he wanted to say something. Claire implored him to speak his mind, and he said, "I know it's terrible timing, but our Romanian team sent us the bill for last month. It was higher than I'd originally calculated because they had to work overtime to complete the UI work we asked of them. It means our burn rate is down to nine months."

Claire sighed. "And remind me again how many more clients we need before we start to turn a profit?"

"Ten. We need an additional ten to make a profit."

"No. We need fifteen more," she said. Sam started to check his math again when she said, "You're not including the salary you're foregoing right now. I promised you that by the time we reach our profit goal it'll include your salary."

Sam shook his head. "Claire, I can wait a little longer. I've got some savings that I built up. But if we don't find some more clients soon, we're in trouble."

Claire looked up at the Thailand postcard that she had tacked on a nearby bulletin board. Thinking of Becks, she said softly, "You never told me that it'd be this hard."

Sam looked over at her with a puzzled face, but she waved him off. She asked him, "What time is it?"

He looked at his watch and replied, "It's almost seven."

"Bloody hell." Remembering that she had a date with Uday that evening, she hurried out the door.

Claire and Uday's relationship grew in a steady rise. At first they saw each other just one to two times per week, and it was only finally in the third week that he kissed her. He kissed her by the boathouse in Gunnersbury Park as dusk was beginning to usher in the closing of the park, and they walked out of the park holding hands. It felt so good to feel someone's lips and hands again, to feel as if the physical touch was thawing her out from the emotional coma that she'd buried herself in since the break-up. She waited for the next step in their relationship, and it finally happened in the second month of their dating. They made dinner at his flat, and as they watched a movie on the sofa she reached over and began kissing him. They were soon undressed, and he made love to her on the floor of the living room. He was gentle and touched her in ways that assured her that he was not a novice. The moment was what she'd been anticipating for weeks, and yet, she felt oddly detached as it was happening. She wasn't sure what it was, but her initial arousal from when they began kissing waned as he entered her. She didn't want to hurt his feelings, so she moaned and breathed heavily. Even so, she feared that he would sense the shift in her desire, and she desperately tried to get aroused. Despite herself, she thought of Becks at the massage parlor in Kilburn. She remembered her cream skin and the shape of her slender hips, and the tingling sensations immediately returned. She thought of her to the very end, and as Uday rolled off of her in a satisfied heap, she lay there in guilt of what she'd done to please the both of them.

She tried to keep her thoughts on Uday in subsequent sessions and failed. Each time she went into the sex thinking that this time she wouldn't have to resort to her head trick, but inevitably her mind would wander to

Becks as she gave her body to Uday. She debated whether to tell her therapist about it, but she was too ashamed to tell Dr. Harris.

Eventually, Claire found herself thinking about Becks not just during sex but at other times throughout the day. She recalled memories of their friendship—snippets of chats, the time in the Cotswolds, their weekend in London. Often, the daydreams ended with her final image of Becks at the coffee shop as they said good-bye to each other in the rain. Claire would often cry in her flat as she recalled these memories, and in the office she would stare at the postcard from Thailand.

This lasted for a few months until one day, while she and Uday were out for dinner and had finished paying for their meal, he quietly said to her, "I don't think we should see each other anymore."

She looked at him in surprise. "What do you mean?" she asked.

"Can you tell me that you don't have feelings for someone else?"

The shock of his words jolted her. Her immediate thought was that he'd been reading her mind all this time. She thought of denying it, but instead she replied, "How do you know?"

He gave her a pained expression at the response but nodded as if relieved by her admission. "I don't know, but I've felt it for a while. You've been distant since our first couple of weeks. Is it that woman?"

Claire said yes, and with the truth confirmed, tears began to flow from her. He was a good man, without the irrevocable flaws of Lewis or her other previous boyfriends, and she knew that he didn't deserve this.

"I don't know what's wrong with me," she said. "I feel like shit. I don't know what's wrong with me. I don't deserve you."

Uday said nothing but gave her his handkerchief. As she dabbed her eyes with it, he finally said to her, "Nothing is wrong with you. You love someone but you're denying yourself, and in doing so, you've hurt me."

The bluntness of his statement stung her, and the tears came out again. A part of her wished that he could have been gentler, but she understood that he was in pain. She reminded herself that she'd been the one who spurred on their relationship after declaring that she was ready to move on. "I'm so sorry," she said. "I'm so sorry."

His expression softened, and he said to her, "This will hurt me for a while, but you've been hurting for so much longer." He was silent for a while and then said, "When I first met you, I didn't quite comprehend what you were saying about a person's sex being irrelevant in a relationship. But now I understand. This One Match program paired you with someone who was right for you, but you won't fully embrace it."

"Why do you keep insinuating that this is my choice? I wanted to be with her, but she told me that she didn't want to be with me."

He responded, "And why did she send you the postcard? And why didn't you fly out to Thailand the moment you received it?"

Her voice rising, she said, "Because you just don't do that. People just don't do that kind of thing."

He paused before saying, "You once told me that we're entrenched in years of social dogma. All of us are, it seems," He got up to leave and said, "Good-bye, Claire. I hope you can set yourself free."

Chapter 44

Claire went home and thought about what Uday had said. He was right in many ways. She had hurt him just like she'd hurt Lewis because she'd thought that she'd moved on from Becks when she had not. She hated what she'd done to him. She knew that an objective observer might consider her to be a careless person, and she didn't want to be careless. She'd cared deeply for Uday, and it pained her that she'd ended up wounding him.

She couldn't take back the emotional pain that she'd brought upon him, but she could follow his advice to seek out Becks once more. She stared at the British Airways homepage on her laptop. She desperately wanted to book the flight, but the practical logistics involved paralyzed her to inaction. To begin with, she had no idea if Becks would still be at Koh Tao as she'd planned over two years ago during their dinner in Hampstead. If she was even there, Claire would have to still find her on the island. If she then found her by some miraculous chance, she'd have to hope that Becks wasn't seeing anyone else and was still interested in Claire. And, while this was all going on in Thailand, she still had her fledgling business in London that would surely fall over in her absence.

The obstacles were too much to overcome. Besides, no one, not even hapless romantics, just flew across the globe to express their love to someone they hadn't seen in ages. If she'd watched a movie with such a plot, she would have snickered at the preposterous storyline. Convinced that she was making the right decision, she shut her laptop off and called it a night.

When the weekend passed and Monday came around, Claire was in a miserable state as she trudged up the stairs to her office. Her emotions were still raw from her breakup with Uday, and the thought of dealing with more calls from Mr. Kahn almost made her turn around and walk home.

She somehow mustered the energy to walk through the office doors where Sam was typing away at his laptop.

"Do you ever go home, or do you just sleep underneath your desk?" she teased him.

Sam was in his usual chipper mood. He said, "Came in early to talk with our Romanian devs about the latest specs we sent over to them. They agreed to complete it by end of the month. Also, a Mr. Rashad called for you. Here's his number."

Claire furrowed her eyebrows, as she didn't know a Mr. Rashad. She sat down her purse and gave the number a call. After a few rings, a man answered.

"Hello."

"Yes, may I speak with a Mr. Rashad?"

"This is he. Who am I speaking to?" His accent was thick, and Claire wondered what was in store for her.

She replied, "It's Claire Moore from Moore Analytics on the line. My colleague told me that you'd called earlier this morning."

The man's voice tone immediately changed as he said, "Ah, Claire Moore. I'm so glad that you called. I'm a friend of Mushin Kahn."

At the mention of Mr. Kahn, Claire's heart sank. She wondered what problems Mr. Kahn was about to create for her now.

"Mushin held a large party for his daughter's birthday yesterday. Lovely daughter, wonderful party with lots of people. Anyway, throughout the party he kept raving on and on to all of us about all the work you've done for his little convenience store. So much so that I thought that I might give you a call and arrange for a time to come over and see what you might do for my business."

Claire couldn't believe what she was hearing on the line. She blurted out, "Is this some kind of a joke?"

She heard a chuckle on the other line as Mr. Rashad said, "No, I'm perfectly serious. I'd love to see what the fuss is all about. Is there time this week that I could stop by?"

She told him that Tuesday afternoon would be a fine time, and as soon as she hung up the phone, she told Sam what had just happened.

"Can you believe it? Mr. Kahn referring us?"

"I'd love to have been there," Sam said. "If our calls are any indication he probably talked their ears off."

Sam brought out a bottle of vodka from his file cabinet for a quick toast, and they resumed their work. A couple of hours later, there was another ring on the phone.

Claire picked up the phone and answered it. "Moore Analytics. Claire Moore speaking."

"Hi Claire, my name is Mustafa Ahmed, and I'm calling because my friend Mushin Kahn told me that you might be able to help me..."

Claire was in a daze as she set up yet another appointment with one of Mr. Kahn's friend to talk about the services that her company could offer for his small business. When she got off the phone, she and Sam jumped up and down as they screamed like giddy school children who'd been told that school had been cancelled. They took another round of shots and swung each other around.

"Two potential clients in one day!" she said. "I could kiss Mr. Kahn!"

"He's still the most bothersome man on the face of the earth, but it's almost worth it, isn't it?"

The lunch hour came and went, and they assumed that was it for the day, when they got another call late in the afternoon. Claire and Sam looked at each other before Claire picked up the phone. Unbelievably, it was yet another one of Mr. Kahn's friends who wanted to meet her. This time it was a Mr. Omar who owned a chain of fish and chips shops not too far from their office.

When the day was over, Claire and Sam sat grinning as they emptied out the final bit of vodka in their paper cups. They knew it was just prospective clients, but the thought of potentially increasing their client base by 30% in a matter of days was unfathomable. Claire spied Becks's Thailand postcard at the corner of her desk. She remembered how Becks had once talked about putting all her efforts into her pub without ever really knowing if it would succeed until it actually happened. Claire felt as if she finally understood what Becks meant, and she began to cry.

Sam handed her a tissue box and asked, "What's the matter, Claire?"

Claire shook her head as she accepted a tissue and said, "Nothing's the matter. I'm just so happy. It's finally happening for us." As she tried to dry her eyes, she looked over at Sam. Sweet Sam who had left Wyman to follow her in this mad business venture of theirs. She said to him, "Can I tell you something? About this postcard of mine?"

Sam nodded, and Claire went on to tell him her story of Becks. She told him everything—including the time in the Cotswolds, their weekend in London, the kiss on the rooftop, the last exchange of letters. She even pulled out Becks's final letter from her secret box hidden in her desk drawer and showed it to him. She'd never shown it to anyone before, not even Maddie or Dr. Harris, and she didn't know why she was breaking her vow never to show it to anyone, but for some reason she trusted Sam.

When she was finished, Sam sat in silence as he continued to read the letter. He finally looked up at her and said, "Uday is right. You have to go to Thailand and find Becks."

Claire badly wanted to accept Sam's verdict, but she protested, "Have you not read her letter?"

"It's the letter that has me convinced that you've got to chase after her. Yes, she says that she can't be with you, but she also says that her feelings for you haven't changed. You can persuade her that it doesn't matter that you found each other through One Match."

"Suppose I am able to find her and somehow convince her to give me a chance. What if I end up in Thailand? What's going to happen to the business?"

Sam shrugged and said, "I can manage it for a bit of time while you're searching for her. And if you do end up staying there, we'll figure it out. In the worst case scenario I can always find another job in London."

She hesitated; he made it seem as if it wasn't a big deal, but it was an enormously generous gesture by Sam. They were already very busy dealing with their ten clients, and if they were to bring Mr. Kahn's friends in, Sam's workload would be off the charts without her.

Before she could decline, however, Sam was looking up flights to Bangkok. "I suppose you'll want to stick around this week to honor the appointments with our prospective clients, but there's a non-stop flight out on Monday that looks fairly cheap," he said.

"Sam…"

He ignored her and proceeded with the booking process. Eventually, all that was left to do was to enter her credit card information. He reached out his hand and asked for it.

Out of excuses, Claire was resigned to ask the most fundamental question that had been bothering her: "What if she says no?"

Once she said it out loud, she realized that this fear of rejection weighed the heaviest on her. After all the turmoil and change since she'd tried One Match, a rejection from Becks would feel as if she had traveled a very painful journey only to end up in the beginning again.

"Claire," Sam said, "I left Wyman to join you because I saw the courage you had in leaving Lewis and Wyman. I mean, look at this place. We're in a drab office space that resembles a Taliban prison cell, we're squeaking by on our payments, and we're ecstatic at the thought of gaining three clients. But I wouldn't trade any of this for the world—I have no regrets. If you can leave what you left behind for this, you can certainly go search for the woman you love."

She felt the tears building up as she listened to him. She felt a tremendous sense of thankfulness towards him, and as she wiped her eyes, she asked him, "Why are you so good to me?" And somewhat joking, she added, "Are you in love with me?"

Sam scoffed. "You're too old for me. But I'd like to find someone with some of your traits someday. Now please give me your card."

"I'm not quite sure if that was an insult or a compliment. I'm only thirty years old," she said. Taking a deep breath, she fished out her credit card from her purse and handed it to Sam. He snatched it away from her and typed in the info furiously before she could change her mind.

"It's booked," he announced.

She felt the tumult of excitement and fear upon seeing the confirmation screen. She closed her eyes and took a long deep breath. When she opened them, an idea sprang to mind.

"It's been an eventful day. Let's go out and celebrate."

Forty minutes later they were in Soho, waiting in the long queue to go inside Misato.

"Why did we have to come all the way here? Couldn't we have just eaten at another restaurant closer in Acton?"

"Because it's been ages since I've been in this area, and because Misato isn't just another restaurant, and because you need to get out and explore more often. Someday, by some odd miracle you just might find a woman who fancies you, and you're going to have to know places to take her."

This shut up Sam for the duration of their wait, and after another half hour of waiting they were seated.

Once inside, Sam observed the homely interior of the cramped restaurant. "I don't see what's so special about this place," he said.

"Stop complaining and figure out what you want to order." Claire looked around and saw that it was bustling with people as usual. Unlike some of the other restaurants she frequented with her friends, Claire had discovered Misato on her own, as she'd stumbled around looking for a place to eat one late evening in Soho. She'd been intrigued by the long queue of Asian students lined up for what looked like a hole-in-the-wall establishment, and she'd been delighted to find a comfortable place with cheap, good food. It became a place that she'd occasionally visit by herself, never with friends or co-workers because its serendipitous find made it special to her, and she didn't want anyone to ruin it with snooty remarks. Sam was the first person she'd brought with her.

Their orders of pork katsu curry rice and salmon teriyaki arrived quickly, and they ate their food like wild dogs. Halfway into the meal Sam took a breather to say, "I take it all back. This place is superb. Such large portions too for only ten quid."

She laughed and said, "See, it's a nice place, isn't it?" She gave him a tousle of his hair, and he gave her a warning look. I really adore him like a little brother, she thought. It made her so happy to see him full and content in this special restaurant that she'd never shared with anyone else. She could feel herself getting misty-eyed, but she managed not to cry.

Sam must have sensed something, however, because he asked, "Are you afraid?"

"Of going to Thailand? A little."

"You will find her."

They paid for their meal, and instead of heading back towards the Tube stop they decided to walk down the winding corridors of Chinatown. They walked down Gerrard Street where they passed the Chinese restaurants and grocery stores and the medicine shops that were closing up. They tiptoed past the drunkards urinating against the brick walls and the women in short skirts prancing in their heels to the Soho pubs. They headed south and eventually made their way to Leicester Square. Even on a Monday evening there were groups of people milling about. The two of them sat down to watch a teenage boy strum his guitar for a small crowd. He was quite good, and Sam threw a few coins into his guitar case. Claire realized that it was the first time she'd been at the square since she'd brought Becks. It felt like ages ago.

"God, I hate this place," Sam said. "So many tourists."

"I used to think the same. But Harriet once told me that tourists are a reminder that our city still matters to the world. My view has changed a bit since then."

"Seems like something Harriet would say."

Claire said, "I kind of miss her."

"Jeffrey told me that her retirement party is next week. But he says that she's still every bit the task master to the bitter end."

"I wouldn't expect anything less of her. But I thought she was sticking around until the launch of One Home. It's still scheduled for this holiday season, isn't it? They have to be announcing it soon—we're already in early November."

"Yes, but he also told me that Lewis has just announced that their experiment with One Work has been a success, and they're going to extend it permanently for all future employees who join. They're going to have a big announcement in the papers along with the unveiling of One Home next week. He says Harriet felt that her work was done with the full integration of One Work."

"So, One Work has landed," Claire said. She wasn't surprised, but it made her ill at ease. She knew that both Lewis and Harriet were not thinking deeply about what the technology would mean beyond their family mission. She remembered how she'd given her impassioned speech to Ned, of how she believed that One's end aim was to provide happiness to people in all aspects of their lives. She believed that Jorgen was sincerely pursuing this endeavor, just as Lewis and Harriet were sincere in their efforts, and she hoped that they would all succeed. She could only hope so because they were leading everyone in a certain direction, and their failure seemed as if it would have catastrophic effects that not any of them could fully understand today.

"The world is changing so fast," Claire said.

"Hmm," Sam replied. He remained focused on listening to the music.

As they continued to listen to the music, Claire suddenly felt very sentimental and grabbed Sam's hand. She said to him, "Sam, whatever happens next, promise me that you'll remember today. Promise me that you'll remember that we had a massively successful day like today at work where we could dream of a big future, and that we waited together in a long queue for a table at a dingy restaurant, that we ate good food and drank in each other's company, that we walked the evening streets of this city, and that we are here now enjoying this music with all these other people who are enjoying it with us. Promise me that you'll remember all of this."

"Christ. Claire, it's going to be okay. Don't talk like that."

"Promise me, Sam."

"Yes, I promise."

Sam looked over at Claire with a pensive expression. Claire knew that she was worrying him a little bit, but she felt that he had to understand the importance of days like today because they were precious and not to be taken for granted. The gravity of what she was about to do next week was taking shape in her head, and she felt that Sam's supporting presence was the one thing that was preventing her panic attacks from occurring.

"Do you really think that I'll find her?"

"Yes, I really do."

"And she'll take me back?"

"I wouldn't be volunteering to do all the work while you're gone if I thought it'd be an utter failure, would I?"

Claire grinned and gave him a light punch. "What happened to the sweet and quiet Sam I knew at Wyman?" she asked. "He was so much more pleasant than this snarky Sam."

"That sweet and quiet Sam found his voice in this last year," he said. "And I owe it all to you. Thank you."

Chapter 45

A week later Claire was on a Thai Airways flight to Bangkok. She'd packed just a backpack with primarily three days change of clothes and her Lonely Planet guidebook of Thailand. Only Sam knew about the trip; she so desperately wanted to tell Maddie as well, but she decided to keep silent for fear that Maddie would convince her out of her madness.

Now that she was on the plane, however, she wished that Maddie had been there to stop the trip. She'd bought a one-way ticket because she didn't have the slightest clue as to when she would return home. Finding Becks was also going to be a challenge. She assumed that Becks would be somewhere in Koh Tao, but that was a big assumption, and even if Becks was living there, she'd still have to locate her exact address. But the biggest question of all was what would happen if she were to even find Becks. Claire had not made any plans on what she'd say or do, and her failure to plan started to bore into her in the form of a pounding headache.

The plane was packed, and there were families with small children and crying babies surrounding her in the economy cabin. It was a decided contrast to her trip to Amsterdam on the Gulfstream jet once upon a time, but she tried to ignore the commotion around her. She looked at her watch. It was nine in the evening, and it would be a twelve hour flight that would deliver her in Bangkok at three in the afternoon the next day. She put on her headphones and pulled out her Thailand guidebook from her backpack. She decided that she would learn something about Becks's adopted country before falling asleep for the red eye flight.

The airplane ride itself was a grueling ordeal. Claire had a hard time sleeping due to chatter of the travelers around her and the stress of the journey that awaited her. Several times the plane ran into strong turbulence, and she held onto her seat with clenched teeth as the plane hurled through wind and rain.

After a series of hazy hours filled with half-sleep, Claire finally heard the cabin crew announce the descent to Bangkok. She looked out the window. Beams of sunlight peeking through the clouds penetrated the thick layers of smog below. She saw the miles of Lego-sized buildings and snaking roads that lay beneath her. Even from up high, she could see that Bangkok was densely packed, likely more so than London, and the difficulty of her mission started to creep back into her mind.

Once the plane landed, she waited her turn to step into Suvarnabhumi Airport. There was a long queue to clear customs, but she made it through without trouble. The airport was spotless and modern, and she passed by familiar retail chains as she rode escalators and followed signs to the taxi area. When she stepped outside, the humidity immediately clung to her. Even in mid-November it was hot, and the heat woke her a bit from her haggard trance. There were multiple taxis queued outside, and she showed her destination address to an attendant who directed her into a taxi and gave instructions to the driver.

She'd read in her guidebook that the taxi ride to the city center would take about forty minutes, but due to rush hour traffic jams it took over an hour and a half. During this time she ran through the logistics of her travel plans to Koh Tao. She had the evening free, but she needed to catch the bus to Chumphon Pier at six in the morning. The bus ride would take six hours, and she would then catch a boat to Koh Tao. Once there, she would then have to rely on fate to take over and bring her to Becks. It was overwhelming to think of all these steps that lay ahead in the next twenty four hours, but Claire took a breath and reminded herself to take it one increment at a time.

The taxi dropped her off at her designated location of the Buddy Lodge at Khaosan Road. After paying 500 baht for the ride, she stepped out into the scorching sun. The street was chaotic and filled with people, and she ducked into the hotel. A hotel receptionist who spoke English fluently checked her in and gave her the key card.

When she checked into her room, she was relieved to see that the interior matched the pictures from the website. The room was not big, but it was clean and well-decorated with white paneled walls and dark hardwood floors and chairs that matched. The bed linens looked clean, and as a finishing touch, there were towels twisted into the shape of small elephants on the bed. Claire laid down her backpack and lay on her bed for a bit. The plane had arrived at Bangkok at three in the afternoon, but she'd only finally made it to her hotel at six. She realized that she was starving now and decided that she'd better eat an early dinner and try to get plenty of sleep.

Claire stepped out onto Khaosan Road and was greeted by a cacophonous scene. The sun had just set, but the street looked as if it was starting up for the day. There were crowds of both Westerners and locals pushing their way past street market stands that stood neck to neck with each other underneath canopies and umbrellas. Claire walked by stands of trinkets and clothes and jewelry as the street vendors motioned her to come over and take a look at everything from Thai silk boxing shorts to iPhone cases. She thought briefly about buying a gift for Becks, but the vast amount of selection overwhelmed her and she continued to push on through the street as scooters and auto rickshaws weaved their way through the pedestrians. She looked up to see dilapidated apartment buildings with drying clothes hanging from the balconies, and next to them there were signs on top of signs in both Thai and English advertising everything from Singha Beer to KFC. Between the stands and stores, there were tables on the sidewalks with blue plastic chairs where customers sat and fanned themselves as waiters brought out heaping plates of rice and curry dishes. It felt a bit like the chaos of Leicester Square, but here she was the tourist, and the vitality and sweat of the street enthralled and intimidated her. Part of her wished that she'd booked another night in Bangkok so that she could tour the floating markets, the Grand Palace and the red light districts that she'd read about in her book, but she reminded herself that her objective for the trip was to find Becks. She stopped by a food cart that offered her delicacies of fried scorpions and tarantulas, but not feeling adventurous enough, she settled for a bowl of green curry with chicken.

After finishing her meal, Claire walked north up Chakrabongse Road and cut east to find her way to the Lomprayah bus office for her trip the next morning. She found it, and having confirmed that it was walking distance from her hotel, she headed back to the lodge to retire for the night. In the room she turned on the TV just to have some background noise while she paced about and thought of what she'd say to Becks in their reunion. She pictured how it was done in the movies, where the hero shows up at the door and kisses the girl. Of course, she'd always imagined that she would be the girl getting kissed. But the very idea of doing something so drastic seemed comical to her, and she gave up and tried to get some sleep instead.

Chapter 46

She woke up feeling sick at one in the morning. She felt nauseous and her head started to feel dizzy. Feeling dehydrated as well, she drank some water, but the nausea continued. At first she thought she was suffering a heat stroke from the hot sun earlier in the day, but it became clear as the night wore on that it was something more serious. Claire lay in bed and moaned as her stomach rolled around inside her. She felt her throat heave, and she ran over to the toilet and threw herself down into the toilet bowl just in time as she vomited violently. She continued to dry heave as saliva and bits of her vomit clung to her hair. As she tried to recover, she felt trembling at the other end, and she sat down on the bowl and suffered through heavy diarrhea. I'm going to die in a hotel in Bangkok, she thought. No one knows where I am, and I'm going to die alone.

The clearing of her bowels gave her a slight reprieve. She tried to fall back to sleep, but it was impossible with her stomach pains. She sat up on the edge of the bed, and tried to think about what she'd say to Becks. She pictured Becks standing in front of her in her classic black shirt and blue jeans, and she began practicing the conversation they might have if Claire ever found her.

"What are you doing here?" asked the imaginary Becks. She wasn't angry, but she wasn't greeting her with open arms either.

"I came here to see you. I missed you."

"You shouldn't have. Didn't get you get my letter?"

Claire took a breath. The conversation was going as she'd feared it would. She stumbled in her words as she said, "I just, uh, I thought that perhaps you might have changed your mind." But why would she have changed her mind? Claire was beginning to feel foolish for believing that she could just come to Thailand and sweep Becks off her feet.

Imaginary Becks said, "Claire, I'm sorry that you came all the way here, but you shouldn't have come here on a whim like this. You know we weren't meant to be together. It was just One Match deceiving our minds into believing so."

Claire shook her head. "No, I don't believe that. What I felt for you was real. And I believe that your feelings for me were genuine too. You told me yourself in your letter that your feelings for me hadn't disappeared."

Becks looked unmoved. She said to her, "Even if you're right, how could we be together knowing that our feelings for each other were predicted by an algorithm?"

"What does it matter? Couldn't we swallow our pride and accept that we can be predicted? What does it matter as long as we love each other?"

Becks shook her head. "It's more than that, Claire. It's about freedom. The freedom to choose our own course in life. And in some ways, that freedom comes before love."

"We don't even know if One Match was sophisticated enough to actually predict that we would fall for each other. It probably just determined that we had a chance at compatibility," said Claire. She felt as if she was floundering in the same debate that she'd had with Becks and others before.

"It doesn't matter. The fact remains that without One Match we wouldn't have found each other."

Becks then added, "You don't trust the technology itself. Are we forgetting that you left Wyman because they became involved with One? I think you're more aligned with my thinking than you acknowledge."

Claire was taken aback by this turn in the conversation with the imagined Becks. She was starting to sweat from her illness, and she felt light-headed. Her reply felt hollow as she said, "Leaving Wyman was about more than the integration with One. I was leaving Lewis, and I wanted to try starting my business—just like you encouraged me."

Becks said to her in an accusing tone, "You should have stayed. You should have figured out a way to convince them to stop from spreading this technology further. Or, even sabotaged the project. Don't you understand the potential impact of what's happening?"

"Please, Becks—"

"Don't you understand that our future is being decided by reckless people who have no regard for the long term effects for our society and are washing their hands of any moral obligation in the guise of providing happiness for consumers?"

Claire countered, "None of us can really know whether the advancement of certain technologies is good or bad. We can only let them happen and choose whether we'll use it or not. I chose to walk away from One, but we don't know if it'll be beneficial or harmful in the end."

"Billions of fates may soon be dictated by this technology simply for the sake of profits! Your answer is that we can only let it happen?"

Claire fell silent. She understood the concern over the power of One and knew that she had her own misgivings. She was hitting a roadblock in the argument and Becks was slipping away. Her stomach pains were also intensifying, and she felt like giving up in her quest to win her back.

She paused a bit to take a break, and a thought occurred to her. She wondered how much freedom they had to begin with. She changed course and said to Becks, "You believe in God."

Becks looked at her strangely, as if to gauge where Claire was going with the statement.

"And when you believe in God, don't you believe this all-powerful being knows everything about you and even knows what your future holds?"

"Claire—"

Claire continued, "And yet, you still live your life, trying your best to make the best choices you can every day. I'm not sure if I believe in God, but I believe to some extent that my background and environment have already pre-determined my fate. Even so, I live every day believing that I'm responsible for the decisions that I make."

"But this is different. The algorithm tells you explicitly as to what your best choices would be." Even as Becks said this, Claire could see the hesitation in her response. Sensing an opening, Claire got up from the bed and moved closer to Becks.

"One Match introduced me to you initially, that I can't deny. And perhaps through One Home and One Work and other future mutations the technology will overtake our lives completely, and it will be the beginning of the end for all of us. But I believe that our societies would fight back before it's too late. I know our ability to assess the relentless progress of technology is precarious, but I believe with all my heart that we would fight back before it consumes us. In the end, I believe that humanity will be capable of rescuing itself from self-destruction. Maybe it's a false hope, but I choose to believe this."

She moved yet closer to Becks until she was close enough to touch her. She grabbed Becks's hands and put them on her own chest.

Claire said, "I am here, Becks. If you take me now, our story doesn't end. It was started by One Match, but it will not end with it. Every day you and I will have a choice to continue to love each other or not. We will never know how our story ends, and I refuse to believe that there will ever be a technology that will know the final outcome either. There are parts of us that remain unknowable and mysterious."

Claire felt the truth of her words, and now assured of what she might say to her, her imagined portrait of Becks faded away. She sat back down, and the needling pains of her stomach continued to stab away at her. She tossed and turned for a while trying to get some much needed sleep, but the pain was too acute.

Eventually she gave up and looked at the clock by the bedstand. It was almost four o'clock. With only two hours left until her bus ride, she decided that she should try to find some medicine before boarding. She packed her backpack and thanked herself for having packed so lightly. She then went down to the hotel lobby and checked out. She'd seen a pharmacy on Khaosan Road and crossed her fingers that it was still open. She trudged over to the location, and to her dismay, it was closed. Feeling weak and as if she was about to faint, she walked on towards the Lomprayah bus station and decided to wait for the bus.

Once she got to the bus stop, she picked up her ticket and sat by the curb. It was still dark out, and the lights of the streets and the shop signs were still turned on. The cool air made her feel slightly better, and seeing pedestrians walking around this time of day gave her some comfort from feeling unsafe. At a café across the street two men were smoking cigarettes as they ate their breakfast. Claire went over to the café and ordered some hot tea. When the tea came she drank it and sat very still to avoid any further disturbances of her stomach.

After what felt like the longest wait, the bus to Chumphon Pier finally showed up. There was a throng of people, mostly tourists, and she boarded the bus near the back so that she could be close to the toilet. The bus was clean and spacious with large seats that reclined. When the bus took off, Claire closed her eyes and tried to sleep again for the six hour ride.

She woke up an hour later needing to go to the toilet. As in the Buddy Lodge, Claire vomited yet again and followed it up with waves of diarrhea. She continued this pattern several times during the duration of the bus ride, and she felt terrible that she was monopolizing the toilet. Several of her fellow travelers asked her if she was all right, and she weakly nodded her head. One of them, a cheery German woman traveling with her companion, offered her an aspirin, and Claire gratefully accepted.

During the ride, fever begin to set in as well. The bus had provided blankets, so she pulled them over her on her seat while she shivered beneath them. Claire looked down at her arms and saw that she was very pale. The bus driver had turned on a movie on the front of the bus, so she tried to focus on the movie. It was the latest James Bond movie that she'd already seen, and the noise from the TV set only gave her a headache. Instead, she closed her eyes and tried to imagine that she was someplace else. She thought of her old flat in Swiss Cottage where she used to wake up on Saturday mornings and drink her tea and read her newspaper. Autumn days were the best when she could see the red and brown leaves outside her window as she planned out the fresh possibilities of the weekend as she drank her tea. Claire continued to think of her old home, and eventually she was able to fall asleep as the bus drove on.

They arrived at Chumphon Pier just before one o'clock. When she stepped off the bus, it was hot and humid again. The beach and pier lay in front of her, and she could see the catamaran docked ahead. The thought of boarding the ferry for another one and a half hour ride to Koh Tao in her state brought Claire to her knees. She wanted to give up and curl up at a bench on the bus station. I can't do this anymore, she whispered to herself. She needed to see a doctor as her fever punished her over and over. But she looked at the pier once more. The path to the ferry loomed in front of her. She'd traveled thousands of miles to see Becks, and she was so close. To give up now was not an option. Claire decided to soldier on and trudged onto the boarding dock and onto the catamaran.

The entire ride on the catamaran ferry was an exercise in pain tolerance. As the boat surged ahead, Claire battled seasickness with all her remaining strength. As she spat into the toilet, she muttered to herself, mind over matter, mind over matter. She practically crawled outside to get some fresh air. The wind slapped against her face, and she could see the island up ahead. She could make out thickets of palm trees rising up in front of small green mountains. In front of one range was the ferry terminal up ahead. As they got closer to range, she could make out huts and bungalows on the beaches and in the hills. The water was a lucent blue-green color, and there were fishing boats and longtail boats carrying divers. The catamaran slowed down as it neared the harbor, and she saw a thatched building that had the sign, "Welcome to Koh Tao." The end was in sight.

Chapter 47

Claire got off the ferry with the other passengers and tried to orient herself. She was at Mae Haad at the lower western part of the island, and when she'd initially researched Koh Tao at home, she'd hoped that Becks might be located there. She headed into Mae Haad Village, feeling slightly better now that she no longer had to endure the tossing of the boat. The village reminded her a little of Khaosan Road in Bangkok, as if that street had converted to a beach town, but it was not as crowded. The main street was wide and filled with motor bikes and tourists who'd just landed with her. Many of the stores had signs in English advertising bike rentals, diving tours, and tattoos. She saw a bar called the The Dive Bar and walked in. Inside a Thai girl motioned her to a seat. Claire shook her head and took out her phone and brought up a picture of Becks she'd taken at L'Antica Pizzeria. She said to her, "I'm looking for this person. Have you seen her?"

The girl studied the picture and shook her head no. Claire thanked her, and stepped outside. She walked a few more minutes down the street and headed into another bar to ask the same question. Again, the answer was no, the face was not recognizable. Claire started to feel panic swelling up. She knew that she hadn't planned this portion of the trip well, but she'd read that Koh Tao was a small island with just over a thousand people and had assumed that she'd find Becks eventually. She'd also not planned on being immensely sick, and she tried to ignore the nausea and fever that she was feeling again.

She stepped into a pizzeria, and she saw a Westerner behind the counter. She walked up to him and showed him the picture, but he shook his head no. She said to him, "I think she might be running a restaurant or pub here now."

He replied with an Aussie accent, "I've been here for just a few months and haven't seen her. You might want to try Sairee Village just up north. A few restaurants there—maybe you might spot her there."

She thanked him. She thought of asking how an Australian had ended up at a pizzeria on an island in Thailand, but she decided to move on. She hailed a taxi out on the street and caught a ride to Sairee.

Sairee Village looked similar to Mae Haad. The colorful signs of restaurants and gift shops supplemented the bright neon of scooters and Kawasaki motorbikes. Tourists also walked around in beach colors, and Claire felt dizzy from the kaleidoscope of turquoise and orange surrounding her. She began her phone picture routine anew with the bars and gift shops of Sairee, but the results remained the same. It started to sink into her that perhaps Becks was not on the island at all. The postcard had just shown a nondescript island of Thailand. She could have changed her mind about Koh Tao and decided that someplace else in the country would be a better spot for her restaurant.

Claire decided that she was exhausted and needed a rest. She saw a bar called The Biker's Bar and stepped inside. She walked up to the bar and ordered a ginger ale to try and relieve her stomach, and thought of her next steps. She would first try to find a doctor and try to receive some treatment and medicine. Once she was better, she would rest up at a hotel here on the island and email Becks to explain that she was in Thailand and wanted her exact address. If Becks responded within two days, she'd be able to find her, and if not, she would head back to London as long as she felt well enough to do so.

She decided that this was a good plan. She signaled over to the bartender to pay for her drink and noticed in their small exchange about the bill that he was British. Deciding to give it one more shot, she brought out her phone and asked him if he recognized Becks.

By reflex she prepared to put her phone away, but he nodded and said, "Becks Kennedy, sure, I know her. Owns The Happy Clam down by Sai Daeng Beach here."

Claire froze. She said, "What did you just say?"

He said, "Yeah, she opened The Happy Clam about six months ago here. Damn good food. Some kind of Thai-Brit fusion. My mates and I went there about a month ago. Fish and chips there are the absolute best."

Claire grabbed him by the arm and said, "Can you take me there right now?"

He shook his head and replied, "It's dirt roads part of the way there. There was a big thunderstorm two days ago, and I'd bet that they're closed. Even if they were open, they'd be muddy as hell."

"Please, you don't understand. I've come all the way from London. I'm tired and I'm sick, but I have to see her. I won't leave here until you agree to take me, and you're going to have to kill me if you're going to move me."

The bartender looked back at her. He seemed to understand that she was dead serious, because he said, "All right then. I can't leave my post now, but I have a friend here who might be able to take you on his bike."

"Thank you, oh thank you so much."

"But if the roads are closed, there's nothing he can do for you."

Claire nodded and said, "Thank you again. I owe you everything."

The bartender picked up his phone and talked to someone in Thai. Ten minutes later, a Thai teenager with a motorcycle helmet showed up at the bar.

He pointed to the teen and said, "That's Kit. He's agreed to take you there for 200 baht."

Claire gave him 500 baht and said, "I'm happy to give you 500 more if you'll go there as fast you can."

Kit nodded, and Claire followed him out the bar. She thanked the Brit again, and she straddled the bike and held onto Kit as he started the motor bike. She could feel her hopes shooting up again, but she tried to hold it at bay. She would not take anything for granted until she saw Becks in-person.

Kit zoomed the bike down the road as Claire clung to him for dear life. They climbed in elevation as they rode past the lush foliage around them. She felt her fever returning to her, and as she sat on the bike, she prayed that she might see Becks's face one more time. If she could see her face just one more time, she told herself, she'd be satisfied with whatever happened afterwards.

They got to a point where they split off the main road and onto a narrower path. The road was muddier here, just as the bartender predicted. Kit revved the motorcycle hard in different areas as they bumped along the road. Mud splashed up and onto Claire's clothes, but she was feeling faint now and didn't care. She felt weak and felt feverish chills running up her body. She came to a point in which she thought she would fall off the bike, but she hung on with every ounce of her remaining strength. Just as she thought that she might lose her grip, he took her to a clearing. It was a small area by the beach with a few bungalows and buildings. One of the buildings had a wooden sign that read, The Happy Clam.

Claire stepped off the bike and paid Kit another 500 baht to stick around a bit. She trudged to the front of the building and peeked inside, but it looked empty. She saw some tables but no chairs, and there were no signs of customers or anyone else.

She felt a crushing feeling of enormous disappointment building, but she tried to push it away as she walked around the area. Pretty soon, she saw a small shack that was renting out scuba gear and surf boards. She walked up to the stand and saw that it was yet another expat. He was extremely tan and had a heavy beard that gave him the appearance of a castaway on a deserted island.

"Excuse me, can you tell me what happened to The Happy Clam?"

The bearded man gave her a dazed look, as if she'd awoken him from a stoned reverie.

"Huh?"

"The Happy Clam," she repeated herself. She pointed to its location and said, "Can you tell me what happened to it?"

He gave a slow yawn and said, "The woman who owned it packed up a couple of weeks ago. She said she missed home. She was going to London."

Her heart skipped a beat, but she assumed that he was mistaken. "London? You mean the UK? She said she was going back to the UK?"

"Yes," he said.

Claire had begun to think about Becks returning to Bourton when the man added, "Well, London is in the UK."

She must have looked at him strangely because he said, "I know what I heard. She said that she was going to London. Told me that she had to see someone there."

At these words, Claire felt a brief, rapturous thrill that lifted her away from all her sickness and stress. But before she could ask further questions, she fell over and blacked out.

Chapter 48

Claire woke up. She was in a bed in a small room. The room was dark, but when her eyes adjusted to the dark, she saw that there was a figure sitting by her bed. It was Kit.

Feeling weak, she managed to murmur, "What happened? Where am I?"

Kit replied, "You are at my family's house. My mother take care of you. Doctor come in and checked. He said you have food poisoning. Need rest."

"Food poisoning?" Claire looked at her body in disbelief. She tried to remember what she might have eaten that caused it. Was it the udon bowl at Heathrow? The curry at the stand in Bangkok?

"You get better. Need rest." Kit pulled a blanket over her.

Claire remembered what had happened before she'd fainted. She recalled that the man at the surf shack said that Becks had gone back. She could be in London at this very moment.

"I have to go home," she whispered. Even as she said these words, she dozed off to sleep again.

She woke up later in the night to the sounds of chattering outside her bedroom window. It was nighttime and dark outside, but there was a gathering of people outside with torches and flashlights.

Claire saw that Kit was by her bedside. "What's going on?" she asked.

"Loi Krathong festival."

She vaguely recalled reading about the festival in her guidebook, but the details were fuzzy.

Claire said, "I'd like to see it."

"No, you need rest."

"Please, Kit. I think I need some fresh air anyway."

Kit gave her a concerned glance, but then he helped Claire out of bed and supported her out of the bungalow.

They walked outside, and Claire could see the beach was right in front of them. They sat down and saw that a crowd of a hundred or so people had gathered. Some of them had begun placing their little boats into the water, and Claire followed the candle-lit boats as they steered into the sea.

He gestured to them and said, "Krathongs. All your anger and hate float away with them."

"They're beautiful."

Kit gestured to the boats and asked, "You want to light one?"

Claire accepted the offer and picked out a boat. She lit the boat and placed it into the ocean. She didn't know if she had much hate or anger, but she felt peaceful watching it sail away.

Once all the little flower boats were released, work began on the paper lanterns. Each of them were lit one-by-one until the orange orbs dotted the beach. There was a countdown, and the lanterns were released into the air. Claire watched as the lights rose into the gaping black night. When all the lanterns had lifted, the sky became a sea of dotted fire that left her breathless and in awe.

She said nothing as she continued to follow the lanterns until they disappeared into the dark. She felt a fullness of joy, a feeling of gladness that she was alive and able to witness something so beautiful so far away from her home. For a brief moment, she felt as if she was suspended away from her physical body and her own story. All of her feelings of sickness and stress, all her feelings of worry and despair and remembrances of the past and concerns of the future fell away, and she was left with a burning gratitude of what she'd just witnessed.

She and Kit watched until the last of the lights petered out into the darkness, and then finally Kit said to her, "I'm sorry that your friend not here. You are sick and you come all the way here for her."

"No," she said. "I'm glad that I came to Thailand. This was worth it. I will remember this for the rest of my life."

Chapter 49

Three days later, Claire was back in London, and she took a breath as she stared at a door. 22 Holly Mount London NW3 6SG. The address was right in the heart of Hampstead, up on a side street on the hilly northern end of the High Street. It was the address that she'd found on Camden Council's public licensing register. There were no signs outside the building, but Claire knew that she was standing in front of the next rendition of The Happy Clam.

She knocked on the door and waited. There was no answer, so she knocked on it once more. When there was still no reply, she was about to give up and turn back home, when slowly the door opened. Becks stood in front of her.

She carried a paint roller, and she had specks of white paint all over her black shirt and jeans, and even some on her face and hair. Her hair was longer and in a braid, and she looked as lovely as ever.

Upon seeing Claire, Becks's eyes widened and she gasped. She said to her, "Claire! You found me."

"Yes, yes I finally did." Claire felt stiff and shy after seeing her for the first time in nearly two years. Their last meeting felt like a lifetime ago, and she sensed the shyness in Becks as well. Becks asked her, "Would you like to come in?"

Claire nodded and followed her in. Inside, she saw that the pub was very much in the process of being remodeled. The walls had a fresh coat of paint that was still drying, the floors were ripped apart, and furniture and decorations were strewn all over the place. Seeing the unfinished mess and comparing it to the perfection of the original The Happy Clam, Claire felt a bit overwhelmed at the work that lay ahead for Becks.

They were silent as Claire surveyed the scene, but then Becks spoke up. "Claire, how in the world did you find me?"

Claire almost laughed. How could she tell her that she had traveled all the way to Thailand and searched her out in sickness only to find out that Becks had packed up to London? She would provide her with the details later.

"I found out that you were planning a pub in London and on a hunch I thought it might be around Hampstead. I went to Camden Council's website and looked for The Happy Clam under the public licensing register."

Claire could see that Becks was blushing. "I was that predictable, wasn't I?" Becks said.

"It's a brilliant name for a pub."

"It was hard for me to let it go."

There was another awkward pause, and Becks then asked, "How are you? How's Lewis?"

Claire was reminded by the question of all that happened since they last saw each other. She replied, "I'm not with Lewis anymore. I broke off the engagement the night before our wedding."

Becks gasped. "You did what?"

"I realized that we weren't the right fit, and I broke it off. My mum's still furious about it."

Becks had a concerned expression as she said, "Are you okay then? How have you been getting along?"

"It was difficult at first, but I saw a therapist who helped me. Wasn't just about Lewis though, but about Will and the anxiety attacks, too." Claire didn't mention that some of the sessions had involved discussions of Becks.

"Good, good. I'm so glad to hear that you finally received help for your anxiety."

"Yes, so there was that, but I also quit Wyman and started my own analytics firm."

"You did? That's wonderful! How's it doing?"

"All right. We're still navigating our way through. We have thirteen regular clients now. It's not much, and we still need to ramp up our client list quite a bit if we're going to be profitable, but we've just signed three, so we're pretty excited about it."

Becks asked, "What do you mean 'we'?"

"I brought over one of my junior family members from Wyman. He's sharp as a whip and really helping with the business."

Becks gave an audible sigh. "Claire, you can't take on a salary you don't need while you're just getting started. Overspending is one of the biggest mistakes of small businesses when they start off."

"It's all right. He's working for free in exchange for a small stake in the company."

"A small stake? You're giving away shares of your company to your assistant?"

Claire felt that the conversation was heading in the wrong direction. She knew that in due time that she'd want to talk more about her business with Becks, but she reminded herself that it wasn't her reason for the visit.

"Let's forget about my business for now, shall we? I came here to talk to you about something else."

Becks looked nervous. Claire took a breath and said, "I came here because I received your postcard. I eventually went to Thailand to find you and tell you that I'd made a mistake in letting you go. I didn't find you there, but I've found you now, and I'm here because I haven't given up on the idea of us being together. I want to find out if you feel the same."

Becks said nothing, seemingly surprised at what Claire was saying. But eventually tears started to stream down her face. "Oh, Claire," she said.

Claire tried to recollect the words that she'd meant to say to Becks in this moment. She tried to remember her point about how she believed that no one was ever quite free and yet they were all free enough to choose to love each other every day. She'd dreamed of this moment for hours on end, and now that it was finally happening, she was at a loss for words.

Becks continued to cry as she gathered herself to say, "I was such a coward. I'm so sorry for what I did."

Claire was confused. "What do you mean?"

"I sent you the postcard because I missed you, but I was too ashamed to say anything in it. I didn't think you'd travel all the way to Thailand. I can't believe that you did that."

The tears were now flowing freely down Becks's face, and Claire could feel her own eyes welling up. "You missed me?" she said.

Becks could only nod as she shook with her crying. "I came to London to come back to you. I told myself that I'd build this pub to be close to you, and once it was built that I could maybe try to win you back…"

Claire leaned in and wiped away her tears with her handkerchief.

"I missed you," she said to Becks. She pulled in close and hugged her as Becks sobbed into her shoulder. As Becks tried to gain control of herself, Claire held her tightly as her own tears streamed down. So much had happened since they'd last seen each other, and she'd changed just as she knew that Becks had changed. They would get to know each other again and let the pieces fall into place as they may. Even though One Match had made a prediction, Claire felt that their future was yet unwritten, and she felt comfortable in this uncertainty. She felt a shudder, and it was the same charged feeling she'd felt from seeing Becks step off the train at Paddington on her weekend visit to London once upon a time. The hope of the weekend had seemed limitless then, and she felt the same feelings of uncharted possibilities rising again.

Becks wiped the tears from her eyes and said, "So what do we do now?"

Claire said nothing. Instead, she reached out and held her hand and led her out of the building and onto a ledge where they could see the houses and chapels of Hampstead standing tall in the sloping hill below them. The autumn leaves were falling, and smoke from Sunday roasts were rising into the crisp air.

They stared at the scene in blissful silence before she turned to Becks and said, "Welcome home."

ABOUT THE AUTHOR

J.Y. Chung majored in creative writing at Stanford University. J.Y. has lived in London and currently resides in Seattle. J.Y. loves food and travel and writes on the confluence of love, technology, and society. *One Match* is J.Y's debut novel.

A NOTE FROM THE AUTHOR

If you enjoyed *One Match*, would you consider writing an honest review? Reviews are extremely helpful for indie authors such as myself. I also love to read feedback from my readers—it's the reason why I write! Reviews for the book can be submitted on its Amazon Review Page.

Made in the USA
Middletown, DE
10 August 2017